CW01221052

Ghosh in China

JOHN FRANCIS CROSS

This is a work of fiction. Any resemblance to actual events or persons, living or dead, is entirely coincidental.

ISBN-10:150277111X
ISBN-13:978-1502771117

This book is dedicated to its readers.

ACKNOWLEDGEMENTS

Stewart Black, Chris Jones, Cindy McDonald, Mike Russell, Mark Shrosbree, and John Zonn all read and made helpful comments on draft sections; Peter Buckman of The Ampersand Agency Ltd read the whole work and suggested significant improvements. I am very grateful to all of them.

CHAPTER 1
Day 1, Midnight, Beijing

The Minister of Religious Affairs smacked the bottom of one of the five half-naked young women in his bedroom and cried, 'Let's have some fireworks!' It was midnight.

The five women squealed as a service to their employer. The Minister stood up, raising his arms and clenching his biceps, displaying his flat hairless chest and powerful belly of nearly seven decades' strength.

He shouted, 'Canada! Canada! Give me Canada!'

The smacked woman set about getting Canada; two others dragged a box of fireworks from under the bed.

Kicking the firework box, the Minister said, 'Not that one. The big one! Tonight's the big one!'

Four tough, dainty hands grabbed the big one. The Minister flung open the balcony doors to the sub-zero winter of suburban Beijing and checked the weather. Above the Ministry headquarters, the sky was dark and clear, though a strong wind suggested change. Grabbing sheets and blankets for dignity and warmth, four women began setting up fireworks on the wide seventh floor balcony. In a narrow kitchen the woman who had been smacked prepared Canada: extract of premium North American ginseng, smuggled Canadian Viagra tablets crushed to a powder, squeezed root of ginger, and expensive Canadian whisky, all mixed with Canadian spa water and micro-waved.

The Minister sat resting in his dimly lit bathroom. He pictured in his mind how the secret plans of this long-anticipated night would become an orderly and spectacular reality. In front of him in the bathroom, on top of a black marble counter and reflected in a wall of mirrors, he saw a pile of possessions belonging to the five women: down jackets - soft and puffy, wisps of blouses and skirts, sharp dangerous shoes, impractical bags, and pretty cell phones. It was untidy and impossible to know who owned what. The

Minister picked up a phone and weighed it in his hand like a little bird.

Although the Minister was always careful not to show favouritism to those he employed, cash in hand, for private services in his apartment, the woman who prepared Canada was the one he liked best. She was older than she said and looked, and he knew that. She was from a village in a pleasant valley that had no money. At that moment, as she crushed and mixed ingredients, she glanced at the sky and saw stars, stars that her twin sister might also see, wherever she may now be, perhaps waking briefly from snug sleep in a nice clean room, paid for by her good, safe, respectful job that she had secured because of hard study at high school and university, through each day of which she'd been supported financially and emotionally by her unlucky, slightly elder twin. The strengthening wind sent storm clouds sliding across the deep frozen sky, covering the stars. The twin link was broken and the woman became aware of herself, undressed in a rich official's room, holding Canada. She knocked on the bathroom door, pushed it open slowly and presented the tumbler of steaming hot liquid to the Minister.

'Urgh! Canada!' said the Minister, 'I love Canada.' He put down the phone and threw the hot liquid down his gullet. He got up and strode across his bedroom to the balcony where four crouching women were fiddling with fireworks.

The Minister embraced two women in each arm, looked down at the Ministry compound building, looked up to the sky and said, 'Tonight's the night for the big bang!'

CHAPTER 2
Day 1, 12:05 am

When it was first built, in 1951, the Ministry of Religious Affairs headquarters compound had a view of fields north of Beijing, and guests and residents nicknamed the square building *Villa No.7*. It was called a villa because of the green land beyond it, and it was seventh of the places that the restless, revolutionary, paranoid Mao Zedong slept in, shifting suddenly from one to the other. Over six decades later, the Ministry compound had long been reached and surrounded by glass and concrete offices, workshops, retailers and residences, as the city expanded in the post-Mao revolution that declared the profit motive was valid, necessary and worthy. The Ministry had been rebuilt, too, and because it was hemmed in on all sides by other walls and could only go upwards not outwards, ten new stories were added while keeping the original floor plan exactly. In the new four-sided building most of the windows looked inward, down to the courtyard or across to other windows.

On the night of the fireworks, at the centre of the Ministry headquarters, a telephone call came to the private number of the *Konka* i-Phone of the Vice Minister of Religious Affairs, Dong Bing. A voice that sounded as if it were spoken down a sock-covered toilet roll tube, which it was, said slowly, 'Vice Minister, at navigation coordinates North 40.04247411411451, East 116.14104141441414, now, one hundred and forty-seven leading national members of Shining Light of Truth are gathered for a prayer meeting.'

'Who are you? Who gave you my number?'

'I'm now texting you the coordinates on another phone. They are: North 40.04247411411451, East 116.14104141-441414. Approximately forty minutes' drive from the Ministry,' said the speaker before ending the call.

'So many 4s - sounds like death,' Dong couldn't help thinking, though he despised the irrational superstition that gives meaning to the coincidence that the Chinese word *four*, *sì*, pronounced *sir*, sounds like that for *die* and *death*.

Given that the caller knew Dong's private phone number, and given the precise nature of the information, the rumour was convincing. Vice Minister Dong Bing immediately knew that this was an emergency. He felt pleasantly cool and clear. It was 12:07 am. It was time to show his worth. He knew he had to wake the Minister - something he had never done before. He looked for the secret emergency number and dialled.

'Urgh.'

'Minister, sorry to wake you - '

'Stop tickling!' said the Minister.

'Huh?'

'A dream. I'm dreaming,' said the Minister, caressing the buttocks of his favourite.

'Emergency!'

'Has to be.'

'An informant.'

'On who?'

'Shining Light of Truth.'

'Oh hell.'

'Unapproved cult gathering.'

'How many of them?'

'One hundred and forty-seven.'

'Toad shit. Where? Far away, I hope.'

'Forty minutes' drive from the Ministry.'

'We're deep in toad shit.'

There was a pause while neither spoke.

The Minister said, 'OK, send security.'

'How many?'

'For these religious weaklings ten armed men are plenty. Be dead safe - fifty.'

'Fifty.'

'No. Double it.'

'Hundred.'

'No. One each.'

'Armed?'

'Of course. That's normal. And gently, gently. Herd them like lambs. That's what we want. Get them quiet, unhurt and entirely without bleating. First make sure you don't let them cause any trouble and most important of all, make sure you get them. All of them.'

'When?'

'When I say *goodbye*. Goodbye.'

It took fifteen minutes for Dong Bing to get the guards awake, up, dressed, equipped, and in their trucks. It took them forty-five minutes to reach the site, a semi-suburban snowy field. When they got there the wind was even stronger; sudden powerful gusts, like solid blocks of frozen Manchurian air, hit soldiers as they dismounted from the trucks, and if they were unbalanced, it blew them over.

Although the field was covered in a solid foot of snow it was clearly a place for growing cabbages. Administratively, the whole district was still classed as a village, a rural area, but progress had run faster than the naming process and the snowy field's neighbours were factories and apartment complexes - all vague, cold and distant in the night.

In the middle of this night, in the middle of this mixed and transitory landscape, in the middle of the isolated field, stood one hundred and forty-seven believers of the Shining Light of Truth, holding hands. Their way of holding hands was a religious practice, and a sign of who they were. To the authorities, it was a symptom of their criminal disease. They didn't form a circle; they made strings of seven. Seven is the number of potentialities, that is, of luck. At any point, the seven-person string can reach out and become eight, and eight is the number symbol of completion. Eight is the number of fortune and fulfilment, both the fat round rich infinity of the Arabic numeral 8, and the openness, generosity and fertile provision of the Chinese character for eight: 八.

So the Shining Light of Truth believers stood in strings of seven in the snowy field. Seven times seven, times three equals one hundred and forty-seven. Seven strings of seven are doubly lucky. And three is the pyramid, the strongest number, thus creating a solid foundation of strength and luck. *Wait as one and our luck will come* is number seven of the seven key sayings of the teaching of the Shining Light of Truth. They stood in the snow holding hands and waiting for something, or someone, or the son of someone, to fulfil their potential; waiting for power beyond life. As they waited Ministry of Religious Affairs security personnel arrived in six trucks and one 4WD (seven vehicles), carrying guns.

The believers had heard the trucks coming from a distance and stood expectantly facing them as the security personnel jumped out and assembled beyond the wire fence of the field.

The group in the 4WD included Officer Liu, representing the Ministry, Mr Zhang, representing the Communist Party, and Captain Ma, responsible for the security personnel. They all recognized the strings of seven people holding hands as typical of Shining Light of Truth followers from photographs shown in Ministry briefings. Liu and Zhang were ranked considerably above Ma, but he was a veteran of the People's Liberation Army, had actually fought in a war - in Vietnam, in 1979 - and was anyway a natural leader. They let him speak. The Captain stood with the Ministry personnel behind him, the wire fence in front of him and the Shining Light of Truth group in the field beyond. First Ma turned to the men who had been woken up in the middle of the night and driven to a snowy field. He said in a quiet voice audible to them all, 'Good work. Now hold steady, soldiers.'

'Security personnel,' said Officer Liu.

Captain Ma turned to the group in the field and said loudly and clearly: 'Citizens - '

'They are criminals,' said Liu.

'Citizens first,' said Captain Ma. Then loudly again, 'Citizens! For your own safety and for the integrity of the laws of our China, I ask you to follow my instructions.'

There was silence. Ma continued: 'Citizens, I am Captain Ma of the Ministry of Religious Affairs, part of the Government of the People's Republic of China, and a servant to you and all our people.'

The silence resumed. Wind roared into it; a storm was coming.

'Citizens, I ask you to move towards our vehicles, enter the vehicles and accompany us to the Ministry of Religious Affairs, where you will be hosted in the safety and authority of the Government of the People's Republic of China.'

There was no answer; only the wind howled.

'Citizens!' he shouted.

A thin, calm woman's voice came from somewhere in the strings of seven: 'We will not move, Captain.'

The storm blew their voices around, creating peculiar reductions and amplifications of sound, as if everything were being spoken through huge faulty microphones.

'Do not disobey your own laws,' Ma said.

'They are not our laws, Captain,' answered the woman.

This time the listeners could locate the speaker, in the middle of the group in the field, at the end of one of the strings of seven. She was slightly built though even at distance and the dim light of Ministry truck headlamps, her posture suggested assurance and a certain elegance. She was middle aged, perhaps older.

Ma said, 'Any crime is unpatriotic, and denying your own laws - that's treason!' He felt genuinely angry though he also felt duty bound to repeat his request.

'Citizens. Once again I ask you: move towards the vehicles of the Ministry of Religious Affairs.'

Silence. The wind howled a warning about a storm that was tumbling and rushing in a ball of confusion from the vast, empty and frozen northeast of Asia.

'Citizens, for the last time, I ask you, for your own safety, move towards the trucks.'

'We will not move, Captain,' said the woman.

'Do not listen to this false leader!'

'They are not listening to me, they are listening to their hearts,' said the woman.

'You!' said the Captain, pointing at a young man at the end of the nearest string. 'Move now.'

One hundred and fifty security personnel looked at the skinny man wearing thick glasses.

Eventually the skinny man said, 'I am waiting here and will not move from this field.'

'Waiting for what?'

'What or *who*,' said the skinny man.

'I am here and I am telling you to move.'

'I am staying.'

Captain Ma raised his head to shout to the whole group, 'We will use force, citizens.'

The wind was stronger than ever.

'For your own safety, I strongly advise you not to do that,' said the woman's voice. Some of the security personnel sniggered. The wind dropped.

'We will enter the field and arrest each one of you,' said the Captain.

'It will be dangerous, Captain.'

The far distant sky crackled with lightning.

The cult believers looked pathetic, ankle deep in snow, many unsuitably dressed for the cold, holding hands like infants or idiots. Captain Ma turned his head to the men behind him and said, 'Defensive posture'. There was the sound of one hundred and fifty guns having the safety catches clicked off and the security personnel felt warmed by a rush of courage in their veins.

'We will enter the field and take you, one by one, by force, if necessary.'

'Please don't, Captain,' said the woman, 'I'm warning you.'

Soundless lightning flashed a nest of light in the northern sky.

'I'm warning *you*!' This was one of the rare occasions in his entire life that Captain Ma, strong brave honest uncorrupted Captain Ma, felt his professional authority challenged. He was not naïve enough to lack bitterness that his competence and exemplary service record were not matched by their worthy rewards. He knew that he deserved better than his current post and that he should be ranked higher than many others including the merely average Liu and Zhang now with him. He knew that his transfer to the dead end position as head of security at the Ministry of Religious Affairs came about because the folly, immodesty and ambition of his immediate superiors in his army Division was highlighted by his presence. He knew all this and also knew that others were in similar or worse situations and he often told himself, 'I do not wish for what I do not have; I wish for what I have and then I feel content. I wish for my son and my wife, my health and my mind, my work and my rank, and I have them all.' For this attitude, and for his abilities, it was Captain Ma who stood at the front of the Ministry men and decided what would happen next.

Captain Ma announced: 'In the name of the Government of the People's Republic of China, I order the arrest of every person in this field.'

In a solemn voice the slight, elegant woman said, 'Captain, we will not leave the field alive. Any one that you seize will drop down dead. And anyone who attempts to arrest us will also die.'

Some security men giggled again, this time more nervously. The Captain felt far from laughter. 'You threaten the Government,' he said.

The lightning came again, nearer.

The woman said, 'Captain Ma, you are a good man. You are not who we are waiting for. Stay back. Stay back. Remember, any one of us that you try to arrest, dies.'

'I arrest you all,' said Captain Ma. He checked his watch - it was 1:16 am. To his men he said, 'Prepare to arrest all the citizens in the field. Follow us.' He glanced, as if aiming, at the woman who had spoken. To Officer Liu and Mr Zhang he said, 'Lead from the front.' When they failed to budge, he unclipped his revolver and gave it to Zhang. Saying, 'We lead from the front,' he moved and Zhang and Liu followed, both thinking *outdated idiot delusional socialist hero* as they stepped over the field's wire fence that, because of the depth of snow, was just knee height. The security personnel followed in ten rows, wordlessly.

At 1:35, back in his office at the Ministry of Religious Affairs, Dong Bing took the fourth and last phone call from Officer Liu. Liu was saying, 'I am going to arrest the criminals.'

'Where are you?'

'The field. The coordinates you told us.'

Dong could hear sounds of Liu's exertions, his breathing in the cold as he walked, his shoes crunching into the snow, and behind that the wind of the storm. The call was ended.

CHAPTER 3
Day 1, 1:20 am

The senior Chinese Communist Party representative at the Ministry of Religious Affairs, the Ministerial Branch Party Secretary, had his sleep disturbed several times that night. The first was by a noise like war. He had been sleeping in his bedroom in the same massive square concrete compound that was the Ministry headquarters, on the eighth floor of the east side. He heard pain in his head. The Party man woke up. The man beside him in bed did not wake up though he said, in his sleep, in English, and pitifully, 'Oh Lord'.

The Party man got up, wrapped a thirty-year old dressing gown over his pyjamas, shuffled into his slippers, and walked to the window. Fat clouds were churning all over the sky and from behind them came the muffled sound of thunder, but far brighter and much, much nosier were fireworks, coming from a launch point on the side of the compound for Ministerial bureaucrats. He couldn't tell which floor or which room. He tried to locate the sound in his mental map of the large compound. The Party man had a key to open every room and every cupboard. He knew every passageway and obscure door. While calculating, he went to check the green digits of the bedside alarm - 1:37 am. Back at the window, and not enjoying the colourful display, the Party man imagined the scene that might occur shortly after 8 am later the same morning.

The whole Ministry entourage would be there - slovenly cleaning girls, unreliable petit chefs, intolerant clerks, thieving drivers, and the office staff - all unnecessarily present and fidgety. Ministerial higher ups would be there too, with the ambitious ones showing no surprise whatsoever, method acting competitively, organizing people into ranked rows, and snapping at minions to keep silence for no particular reason. In this they would be led by the Vice-Minister, Dong Bing. And the only one of the crowd looking amiable, the only one not ordering anybody else, the one who actually ordered the whole performance, the only one who knew exactly what was going on, would be the old rogue himself, the Minister. Finally the Minister would speak, compelling and confident, and with a certain inarticulate clumsiness that was a sure sign of sincerity, the virtue valued above all by his listening subordinates. And he'd start slowly and apparently haltingly about how there had been an shocking anti-social unauthorized and illicit use of prescribed explosives that disturbed everyone's sleep especially his own and now that he's old if he doesn't get a smooth night - and he didn't - then he gets befuddled like he is now and it affects the day's work like it is now with everyone not having their proper sleep and now neglecting their duties by having to attend this meeting, too. And more than these personal inconveniences don't forget there is *danger* and *criminality*. And illegal explosives threaten the lives and safety of everybody and hinder the work of the Ministry and anyone who does criminal activity is a terrorist and an enemy and a personal enemy of mine and of the Ministry and of the entire Chinese Government that governs the motherland and also of the Chinese Communist Party that (here looking sincerely at the Party man) with its bravery, wisdom and experience leads the Government, and an enemy of all the Chinese people and all China, and anyone who is an enemy of China is a supporter of the enemies of China and *is there anybody here* who supports the enemies? Is there anybody here who wishes that the enemies of the Chinese people would triumph? Is there anybody who wishes the Japanese had won the war with China? Is there? And under the leadership of the Party, the Ministry is a servant of the People, and as the chief servant I will not rest until I find the perpetrator. And I will find the perpetrator. And I will punish them. They will be punished. You understand me.

The Party Secretary also imagined that when hearing the Minister's speech, he would understand, deep in his heart, that it was the Minister himself who had illegally bought the fireworks, brought them into the Religious Affairs Ministry compound, and set them off. As he watched the fireworks in the cold midnight, the Party man imagined this is what would happen at eight in the morning. And, indeed, this is exactly what did happen.

Despite the Party man's proven knack for prediction, even he could not have guessed the second and third incidents that, later the same night, were to disturb his sleep and that of everybody else in the Ministry of Religious Affairs compound. Nor could he guess their complex and profound effects.

CHAPTER 4
Day 1, 1:30 am

Less than five minutes after his last call from Officer Liu in the snowy field, Vice Minister Dong Bing phoned Liu. There was no answer and no connection. He rang Captain Ma. His line was also not available. Dong found numbers of other members of the security personnel - sergeants, corporals and other ranks carrying cell phones. At each number dialled and no response gained, Vice Minister Dong grew more perplexed and more afraid. The situation had started as an emergency, and he had then acted, and now it was out of control. He acted again. This time it took only seven minutes to get another one hundred security personnel awake, equipped and in vehicles. The men were hurried by his intense anxiety. The Minister was informed. Dong's fear communicated itself to the Minister. The Minister said, 'GO! GO! GO!' Leaving the recumbent women in his gunpowder-smoky room, the Canada-powered Minister ran down many stairs to the Ministry's main office wearing nothing and holding a blanket. He said 'Call the Party Secretary!' When Dong got the number of the senior representative of the Communist Party at the Ministry, the Minister grabbed the phone and shouted information. When the short call was over, Dong was already gone, having driven away using any available vehicle including his and the Minister's own cars. The Minister, noticing for the first time the cold and his nakedness, now that he was alone, shivered uninhibitedly.

CHAPTER 5
Day 1, 2:55 am

Marcas Ghosh, aged twenty-seven, a young British man of under-exploited talent, walked comfortably and drunkenly along a large suburban Beijing street at 2:55 am with nobody else around. It was minus 10ºC and an awful windstorm had blown through not much more than an hour ago. Here and there were piles of mucky slush, re-frozen. On a foolish whim he had got out of the taxi that was taking him home and started walking. His feet moved in inefficient diagonals across contrasting areas of light and dark characteristic of city streets throughout China - areas of brightness lit by private neon and areas of publicly maintained darkness. The sky was black or orangey-grey or entirely gone depending on when he looked. It was the end of a long and complicated working day for Ghosh involving stamina, self-control, frustration and alcohol inappropriate in quantity and purpose.

He said, 'Unaccustomed as I am to public drinking - ' and found it impossible to invent anything to follow. He liked the start, and he said it a dozen times. An Audi 6 with blacked out windows approached from the distance at high speed. It looked sleek and glossy. It looked, to Ghosh, a beautiful and evil car.

Thick snow started to fall and Ghosh gestured at it as he finished his sentence at the thirteenth attempt: 'Unaccustomed as I am, to public drinking, I'm thinking I'm doing it pretty well, thank you!'

In a total of four years in China, he'd never been so drunk. In his student days, he'd spent spare time practising the language, and these days, as an intern, he read history books as if preparing for a quiz, otherwise hanging out on *Weibo*. He wasn't a practised drinker.

The black Audi braked without a scream, left the highway, rolled onto the pavement, and drove at Ghosh slowly and steadily until the fender knocked his shins and he had to balance himself by putting his palms on the hot black bonnet.

'Get your fucking hands off state property!' said a fierce shaven head sticking out of the car window. The head, and its body, got out of the car. Another, bigger, man also got out. Each grabbed a Ghosh bicep. He was pushed into the back of the car and they sat either side of him.

The driver said to the leader sitting in the front passenger seat, 'Looks like a terrorist'. He drove off fast. The car was warm and had wonderfully comfortable seats. Ghosh's day was becoming even longer and more complicated, he thought.

Ghosh said 'Er . . .'

'Shut your mouth!' said the driver. Then to the bigger man: 'Ask him if he can speak Chinese'.

'You!' said the bigger man, 'Can you speak Chinese?'

So far, the whole exchange had been held in the Beijing dialect of Modern Standard Chinese, which Ghosh spoke well. Ghosh thought about his answer for a while before coming up with, in Chinese: 'A little'.

Ghosh laughed. Being sleepy and drunk he only noticed the slapstick element that comes with threatening and unpredictable circumstances. He also felt the confidence of being British, which made him feel like an insignificant and invulnerable observer.

The driver said to the leader, 'So, not only a terrorist, but also a spy.' And he said to Ghosh, 'Where are you from?'

Because he was drunk Ghosh said, *'Pòcìmáosī'*, signifying *Portsmouth*, which was true enough.

There was a wilful mishearing: *'Bājīsītǎn?' - Pakistan.*

'No, no,' said Ghosh. *'Yīngguó' - England*

'Don't look like it,' said the driver. 'Too dark.'

'Yīngguó,' said Ghosh.

'Pakistan,' said the driver.

Ghosh wasn't spoken to again. The leader in the back had a whispered phone call. Ghosh caught, '. . . our side one hundred and ... the other, one hundred forty seven . . .' It sounded like the score of basketball game. They drove fast to the compound of the Ministry of Religious Affairs.

The men in the black Audi took Ghosh to an office in the Ministry. He was frisked and made to stand at the back. In the office there were black leather-look chairs swivelling on silver pedestals and running on black casters, and desks, the top of each desk covered in a sheet of glass, name cards held under the glass. There werc black leather-look sofas around low, glass-topped tables, full ash trays on the tables, also tea cups with dried tea stains and parched, used tea leaves, and plastic bottles of water. Many people were talking - to each other, at the same time as each other, and on cell phones. To Ghosh the workplace scene was familiar, typical - even comforting.

Ghosh thought he was at another Beijing meeting at which his presence as a junior staff member was required by protocol although nothing he said would be considered of importance, however wise or frivolous. At home he was a minor expert; in China he was a know-nothing. And because he was never asked, or when asked he was never considered seriously, his feeling of importance became aggravated and increased: he wanted to say something and show what he knew.

In the Ministry office, the man behind the main desk, the obvious boss, was the Minister of Religious Affairs, though Ghosh did not know that yet. Around the Minister, many people were busy, mainly men in dark suits with white shirts, all ignoring Ghosh.

In that state of being ignored, standing up, halfway between consciousness and unconsciousness, Ghosh contemplated the Minister.

Ghosh saw the Minister had a rough-looking head topped with salt and pepper hair, cut short and sticking up like brush bristles; he had bushy eyebrows over round eyes that had red veins in them and dark bags under them; he had a fat red nose, thick purplish lips, and yellowish leather cheeks bristling with stubble; all features on a rough block frame, a chunk like the starting point for a heroic sculpture.

The Minister's hands were clutched together in a fist without the fingers tucked in, making Ghosh think *trotters*; the hands had moles, blotches, freckles, age spots and some hair between knuckles and joint. The fingernails were thick and yellow. The Minister was wearing long johns under his trousers, and they were visible in a crumple at his ankles.

The Minister looked at the leader of the Audi group and said:

'Find anything?'

'Not much, Minister.'

'Well? What?'

'One of the misbelievers was holding piece of paper, in front of her, tightly, as if it was important. There are photos on my phone,' said the Audi 6 group leader.

In the car, squashed next to him, Ghosh had not been able to look at this man clearly. He now saw that the man was tall, broad shouldered and athletic-looking, about forty-five. The front of his hair was neat while the back of his head looked brutish. In the presence of the Minister he held his face in a wide, aggressive smile. This man was the Vice-Minister, Dong Bing.

On the phone, the Minister saw photos of indistinct clothed lumps in snow - they were bodies. He said, 'Dead pigs!'

He saw a photo of a dead woman. It was the one who had spoken from the field to Captain Ma. The Minister swallowed and said, 'Ah, ah, ah!'

The woman, in death, had a face like a carved artwork: regular, simple, attractive, austere, and refined.

Dong said, 'She's the one who held the paper. Held it in front of her.'

'Urgh. Did she? Did she? It's an ugly situation. Ugly,' said the Minister. 'Show me the paper.'

Dong gave him a square piece of paper, about four centimetres each side, folded four times, and soft from being handled often.

'Ugh!' said the Minister, admiringly. 'Small. Bloody small. Which soldier found this?'

'This one' said Dong Bing, whose given name, *Bing*, means *soldier*.

'China would not be what it is without soldiers like you, Vice Minister Dong.'

'If that was intended as a compliment, Minister, then thank you.'

'What makes you doubt that it was?'

'Modesty.'

'A virtue incompatible with your age, position and ambition.'

'You overestimate me, Minister.'

'I try.'

The Minister opened the folds and saw the writing.

Chairman Mao's Positive and Negative Map of a Four-Sided Building

Beaten by Father
Lose mother
Learn violence
Lose wife
Make Zhou mine
Defeat Jiang
Lose son
Stung by 7,000 insects
Start Cultural Revolution
Betrayed by Lin
Plant seed of truth

The Minister's face showed nothing, which was a sign of something serious.

He stopped reading and said, 'What's *7,000 insects*?'

In the short time that the Minister had been quietly reading, Ghosh slipped into a state close to sleep. Rarely visited childhood memories of his bickering parents blended with the confusion of raised voices he heard around him in the Ministry office. At home, in the kitchen, as he did school homework, ate dinner on his own, or fished for badminton gear from dirty laundry in the washing machine, his parents argued about food, the worst points of England, or summer holiday destinations. His Indian father would be frying potatoes in a specially made chip pan full of solid beef fat, saying *there's nothing so French as chips*, and his French mother would be microwaving a supermarket ready meal, usually *Weightwatchers Chicken & Lemon Risotto*, and one of them saying *what's wrong with paigle* and the other one saying *nothing wrong with paigle* - Marcas Ghosh was eleven before he realized *paigle* was the French sound for Wales - and always someone brought up *vomiting moules marinières all over the tent* and disputed who was *truly responsible for the vomiting*. Ghosh felt sick.

Nobody answered the Minister.

The Minister said again, 'What's *7,000 insects*? What is this paper?'

'It means something,' said Dong. 'I'm sure you know - '

'Know what!' said the Minister.

'This building,' said Dong.

'What?' said the Minister.

'Is built on the site of - '

'I know,' said another official.

'Chairman Mao's plan,' said Dong Bing.

'I know,' said a third.

'To the same basic room plan except bigger and better - '

'Taller and - '

'But what's *7,000 insects*?' said the Minister.

Ghosh woke from his nauseous drowse and hearing *Seven Thousand*, said, 'Sixty-two!'

'Who's this!' said the Minister to Dong Bing.

'A suspect.'

'Of what?'

'That hasn't been determined. He was near the site. There may be foreign involvement - there often is with these cults.'

'Can he speak Chinese?' asked the Minister.

'That hasn't been determined,' said Dong Bing.

'One thousand nine hundred and sixty-two,' said Ghosh, in Chinese.

'What did he say?'

'Sixty-two,' said Ghosh.

''Sixty-two' perhaps, Minister.' Said Dong Bing.

'*Sixty-two*! What the fuck's that!' said the Minister.

'Shishty-too,' said Ghosh, who was still drunk. 'Clever map. Says where.'

'Where's he from?'

Dong said to Ghosh, '*Pakistan*?'

Ghosh said, 'Huh?'

Dong said to the Minister, 'He doesn't understand.'

The Minister said, 'Nobody understands that.' Then to Ghosh, 'Urgh. You! Where are you from? What are you doing here?'

'I've been arrested.'

'What country are you from?'

'England.'

'England! You don't look English.'

'Er, thank you.'

'He's an idiot. Get rid of him.'

'Kill?' said Dong Bing.

'Out of the room, egg fucker!'

'Why did he say 'sixty-two'?'

'Fuck twenty-six. We're in the middle of the biggest religious crisis in the last ten years and we're pissing about with some random foreigner. Take him out. Put him in another room. Lock it.'

'The year one thousand nine hundred and sixty-two,' said Ghosh, 'when seven thousand cadres gathered in Beijing and forced the Great Helmsman, Chairman Mao Zedong - '

'He's drunk,' said Dong.

'You don't know the Conference of the Seven Thousand?' said Ghosh, as he was being dragged away by the fierce-looking man with the shaven head.

'Never heard of it,' said Dong.

'Important! Map information,' said Ghosh. 'Hishtoree'.

'Foreigners never understand Chinese history,' said Dong. 'It's too complicated.'

'Dead right,' said the Minister.

Dong said to shaven head, 'Put him in an empty room for now.'

'Numbers! Sixty-two!' said Ghosh.

The fierce shaven headed man grabbed and dragged Ghosh more roughly than necessary out of the office, along long corridors, up many stairs, and shoved him into empty Room 62 in the Communist Party wing of the Ministry of Religious Affairs building.

Back in the Minister's office, the Communist Party Secretary appeared unannounced, like a ghost. He looked paler than ever. Everyone went quiet.

The Minister said, 'We've got hundreds of dead bodies.'

'I know,' said the Party Secretary. 'One hundred and forty-seven believers.'

'One hundred and fifty Ministry officers' said the Minister.

'All dead in snow,' said the Party Secretary.

'How do you know?' said the Minister.

'I sent some people, too.'

'What - after the Ministry cars?'

'The Party has its own resources.'

'To see Vice Minister Dong Bing's footprints all over the place.'

'It wasn't too bad, apparently.'

'He's a neat investigator,' said the Minister.

Dong said, 'Thank you Minister.'

The Minister looked at Dong then said to the Party man, 'Find anything else?'

'No.'

'Oh,' said the Minister.

'I didn't. Vice Minister Dong did,' said the Party man.

'Urgh, yes.'

The Minister took the paper showing 'Chairman Mao's Positive and Negative Map of a Four-Sided Building' from an inside jacket pocket and passed it to the Party Secretary. The Party man lifted up his spectacles and looked at the paper, reading the words without understanding their meaning.

He said: 'This may be irrelevant. We need something quick - very quick. We need to find out what happened and do it fast. We've only got days. This is not like the old times. Computers, internet : they will get the word out. There's an uncontrollable openness, and somehow the news will break. I've had big people on the phone - very big. People who have never called me before. They reckon we have four days to postpone exposure and scandal. Four days before rumours will reach a critical mass. Four days of official silence. When that time is over, if we haven't found an answer, we are doomed. The State Council meets in six days. We are under intense pressure. Fail at this and our careers are over.'

CHAPTER 6
Day 1, 3:44 am

As far as the Ministry of Religious Affairs was concerned, the Shining Light of Truth was an especially vexing phenomenon. Three or four years previously, when the Shining Light of Truth began to attract the attention of the Ministry, it was assumed there was an organizational hierarchy and the Ministry arrested the people who appeared to be the leaders, that is, the ones posting the most messages on-line and talking most at meetings. Yet numbers of gatherings grew.

Once it was clear that arresting 'leaders' was unproductive, someone in the Ministry - no less than the Minister himself - had a Canada-inspired brainwave: 'Urgh. Ah-ha. Cell pattern. The classic cell pattern! Catch one and they'll lead you to the cell ringleaders.'

They didn't. Sometimes they lead to others, though it was always sideways, never up.

'It doesn't matter who you arrest,' said the Minister, 'Use a big net, throw out the dross, and squeeze the catch till the squeals take you to the top.'

It didn't work. Government action failed to stop the organized gatherings and the contagious spread of the SLT.

'It's a disease!' said the Minister. 'Don't know who's going to be the next.'

'Next what?' said Dong Bing.

'Next sick victim! We arrest large groups and still it spreads.'

'The practitioners are like bacteria', said Dong Bing, 'which may multiply until there is no food source and all die.'

'Cheerful.'

'In what way?'

'They die in the end.'

'Bacterial *spores* can remain after bacteria are dead and in the right conditions can come back to life hundreds, thousands, maybe millions of years later,' said Dong.

'Urgh. Don't know if that's cheerful or not.'

The government does not fear religion, it fears rivalry for loyalty and power. The believers in the Shining Light of Truth feel they have little to lose by rivalry to the state, having already lost so much in their own nation. They are young, old, poor and rich, and come from the north, south, east, west, cities and countryside and are linked by the internet, the alternative state. The people and their pains are many and what they get from belief in the Shining Light of Truth is, first, what they need - solace, and, second, what they want - respect: respect from co-believers and respect for themselves.

Believers says there are elements of truth in many faiths, and that they coalesce in the Shining Light of Truth. And the truth can be passed on: *Hold hands and make connections* is saying number five of the seven key sayings.

Believers say the truths belong to everybody and everybody can know them. It only requires listening with your heart. Being still. Avoiding the distractions of moving images, of pixels, radio waves and of artificial pulses and beats. *In emptiness flows truth* (saying No.2). It's not that the Shining Light of Truth has taken truths from other religions, it has found them independently, by listening, as others have listened before. These are the Seven Sayings of the Shining Light of Truth (as of today):

> Truth is shining bright
> In emptiness flows truth
> Truth is simple
> In dark and silence hear truth
> Hold hands and make connections
> In truth we live forever
> Wait as one and our luck will come

No one person created the Sayings as a complete set. The Sayings were each just things said, once, in emailing or messaging or chatting: *memes* that spread. Later they were said again in the same words, more or less, and repeated, then lost to deletions and government shut-downs; next, recreated, passed on, changing, and evolving like a language, until, one by one, they reached their present state, easy and ready to change again.

The truth is so simple that it seems trite and untrustworthy. You need to be weak, humbled and ashamed, and a little bit stupid to see it. Other kinds of people, the brave, proud, confident, clever people, can convince themselves of anything - and there are plenty of those kinds of people in China, too.

CHAPTER 7
Day 1, 3:45 am

Ghosh was manhandled out of the office of the Minister of Religious Affairs and dragged by the fierce shaven-headed man to a concrete-floored room. He was pushed in and the door was locked. The room was dark and Ghosh was alone. Tired, he sat down. He touched the fine grit on the floor. 'There's something so very Chinese about this floor grit,' he thought to himself, mistakenly. The floor was cold so he got up and looked for somewhere to rest. It was dark and he couldn't see any light switches. Faint greyness came in through the windows from outside, where snow was falling. His eyes adjusted to the interior. He saw a huge floor-to-ceiling built-in wardrobe. In it he found blankets, thin folded mattresses and pillows, all neatly piled to head height. He took some items from the top of the pile and searched the room. There was no furniture. There was another darkened wardrobe adjacent to the first, this one empty. He put a mattress and blankets on the floor of this empty wardrobe, making a bed in there. He lay down. Then, by putting his fingers in the space between the gritty floor and the bottom of the wardrobe door, and by dragging slowly, he drew the door almost to a close. In the wardrobe there were two lines of grey light, a horizontal one between door and floor, and a vertical one between door and wall. The lines made an 'L' shape that showed part of the room beyond. There was nothing to see. Ghosh fell asleep.

Minutes later he woke up to the sound of grit. He saw part of a shoe in the horizontal grey line. It went; another came; the sound was painful in his head. He heard the other wardrobe door being opened - things being pulled out. He heard a metal sound. He shuffled his shoulders a fraction higher to get a look along the vertical grey line of light. He saw part of a man bending over and unfolding a camp bed that had a metal frame and a canvas covering. And a second bed. The man seemed big and moved somewhat stiffly, as if middle aged. He was in deep shade and his features couldn't be seen. Large, square hands with square fingers laid sheets and blankets on the beds accurately, and tucked and folded them neatly, ready for use. Two of the man's fingers were taped with white bandage. The man coughed and stood up, trying to muffle the cough. He coughed again, this time almost completely stifling the sound. The stifled coughing continued, quietly, seeming to go deeper in the man's chest. Ghosh still hadn't seen his face and could now only see shins and knees in old, clean jeans. In Chinese, Ghosh knew, jeans are *niúzǎikù*, meaning *cowboy trousers*. The man panted and Ghosh had the impression of a large chest frame in lightweight metal, like the fold-up beds, and the lungs of the man like dusty canvas, wheezing when breath blew through them. After a minute of the suppressed wheezing, the man folded his body down to the level of one of the beds and his hands pulled back tidily prepared blankets and he got in bed. As he did, his face passed for a moment though the vertical grey line of light and was revealed. Ghosh was shocked by what he saw. It wasn't just that it was a white Western man's face - though that was surprising enough - it was the age of the face. It was a face like a rock - rocky jaw, chin, and nose, and flat rock forehead, like Tarzan in, say, a 1948 Tarzan movie, and 1948 was about right because in that year this man would have been a young man and now he was a so much older man, essentially the same man, though a tired man, and, at this moment, from the steady breathing sound of it, a sleeping man. Ghosh slept, too.

CHAPTER 8

Day 1, 4:20 am

The pressure on the Ministry of Religious Affairs, in particular on its highest leaders, the Minister himself and the Party Secretary, was increasing with each piece of information about the Shining Light of Truth and the security personnel in the snowy field.

'No bullet wounds?'

'That's correct, Party Secretary,' answered Vice-Minister Dong Bing.

Information from the field was bad. Extremely bad. It was Vice-Minister Dong Bing who had first brought it, by mobile phone, to the Minister. Dong had called from his Audi 6, parked beside the field where Captain Ma had lead his one hundred and fifty men, as well as Officer Liu and Mr Zhang, to arrest the hand-holding Shining Light of Truth believers. All of them were dead.

The Party man asked the Minister, 'Why did you send one hundred and fifty men?'

'Those cultists are baby rabbits. Never resist arrest. In four years they've never hurt anybody, not even squashed mosquitoes. Hundred and fifty is plenty. One each. Send more and you cause a noise.'

'Caused a big noise now.'

'My ears are bleeding. How could I know? How could anybody - '

'This isn't a debate. It's time for work. First: secure the site.'

'Move the bodies?' said the Minister.

'No. The snow that's falling now will keep them fresh. For a day or two. We could learn something for a detailed daytime investigation. Second: no news is to get out.'

'Easy to say.'

The Party man looked at the Minister, who said, 'Urgh. I'm just talking, I'm not arguing. I'll do it. You know me.'

'Third,' said the Party man, 'get investigators. The best - medical and police.'

'Shanghai?'

'Yes.'

'Won't that spread news?'

'It's our job to make sure it doesn't. And that's why we need the fourth tactic. The fourth thing we have to do is find a cover - a disguise investigation to hide the reason for all this unusual activity.'

'Urgh. Just might be able to cook up something.'

'I never doubted it.'

Dong said, 'Minister, should we arrest all the misbelievers?'

'Urgh? What? The dead ones?'

'No,' said the Party man.

Dong said, 'I don't mean - '

'Yes, we know,' said the Party man. 'It's an obvious thought. However, the more productive behaviour is to observe. And that is our fifth task: observation.'

'Observe?' said the Minister.

'Based on the current monitoring evidence, no other cult members know what has happened. The people in the field did not communicate with anyone.'

'Urgh. Our little secret.'

'It's also our big advantage,' said the Party Secretary.

'Won't last,' said the Minister.

'I have already asked you to keep matters quiet.'

'Urgh.'

'And as other cultists do not know what happened, there is no point alerting to them the fact by making mass arrests nationwide. We should observe them. Monitor their chatting and gathering. Hear what they know; see when they get the news. Don't let's tell them anything ourselves,' said the Party Secretary.

'I see,' said Dong. 'That's clever.'

'Results will show whether or not it's clever. Let's begin.'

Officials started moving around the large office, finding contact details, telephoning and emailing, copying messages, making notes and comparing them with other notes. There were spirals of activity around the Party man and the

Minister, who themselves each spun purposefully, occasionally coming into each other's orbit, communicating, and then spinning off, each individually, to other tasks. They worked this way through the early hours of the morning.

Vice-Minister Dong said, 'Wait! What if the incident in the field was planned from outside?'

'No,' said the Minister. 'No use blathering about what might be and might not be. Work - that's what we need to do. And work starts with fuel. Eat. Let's eat. Breakfast. Eat. Eat.' He made big gestures towards the door as if directing chickens.

Nobody moved and Vice-Minister Dong Bing stared at the Minister, who said, 'What you looking at?'

'Nothing.'

The Minister did not like being thought of as 'nothing'. At the moment what could he do about it? Nothing.

The Party Secretary glanced at both, looked at his watch and said, 'Enough for now. It'll soon be six o'clock. The first stage is over. A meal now is correct.' He walked towards the door and they all went to breakfast.

CHAPTER 9
Day 1, 5:57 am

Ghosh was woken once more by the painful sound of shoes on grit. Though the footfalls were lighter than those previously they were more painful because of the development of Ghosh's hangover. The grey light seemed harsher. He saw a black, polished, man's shoe, and another, then none. He heard the creak of a bed as the new person sat down. He heard shoes being taken off and more bed creaking - presumably the new man lying down.

A voice said in English, as softly as blowing smoke rings, 'Bill.'

There was no answer. The first man coughed, in his sleep.

The new man breathed softly, '*Bill*'.

Into Ghosh's vertical grey line of light came for a moment a hand, and a wrist. The hand was small and delicate yet strong, Ghosh thought. He could see the cuff of a white shirt and of a greyish sweater. The wrist moved slightly and continued to move in a simple, regular pattern. The word 'Bill' was breathed upon the air of the fading night. Ghosh couldn't see, but he knew that the hand attached to the wrist was gently and carefully stroking that rock face, the face that belonged to sleeping Bill.

Gritty dust tickled Ghosh's hangover-sensitive nose: 'Aaaa*SHOO*!!!'

The door of the wardrobe was flung open. A man stood over Ghosh, silhouetted in the grey light coming from behind. The man looked down at him steadily for a long time.

The man said, to both of them, 'I haven't seen you. You haven't seen me.' The first man on the bed was still sleeping.

The second man, lowering his eyes slightly in reference to the sleeping *Bill*, said, 'You haven't seen anyone.'

CHAPTER 10
Day 1, 6:20 am

Vice Minister of Religious Affairs, Dong Bing, was one of four vice ministers, the other three being variously: one - entirely incompetent and generally absent; two - currently studying an MBA at MIT, Boston, Massachusetts; and three - present and completely manipulated by Dong Bing, a man who did not like to waste time. In spare moments - which were few because Dong was hardworking himself into a glorious future career - he had recently begun to compile a list.

'The list has three purposes,' Dong spoke to himself, silently, in preparation for a possible future public explanation.

'First, it is an activity to engage and exercise my mind when it is otherwise less than fully occupied, thus increasing my mind's strength and stamina. Second, it will feed and develop a sense of pride in our people, history and nation, thus bolstering my patriotism and, if broadcast publicly, that of all my compatriots. Third, the list will educate and improve others' level of culture, thus enhancing the quality of civilization in our nation.'

Dong Bing wrote:

'A List of Chinese Inventions

1. Walled cities
2. Writing
3. Paper
4. Printing
5. Gunpowder
6. Compass
7. Stirrups'.

Dong stopped writing at seven and went back to work.

CHAPTER 11
Day 1, 8 am

The Ministry of Religious Affairs had five thousand staff in its Beijing headquarters and most of them were ordered into a huge auditorium to hear the Minister's speech about fireworks, terrorism, patriotism and justice. Following the speech, Ministry and Party leaders reconvened at 8 am in the Party Secretary's office. When making tactical decisions, the Minister's key debates were with the Ministry-level Party leader, the Party Secretary, who answered to his own superiors in the Communist Party stratosphere, who have their own priorities - enforcing policies and keeping power. On the way to the office, ahead of everybody else, side-by-side, the Minister and the Party Secretary whispered to each other. The Party man said:

'Some people might say having a criminal incident in the Ministry compound this morning was convenient.'

'So we can hide something more important, uh?'

'Using the fireworks investigation to distract attention from the other was certainly flexible thinking on your part.'

'That was my plan.'

'Really? From when?'

'Urgh. In the talk just now. A case of doing a small bad thing to get a big good thing. It's like they used to say in the old days: without the Japanese invasion, the Party would never have taken over China.'

'Don't let Dong Bing hear you say that.'

'Different generation. Born twenty-five years after the war and hate Japan more than those who fought.'

'Careful,' said the Party Secretary. He raised his voice to normal level, 'Concerning soldiers - '

'Yes, of course' said the Minister, as they slowed down to enter the office, with Dong Bing close behind them.

'Beijing Municipal Government reserves.'

'I will call them,' said the Party Secretary.

They entered the office and began contacting Beijing city administrators, arranging armed guards for the snowy field, and began the difficult task of contacting Party and government colleagues and superiors outside the Ministry, informing them and asking for advice. As much as possible, they wanted to prevent any higher authority hearing the news from a secondary source, such as a rival ministry. They were not always successful. It was a difficult morning.

Marcas Ghosh was removed from Room 62 and, briefly, brought into the Party Secretary's office. He saw officials crowded around low glass-topped tables, busy with phones and laptops, and he saw some men he already had seen in the early hours of the morning. Many of them had been smoking cigarettes constantly since that time and the smell of the smoke permeated the room on three levels, like the three levels of distance in a traditional Chinese landscape painting. In the foreground was the fresh smoke; in the middle distance was stale smoke; and in the far distance was the equally powerful permanent stink, deep in the grain of the furniture and securely attached to the minute fibres of fabrics, wall coverings, bindings and papers. In traditional landscapes, the far distance leads to infinity. There was such a painting on a wall: a tall black ink scroll depicting the essence of *Huang Shan*, the most famous holy mountain in China. It was after all the Ministry of Religious Affairs. Nobody was paying attention to the painting.

Among the men that Ghosh recognized from his interview earlier in the morning was the leader of the Audi group, Dong Bing, and his boss, the Minister, standing by the main desk. Next to the Minister, in the big chair, behind the desk, king in his own throne room, Ghosh saw another man, the Party Secretary. Ghosh looked at this man's smooth, pale face decorated with neat features - a thin nose, thin lips with soft curves, thin eyebrows arching over clear narrow eyes, an unlined forehead, and flat black silky hair parted exactly at the point of the head called *seven tenths*, stiff and careful hair, and at the crown a circular bald patch like a little halo. The man's hands were clean and delicate enough to be *Guanyin*, the goddess of mercy. The nails were white at the ends, the cuticles clean and rounded and there was no dirt or blemish. Ghosh recognized the hands. This was the man who had said, 'I haven't seen you.' He was staring hard at Ghosh. Ghosh noticed and immediately averted his eyes.

'Who's this?' that man said.

Dong Bing read: 'Foreigner. UK passport. UK birth. Aged 27. Third entry to our country. Visa type Z. Valid. Work unit: Red Cross (International Section) Development Office. One-year intern contract. Eleven months completed. No criminal history. No medical history. Arrested 3:01 am, today, District 4, Hei Wan Lu.'

'Why?'

'He's a suspect.'

'You arrested him.'

'Yes, Ministerial Branch Party Secretary.'

'Was he drunk?'

'Probably.'

'Get rid of him.'

'Get rid?'

'Deport him. Get him on a plane. Now. Do it yourself. Quick.'

Ghosh was taken out and Dong Bing went with him.

The Party man said quietly to the Minister, 'I disapprove of time wasting and I disapprove of arresting random foreigners.'

'Yeah. Yeah.'

'Thoughtless; in a panic.'

'Yeah. Yeah.'

'Arrests a foreigner based on a resemblance to a villain in a schoolboy's computer game.'

'Don't loose your temper. You know he's a cow arse.'

'Dong Bing? He's your problem,' said the Party Secretary.

'Tell me about it. He makes my stomach ache and farts stink,' said the Minister.

'He'll eat you.'

'Not yet.'

'He's close to everything.'

'Too close. If he hadn't been in the field with his car I could've lost him on the fireworks investigation.'

'You're wrong. And that wouldn't help you anyway.'

'Fuck him - we are busy going nowhere. We had no warning those idiots were meeting in a field. We have no idea why they were meeting, no idea why they are dead - '

'How they are dead - '

'Why they killed our security personnel - '

'If they killed them - then how.'

'Too much we don't know,' said the Party Secretary. 'And it's all too unorthodox.'

'Nobody can tell us. We are crippled by the need to be top secret. We can't just talk to anybody.'

'We need something unorthodox.'

'Somebody unorthodox.'

'You mean - '

'I don't mean anything. But any puzzle - he'll solve it.'

'Nelson?'

'Nelson? The idiot genius? It's your call,' said the Minister.

Dong Bing came back in the room and sat by the desk to catch the quiet talk.

'A special time and a special person,' said the Party Secretary.

Dong said, 'Special? You're considering calling someone special.'

The Minister looked at Dong.

Dong stood up shouting 'Stand up! Everyone out!'

All Ministry staff seated at the low glass tables stood up; those already standing, talking or mid-errand, stood to attention. The Minister looked at the Party Secretary, who twitched an eyebrow and Party staff stood up. Dong marched out of the room followed by all except the Minister and the Party Secretary. Dong came back in.

'Everyone out?' said the Minister.

'Yes, Minister.'

'Why?'

'That 'special person' . . .'

'What?'

'May not be suitable.'

'Certainly isn't.'

'For all except senior leaders.'

'Indeed,' said the Party Secretary, 'So leave us, Vice Minister Dong.'

Dong looked sharply at the Minister, who looked away. Dong left.

'He thinks we're calling the President,' said the Minister.

'Luckily for us,' said the Party Secretary. The Party man got up, walked to a window and made a gap in the blinds. Looking out and down to the large concrete courtyard below he said, 'Do you know who that is?'

The Minister came over. Looked down. Saw a tall old white foreigner in shorts and T shirt, his knees strapped with bandages, walking stiffly across the concrete, bouncing a basketball slowly and steadily as he walked, the ball sounding like a charmless gong in the courtyard. The man reached a spot where a rusty hoop was fixed to the wall. He bounced the ball and threw it. Basket. The ball bounced back to him. He threw again. Basket. And the next. Young kitchen staff with floppy chef's hats ambled out of a doorway. A basketball game started, apparently without words. The old foreigner was fast. The chefs were faster. The foreigner was more accurate.

The Minister said, 'Urgh. Him. Yeah, right. I know. Ministry hired him to teach English to service staff. Local wage. For English teaching. He's Christian. Never converted anyone. Gets them to play basketball. Older than me. Moves OK.'

'Hmm,' said the Party man, turning away from the window, 'As long as you know.' The man in the courtyard was Bill, his own Bill.

The Minister picked up a phone on the desk and put it down again. From his pocket he took a cell phone and a small folded piece of paper and, looking at the paper, he dialled a number, slowly. It was soon answered by a voice saying, 'So how did you get this number?'

The Minister said, 'Nelson. This is Wang Min, Religious Affairs.'

'Who gave you this number?' said Nelson.

'It's something serious. Someone we both know.'

'The whole of China is a leaky sieve. Much quieter here in Japan.'

'Come back to your own country.'

'My own people never wanted me, did they - uncle?'

'Don't call me uncle - not true I swear. And why Japanese - of all our enemies?'

'They never attack *me*. And so many good things.'

'Anything good they have is stolen from us. And China is developing. Economy, civilization, culture. We'll be number one.'

'Developing? Culture, you say? When the girls in the streets of Beijing are as cute as the girls in the streets of Tokyo, then I'll believe you.'

'Fuck girls on the streets!'

'Stop!' said the Party man. 'Stop this nonsense.'

'Is that the Party shouting in the background?'

'It is.'

Nelson said, 'Giving leadership. You should listen. What's this call about? Insider information on your speculator property portfolio?'

'No! Shut up about that. This is Shining Light of Truth. Mass deaths.'

'Suicide?'

'Maybe. Maybe on their side. Also a hundred and fifty dead on our own side.'

'*Our*?'

'Ministry.'

'How many soldiers does the Ministry of Religious Affairs have?'

'None. Four hundred security personnel.'

'With machine guns.'

'Of course.'

'And armoured vehicles.'

'I could only get nine.'

'Ah. Poor you. And so four hundred became two hundred and fifty. What do you want me to do?'

'How did they die? Why did they die? And - '

'Mmm?'

'Who knows about it?'

'Knowledge a dangerous thing. And what's it worth to me, this request?'

'The gratitude of your people. *Serious* gratitude.'

'Ah, *money*. Money is everywhere. I'm a busy person. Why should I do this?'

'Urgh. I'm going to send you a photo. The leader of the cult group. The dead leader. Just you wait.'

The Minister manipulated his phone and said, 'And, yes, I know I'm a bastard.'

Nelson looked at his phone, in his luxurious apartment, with the Tokyo winter sunshine sparkling through the window from the unblemished blue sky of Japanese exile.

The photo arrived.

Nelson said, 'Ah.' There was a pause.

He said, 'Call me back in an hour with all the details. Not you - a scientific person.' The phone was turned off.

'What happened?' said the Party Secretary.

The Minister said, 'We got him interested. That cult woman. Dead one. It's his mother.'

CHAPTER 12

Day 1, 8:08 am

On February 4th the Ministry of Religious Affairs authorized a feature article to appear in national dailies on the topic of new cults with particular reference to the Shining Light of Truth. An English-language version was published simultaneously on-line by *Global Times.*

China>>Society>>Update

Cult Scams Exposed

Xinhua/ Global Times
[08:08 February 4]

China's government has been taking strong measures recently to protect society from the menace of both home-grown and foreign-seeded cults.

'There have been many hard won and notable successes against these uncompromising dogmatists', noted Li He, Director of the non-governmental Beijing Anti-Cult Association (BACA).

In 1999, China identified and uprooted the cult known as *Falun Gong*, seven years after it was formed. At the time, it had around 2 million followers and had resulted in the deaths of about 1,700 people, official numbers show.

Such cults promise good health or security to its members to lure them in, and then gradually begin to exert mind control over them through brainwashing or threats while the leaders accumulate great wealth in the process, explained Yu Jianping, deputy secretary general of the China Anti-Cult Association that was founded back in 2000.

'Cults usually cause physical or psychological harm to the followers, and oblige them to engage in immoral sexual conduct or in extreme cases commit mass suicide,' said cult expert Yu.

'There is no doubt that these cults are not religions, but rather use the name of religion to control people from afar and achieve other purposes, often detrimental to the nation as a whole,' Yu added.

CHAPTER 13
Day 1, 10 am

Ghosh's father was Indian and his mother French. His father was an English-educated Francophile Hindu of a Kayastha family from Bombay. From his father came his family name, *Ghosh*, pronouncing it *gauche*, or like *ghost*, with *sh* for *t*, though other people usually said *gosh*. His father had frequently annoyed his son by claiming the early nineteenth century French novelist Balzac said it all, about everything, everywhere, especially modern Chinese history. It was his mother from Tours who was the successful one in contemporary economic terms. She owned the Portsmouth family house where Ghosh grew up. His parents split - his Dad's idea and his regret because he was the one who suffered most. The big house was rented out and brought a decent income to his mother, living in a top-floor studio, with Ghosh rent-free, whenever he wanted, in a ground-floor flat.

As a boy Ghosh played football and rode around Portsmouth on his bicycle. He liked school because there were more people to play with and more games to play. He was well-behaved and did his assignments whether he understood them or not, and was respectful to teachers though not friendly because he never thought school teachers could be friends. He also liked school because of the simplicity of tasks and lack of discussion: do this; don't do that. It was better than home where his isolated parents argued between themselves or with the world, which never listened. At fourteen he joined St John Ambulance as a cadet, ignoring its abstract code about serving God and being loyal to the Queen, instead being impressed by its uniform and motto *to be thorough in work and play*. He also played badminton, later squash, and did his school work with enough attention to qualify for an International Relations course at a university in London. At university he made two changes: he took up indiaca and began learning Chinese.

At university he was sociable but didn't make strong friendships. He lodged in Peckham with second cousins who called him *swotty country boy*. He took to reading in the evening, and as he was learning Chinese, he read the history of China. It became a habit.

The language was an option on his course and he kept going without deciding whether he liked it or not while enjoying the difficulty and difference. By doing so for two years he came to qualify for a year's study in China. It suited him. He felt like he had done at primary school - the place gave him a place and a purpose.

China offered a nourishing rigour that his life had lacked. He found an appeal in studying the austere and difficult text of the written language, in recognizing the rigid structure of family and social links, and in learning details of the state with its two-part government framework reaching everybody, everywhere.

And there was a comfort based on his looks. Like others with faces different from most Chinese, he was given a public identity as a foreigner based on his appearance, and that was a kind of equality. Ghosh in China was *lǎowài*, Mr Foreigner, the same as the other British, and the same as the French, the Indians, Americans, Germans, Australians, Brazilians, Russians, Mexicans and many others.

In Portsmouth he'd always got stick for his looks though he was born there and spent most of his life there. He'd never been to India and his dad hardly ever talked about it. He'd been to France to visit his mother's relatives and he certainly wasn't French.

During his year as a foreign student Ghosh became committed to language, to the country and to the belief that he had a place in it. He came back to England to find his University had closed the Chinese language option. It was too late. He was already spoke well enough to explain indiaca as *déguó yòng shǒu yǔmáoqiú, méiyǒu qiúpāi*, (*German badminton using hands, without raquets*), and he had read enough history to compare indiaca to *jiànzi*, a traditional Chinese shuttle-kicking game.

As soon as he graduated he tried to find work in China. He had been a serious student, made employment-skill-enhancing use of holidays and was still a member of St John Ambulance. He got an internship in Beijing for a year. When it was finished he went back to Portsmouth and worked six-days a week at a DIY chain store, paying off debts. The week the store offered him a supervisor position he found another internship in Beijing. When that finished he landed the International Red Cross internship through the connection of a friend of the father of a former fellow St John Ambulance cadet. Ghosh again promised himself *to be thorough in work and play.* He returned to his history reading habit, focussing on China's twentieth century adventure, his eyes tracing different paths across the same stories, seeing and remembering more. The discipline brought knowledge and the knowledge gave him confidence.

Yet he was still no more than an intern, a decorative, dispensable dogsbody, four years after graduating, in a career going sideways. He was a reader of reports, a translator and summarizer of blogs, a scholar as much as a participant, an absorber of data, and a figure that was static not radical. That's how he felt.

After quiet, desk-bound, computer-facing days, his work included evenings of official entertainment duties. This meant eating, drinking and, more importantly, talking and networking in huge restaurant rooms or halls hired for the purpose. The previous evening, he had sat to the left of two middle-aged female colleagues who were his workplace superiors and thus eligible to use Ghosh as a topic when there was a conversational lull. To his own left was the vice-director of a property development company, nominally responsible for the company's support of non-governmental organizations, hence allocated a seat next to International Red Cross employees. As on previous occasions, fellow diners seated around his designated round table referred to him as 'he can speak Chinese relatively well,' and otherwise made some remarks about his skin colour, face, hair and slightly surprising lack of smell, and mainly ignored him.

There were regular cries of *gānbēi* and Ghosh was obliged to drain his always-full glass of beer, again and again. Ghosh wasn't a person who could hold his drink. He knew he had no ability to go beyond two glasses of anything. But, as so often, he couldn't calculate how much he had drunk. It was always the same glass; always full.

Feeling isolated and intoxicated, he began to dwell on his perception that his work colleagues were disturbed by his ability to speak standard Chinese and disqualified him from all serious talk of Chinese society because of his non-Chinese nationality and birth.

In his mind, Ghosh piled up the reports and history books he had read and felt disgruntled. There was another *gānbēi!* Ghosh's Vice-Director neighbour noticed his sulky sip and started conversation, in English.

'You foreigners always want to find bad things to say about China.' It was that stage in the evening when people felt the need to be frank to those less important than themselves.

'Tell me the bad things about China,' the woman said.

Ghosh breathed out for at least ten seconds: 'Haaaaaaaaaaaaaaaaaaaaaaaaaaaaa.' He said, 'There are bad things everywhere in the world.'

Vice-Director Shen took this as a graceful retreat in the face of attack and retreated somewhat herself: 'Living here, you must be homesick for your family and food.'

'Nmm,' said Ghosh. 'Not really. My family are fine without me; the food is good here.'

'What things are not good?'

'Most things are good.'

'What things are not good?'

Alcoholic depression of his usual control allowed Ghosh to say: 'I don't like people shouting at me when they see me. *Hailou! Hailou!* From motorbikes or buses or just walking by in a group. It's not a greeting, it's just shouting. *Hailou!*

Hailou! They can't even speak English. Except *hailou! Hailou!*'

The Vice-Director of Seven Star Property Development Conglomerate looked suitably offended. 'These are not native Beijingers. They are not educated people. They are people without culture from outside. Beijing is a very cosmopolitan city, you can see foreigners everywhere. There are thousands.'

'Yes, thousands', said Ghosh, and didn't say, *in a city of ten million*.

The Vice-Director of Seven Star Property said, 'Chinese people love foreigners and are always very friendly to them and treat them well, especially Westerners. A Western man in this world dominated by Western men has nothing to complain about. Even you if you just have a British passport. Chinese young girls love foreign men. You must have many girlfriends.'

He knew some Western men who collected Chinese girlfriends like disposable accessories they treated shabbily, or at least they boasted of doing so. Ghosh had no girlfriends.

There was another call to *gānbēi* from someone at the table who sensed disharmony started by the foreigner. Ghosh was pressed to drink and not otherwise spoken to from then on. The frustrated conversation, and his general frustration lead to him drinking more and to drunkenness. He left late, almost last, entirely alone and on a whim went to a loud and shouty 'pub'. It was a mistake. He sat on a high stool alone for an hour in the dark and flashing lights with one drink he didn't touch until he woke up from a five-minute sleep, downed the beer, and left the bar.

He got in a taxi.

He said, 'I want to walk!' He got out of the taxi. He started walking in the dark. He talked to himself. He was noticed and he was arrested at around two thirty in the morning and his evening was ended.

In his life now, five security personnel from the Ministry of Religious Affairs were accompanying him to his suburban apartment. They opened the metal gate covering the front door and the three locks on the door itself, and entered immediately into the low-ceilinged living room where the way forward was obstructed by bulky, cheaply made furniture including a large leather-look black vinyl sofa and armchair. The sofa and its sidekick armchair were made of cuts of medium-density fibreboard nail-gunned together, with fabric tacked on top, and were hollow inside. Both were cold to the touch in winter. History books were stacked in columns on the floor. On the sofa were the things he had thrown there the previous morning. He had gone to work, stayed all day and in the evening went directly to his entertainment duties.

The security personnel called him 'the drunken foreigner'. They got his passport, and a carrier bag of belongings, and headed to Beijing Capital Airport. Ghosh was taken through private doors and corridors to a First Class seat on flight CA374 to Heathrow. Although his drunkenness was long gone, his lack of sleep and hangover and the unprecedented strangeness of the events leading up to and including the present moment greatly lessened his awareness of the seriousness of his situation.

The plane drew smoothly toward a thick white sky and Ghosh's tired mind began to drift towards sleep, to thoughts of his old home. In his old home was his mother, a calm and lonely drifter who stopped drifting geographically because she was too clever not to know that anywhere is as good as anywhere else and that drifting is just another way of avoiding that fact. And so as a young woman, his mother had drifted for a short while then stopped and never moved again. The drifting happened one summer when she and her friend, both aged seventeen, aimlessly hitchhiked around west France from their hometown of Tours and ended up in Cherbourg sitting on the old harbour walls and saw a ship going to England.

Her friend said, 'Let's go there,' and Ghosh's mother said 'Yeah,' and went on the next ferry but her friend didn't. As the big boat sailed away her friend waved goodbye from the shore thinking there are things more important than spontaneous verbal suggestions and Ghosh's mother on the ferry deck was waving back thinking one idea was as good as any other.

CHAPTER 14
Day 1, 11:15 am

'Nelson - who is he exactly?' asked the Party Secretary. He and the Minister of Religious Affairs were alone.

The Minister said, 'It's complicated. Related to his mother.'

'The dead cultist?'

'Yeah. Reason to call him. Personal interest.'

'Who is she?'

'A beauty. A brain. A Party member.'

'And the boy? Nelson?'

'Protected. No one knows who the real father is. Could be anyone - the highest. Spoiled. Ruined. Grew up fast and bad. You know there was all kind of trouble when he was a kid - motorcycles, delinquency. And aeroplanes.'

'Aeroplanes?'

'He's not like other people. When you see him he looks like a freak. When you talk to him you think he's an idiot. But what he does - he's something else.'

'What do you mean *freak*?'

'Skinny with a big head. Hair. Weird hair. Like a girl.'

'Like a girl?' said the Party Secretary.

'Shiny. Soft. Wierd cut. He made millions on the Shanghai stock market. Underage. As a teenager. More or less legally.'

'How?' asked the Party Secretary.

'Numbers. Predicting big numbers. He's a predictor.'

'A genius?'

'Sure, yes. But unreliable, unsound. More like a bastard monster.'

'How are you acquainted?' said the Party Secretary.

'Keep dangerous things close where you can see them - that's what I say.'

Dong Bing entered the room. He was the scientifically minded person the Minister had found to telephone Nelson. An hour had already passed since the first call.

The Minister said, 'Let's talk to the genius monster.'

Dong held the cell phone and the Minister and the Party Secretary stayed listening in the same room.

Nelson's voice answered the call, 'Who are you?'

'Dong Bing, Vice Minister of Religious Affairs.'

'Are you scientific?'

'I hope so.'

'You said it, dear Dong.'

Dong, now slightly humiliated, felt the situation was beyond his control and the crisis was beyond his experience. He was at a depth and in a place he could not manage and it was a strange desperate place. The only positive aspect was the knowledge that the Minister and the Party Secretary were also beyond their depth, desperate and unable to manage. In this he had equality. He now also had ambition and energy. The momentum was his. Eager to talk of scientific details, he began the story of the field.

Dong Bing described how he led two Ministry Audis to the snowy field northeast of suburban Beijing. And how they drove to the scene at optimum speed. He said that when he arrived the main impression was of snow and silence. A mass sleep. The sky was black and the ground was white and the bodies seemed black like bits of the sky fallen down, though Dong didn't say that. As Audi headlamps went slowly across the field and his eyes followed, going from one motionless body to another, the people seemed less like sleepers and more like corpses. The headlamps cut two routes through the darkness, gradually weakening and widening. Dong and the other officials got out of the cars and started to walk in the light. They crunched on the snow, which had fallen before the bodies had. It was cold. About minus 12ºC. Nobody spoke. They reached a barbed wire fence. They stopped. Officer Pan Yipeng cut the fence in several places, and they all walked into the field. Officers Yang and Xiu held torches. The first bodies they came to and inspected were all security officers. Officer Wu checked the first ten for a pulse, and after that did not bother. Footprints in the snow suggested the deceased security officers had all crossed the fence at a point twenty metres to the right (or east) of the investigating team and they had not cut the fence, probably, said Dong, on the principle of not damaging private property whilst on state business.

('Don't you worry,' said the Minister, in the background of the phone dialogue, 'They'll all get a medal.')

Dong said that, roughly speaking, the deceased security officers had made a half circle around the misguided believers. The misbelievers were in a circle at approximately the centre of the field. They were distinguishable from the security officers because they were not wearing uniforms.

'Were they dancing?' said Nelson.

'No. Well. Yes, it's strange you should say that.'

'Not strange at all.'

'The misbelievers were all holding hands - it's part of their perverted ritual - and of course the security personnel weren't - and they were all on the ground, fallen dead - but many had their knees raised and elbows bent.'

'Dancing, then.'

'That's not an appropriate description of our brave defenders!'

'Science is never appropriate. The religious ones - were they carrying anything?'

'No.'

'Any ID?'

'Yes, their identity cards.'

'Known to the government?'

'No. Except the leader. We know her.'

'Me, too. The others?'

'We don't know them.'

'Describe them.'

'They were all ages: young ones, middle-aged ones, old ones. I saw some about eighteen or nineteen; I saw some about seventy.'

'So, the adult population of China.'

'Men and women. Some were city people with smooth faces and white hands. Wearing city clothes and down coats.'

'No gloves?'

'Yes, gloves. I took them off to look at the hands. Some were from out of town - rougher faces, red hands. Wearing cheaper clothes and more of them.'

'The usual mix of believers.'

'*Misbelievers*. There were no marks on the bodies. No sign of fighting. No weapons had been fired, many weapons not even ready to fire, still in holsters or strapped to the back. No obvious sign of danger. Some of our men looked, how can I explain it - well - surprised. Not the misbelievers.'

'No bruises, no blood.'

'No.'

'Not angry or frightened looking?'

'No. To tell the truth, we were frightened. It could happen to us. If it happened to them. Though I know this is irrational and not necessarily scientific. And I thought about terrorism. The corpses in the snowy field - was that terrorism? Will it spread?'

'What did you do?'

'Made calls. Drove back here.'

('Ask him,' said the Party Secretary, 'about the paper.')

'The paper?' said Dong. 'Oh, the paper.'

'What paper?' said Nelson.

'Oh, some paper was found.'

'Anything on it?'

'Doesn't make sense.'

'That's what you think.'

(The Minister said, 'It's nonsense.')

(The Party Secretary said, 'We can send a photo of it.') They did.

Nelson looked at the photo of the paper and said, 'Interesting. Anybody any ideas?'

(Minister: 'Nothing.')

Dong: 'The foreigner said - '

('Shit. Talking shit. He was drunk,' said the Minister.)

'What foreigner?'

'Oh, when we drove back here. We picked up that drunk foreigner.'

'Why?'

'You know I said we were irrational - worried about terrorism. I made them stop the car. It was his face. His location. Ten minutes from the field. He was acting suspiciously. We - I mean me - as soon as I saw him I thought he looked like a terrorist.'

'What kind of terrorist?'

'Al-Qaeda. A separatist.'

'Xinjiang?'

'Too smart looking.'

'Terrorist expert are you?'

'No. But - '

'You let him go?'

'Brought him here.'

'Tortured him?'

'No. He was drunk and said something about twenty-six.'

'Twenty-six?'

'Or sixty-two. He was drunk. It didn't make sense.'

'If you had any idea at all about sense and nonsense, you wouldn't be bothering me. Now I'm getting annoyed. First, you didn't tell me about the paper you had. Second, you start making judgements about what makes sense and what doesn't. Your third mistake is looking for causes in coincidences. There are lots of people dead; the people are in a religion and so you say: the religion caused the death. You've got no evidence. You don't know what you've got. I'll tell you: you've got questions. And you're making up answers before you've made your questions clear. The basic questions are: How did they die? Was it deliberate? If it was, who did it and why did they do it? Can they do it again? Now, around that field where they all died - there must be somebody who saw something. Find that somebody. A farmer. Nearest farm. Can't sleep. Or he's up to no good in the middle of the night. And one more thing - that foreigner, he's right. And he knows something you don't. When you call back, have the foreigner ready to talk to me. That's the end of this call. I'm going to think.'

CHAPTER 15

Day 1, 11:39 am

Nelson and his mother, Li Honglan, were both fruits of the elite - fruits grown in nets. Honglan's life was protected and privileged because she had been loved by elite men. From age twenty-one to her death at sixty-six she saw power in its processes whether she wanted to look or not, and it revealed itself in what was done to her through and because of the desire of two men. These two men were rivals, comrades, co-lovers of the same woman, and therefore enemies. She married the first when she was twenty-one. She met the second when she was twenty-eight, seven years married, and never more beautiful. Now one of the men was dead and the survivor was a powerful man indeed, the Minister of Religious Affairs. The former - the departed, remembered man - was he who Nelson called father, though this man was dead before Nelson could form a conscious memory of him.

Wang, the future Minister of Religious Affairs, had noticed Hónglán, *Red Orchid*, because she was the wife of a more powerful and celebrated politician. It was when the future Minister first came to Beijing, young and provincial enough to be impressed by the woman who was the prize flower of the prize man, her husband.

The prize man was compared to a young Zhou Enlai, the incongruously gentleman-movie-actor-looking Prime Minister. His dark bushy eyebrows were full of liveliness and he was ardent in most things including romantic love, although the target of the ardour was, Honglan soon sensed, adjacent to herself. The prize man's eyes were the sweet brown colour that was the caramelized essence of future socialist visions, and they were intrinsically unable to focus correctly. His gaze fell, she felt, on a shadow or reflection: near her, resembling her without actually being her.

Maybe it was fate that caused him to be crippled in an accident in a remote mountainous area, and maybe it was the incorrect sight of his eyes that could not see this cloud on the horizon of time, looming dark and large like a typhoon from the south.

Those who saw the accident said his rushing truck left the narrow precipice road and carried on so straight that for a moment they thought - but did not later admit - that the blessed man's truck was truly able to fly and would keep going straight to whatever its final destination was supposed to be. In mid-air the truck stopped and dropped and when it was found later upside down among a lot of tall trees most of its cargo of important supplies of bottled medicines for poor mountain villages were broken and everyone inside, including the driver whose hands still clasped the steering wheel, seemed to be dead.

It was found he had been driving too fast and recklessly. The crash was the proof. More seriously, his power and glamour had frightened local Party officials and they reported that he was excessively leftist. The officials did not know that their judgement was made at exactly the time that political forces in Beijing were happy to hear it.

Back in the mountains, the treatment he received meant the previously prize man existed while his condition did not much improve. Politically, he was quickly tried, found guilty and sentenced to house arrest. He stayed in the same village and the same hut that was his 'hospital' because it was two years before he had the strength to leave the hut, and it was clear he couldn't get far. He was so useless, he wasn't even made to work, a rare occurrence in a mountain village.

Meanwhile, future Minister Wang, used all his efforts to place himself in the sight of Honglan, wife of the *more or less dead* man whose power had suddenly gone. It took time before she noticed the man behind the position and provincialism, and some time more before she admitted to herself that she had noticed him. Honglan could be weak, unreliable and unfocussed. When she did focus, she was obsessive. If life is a burning flame, hers seemed to burn more strongly than most, which phenomenon was attractive to moths like future Minister Wang.

At the end of 1984 the former prize man was allowed to come back to Beijing and to lie at home, where he died within twelve months, just after Nelson was born. In the contours of the caved chest of his corpse the shape of the truck steering wheel was still vaguely discernible.

Honglan, his wife, mourned truly and officially though she was long used to life without him. People said she had her son to think of, and as months and years went by she eventually she did think of him, noting that he was more correctly sighted than his father had been and that he saw her entirely, including her long period of distraction and slight neglect. He loved her, exactly her, though he could live without her. They were two people who could love each other without one ever relying on the other. Nelson was ardent about nobody and nothing except the excitement of speed.

He started with bicycles, first a child's, later an adult's, far too big for him, that he rode with his body slanted under the crossbar because he was still too small to reach the pedals if he sat above. At eight he moved to motor scooters. And later motorcycles. He rode an illegally imported Japanese bike that was faster than the official law officers' vehicles. He would taunt the police by riding past them and shouting. They chased him - unless they knew him - and they could never catch him, not even when they got their own illegal imports. And one night his motorbike's front wheel hit a hidden hole on a dark stretch of road. The chasing police picked the bloody fourteen-year-old and took him, slowly, to hospital. His mother visited him having used her connections and paid handsome financial apologies to the police. She told Nelson that his motorcycles were forever banned. He said nothing and waited because he knew her too well, her resolutions, her guilt and her indulgences. She was annoyed at his unsuitably confident foreknowledge, and at her weak self. She threw a bunch of keys on the hospital bed and left in a huff.

Nelson closed his eyes and felt the bunch in his hand to test if he could identify the brand of car from the shape of the keys. He could, and he was satisfied with the choice of Mercedes Benz as a substitute for the banned and damaged Kawasaki racing bike.

Through the years of Nelson's movement from bicycle to Benz, the future Minister, already married of course, pretended to court Honglan's younger sister, Hongmei, a prettier woman, lighter in personality. No one suspected, not even Hongmei, that the true object was Honglan. Hongmei was popular and sought after by several powerful men, and this pleased the future minister because it further obscured his real purpose, although not, of course, from Honglan. They were lovers.

As the years went by Honglan's dead husband was rehabilitated as a hero, and Wang Min became Deputy Minister and then Minister. Honglan's life as a loved, protected and privileged creature became to her less and less fulfilling. The Party and its power held her. She wanted to hold herself. She took gradual, secret steps towards a source of strength. From Minister Wang she had learned the techniques of secrecy and put them to good practice. The Minister was useful and helped her; he didn't know he was helping her to escape from the Party, from him, and from her life.

She went to temples, freshly painted or decrepit. She went to shrines, orthodox or esoteric. She went to public Christian churches, empty shells of white plaster, and to private churches in cluttered, undignified homes. Her travelling did not take her to the destination she sought; though it did put a distance between her and the busy Minister. She became a less loved and more respected, and a more emotionally neglected creature. Their relationship cooled and was less physical. The change did not displease her. She took to visiting holy mountains, either crowded with loud and littering trippers, or remote and treacherous places where, on one retreat, she slipped, broke a wrist, and caught an inexplicable fever from leeches.

She lay long in bed. Although this worried the Minister it was all fine until he made a fatal error. He shared with her his secret understanding of the internet . Nobody knew he was adept, an experienced user. It was part of his carefully maintained tactics to display a weakness that didn't exist. For Honglan, it was a powerful secret. In bed, immobile, with hours to spare, she found many things, and, eventually, the Shining Light of Truth.

CHAPTER 16

Day 1, 11:40 am

During an early lunch break called by the Minister of Religious Affairs on Day One of the investigation into the multiple deaths, the Party man said to Bill, 'He knows about you. About us. About our special room.'

'The Minister?' Bill stopped kneading the Party man's shoulder muscles and started chopping movements, like a trained sports masseuse, which he was. Bill said, 'How much does he know?'

The Party man was flat on his stomach on his bed in his room, wearing only large white underpants. The clothes he had taken off were neatly folded on a chair.

He said, 'He knows your details and he recognizes you. Now I wonder if getting rid of that foreigner so quickly was wise.'

'How did that boy come to be in the same room as us?' said Bill.

'They sent him to an empty room because they couldn't decide what to do with him and felt that removing him from their sight was equivalent to solving the dilemma.'

'But *our* room. They choose our room.'

'It was coincidence. I believe that and you have to believe it. I sent you there after the first call about the snowy field bodies and when it was clear it would be a busy, sleepless night.'

'I was sleepy enough not to notice another man in the closet.'

'You were still sleeping when I came in.'

'You're always silent.'

'That was when I thought I could sleep. We'd done all we could for the night and the Minister was chomping his breakfast.'

'And you found the foreigner.'

'He gave himself away.'

'He's gone now. Far away.' Bill massaged the Party man's soft, pale biceps and said, 'Nothing to worry about.'

'Almost nothing. He is next to nothing, that's right. No more than a speck. But it's not tidy.'

'I'm dangerous.'

'No. You exist. I exist. We exist. This is the truth. We should protect the truth from danger.'

'What can you do?'

'I can make sure he never comes back.'

'He's been deported. He'll never get a visa. He won't *want* to come back.'

'Those are minor objections. The Minister could arrange it.'

'Why would he?'

'That foreigner knows something.'

'He was intoxicated,' said Bill. 'Unreliable.' He started pressing his thumbs either side of the Party man's spine, top to bottom.

The Party man said, 'The Minister will think the foreigner knows something, whether the foreigner is aware of it or not. The Minister will think that's a risk.'

'The foreigner's more dangerous to us.'

'Exactly. So we have to stop him coming back here.'

'How?'

'Ahh,' said the Party man as Bill applied pressure, gradually, with the heels of his large old hands, to the Party man's lower spine. Bill released the pressure, and the Party man breathed in and said, 'I will firmly suggest bringing the foreigner back.'

'Ey?'

'And the Minister, if I judge him correctly, will be bound to object. I will counter. He will object more strongly. And so on. If I play delicately enough, we can be sure that foreigner will never come to China ever again.'

Thirty minutes later, after a short lunch break, a cool, refreshed and relaxed Party man made a casual, off-hand suggestion to the increasingly grumpy, sleep-deprived Minister as they discussed the deaths in the snow. The Minister was desperately missing his usual early afternoon nap and looked at the Party Secretary through eyes that were redder than ever.

The Secretary said: 'Retrace our steps, bring everybody back and talk to them again. Dong, his car crew, all the security personnel who went with him, anybody around, living in the area, walking in the area - even that drunk foreigner - call them all back.'

'No need for the foreigner.'

'Oh every little person counts.'

'No. He's gone.'

'You could bring him back.'

'What for?'

'Almost certainly nothing. It's just because this affair is huge and we need to avoid assumptions and we need to look at every tiny thing.'

'That's true.'

The Minister was suffering from lack of sleep, dehydration, a slight chill and an amorphous sense of loss. His head was tight with ache, his bladder felt hot and raw, and his muscles were indicating their existence through pain. The Party Secretary's calculation that the Minister would object to anything he proposed had been correct, and he felt the Minister's weakness at this point in time would only help achieve the outcome he wanted, so he pressed the point and said: 'So you'll call him back?'

'No, no. Not him. Wasting time. Need to act quick. Any action,' said the Minister.

'Let's make it the first.'

'No! Damn! I'm dying for a piss. Ay ay! Canada! Canada! I need you now! Oh fuck it! Do what you want! OK, bring him back - bring anybody back.'

He rushed from the room shouting, 'Hear that everybody! Bring everybody back! Drunk foreigner! Anybody! Everybody! Bring them back!'

Later, the Party man explained to Bill, 'I was outmanoeuvred by the Minister's own hangover.'

As a matter of fact, the Minister was desperate to send someone to England to bring Ghosh back. Nobody could go there without the Party man finding out, and the Minister did not want to ask permission to send a Ministry official to England because that would show his anxiety, and anxiety is a kind of weakness, and showing weakness before your opponent when you're playing a game is a first step to losing. Yet he wanted an officer to go to England immediately to bring Ghosh back. Nelson in Tokyo wanted to speak to Ghosh and Ghosh seemed to know something even if he didn't realize he knew it - the kind of knowledge that is the most dangerous. The Minister wanted to know what Ghosh knew about the messages on the folded piece of paper, and how he knew. Did anybody else know? Could they find out the same way Ghosh found out? Ghosh had to be made to talk and then made silent.

CHAPTER 17
Day 1, 12 noon

The Minister rushed to his private rooms and the five young women waiting there cheered when the saw him enter. They were sitting in bed watching TV and eating strong-smelling snacks. These were the activities that took most of their work time though they were also expected to have sex.

'Canada! Canada!' the Minister yelled. His favourite clambered out of bed over two other women. For two minutes the Minister lay in an armchair with his feet on a table. Through the windows he could see the weather was calmer with no hint of storms. When Canada was ready and brought in from the kitchen he drank it without smiling. The women all cheered again. He looked at them in bed and said, 'No, no, no! Other things. Big things. Just wait.'

'We're starving,' said one. She slunk across the room, stood before the Minister and holding one arm of his chair for balance raised her right leg to stroke the Minister's cheek, gently, with the inside of her calf. 'Playtime?' she said.

'Ahhhhhh, no playtime. I'll send some food. Don't show yourselves.'

He called the main Ministry compound staff kitchen and ordered a big meal. 'I'm busy working. Door's shut. Leave it outside. No knocking.'

The chef who took the order said, 'The Minister says his door's shut and there's to be no knocking today.' The whole kitchen laughed. They liked the Minister.

Fortified by Canada, the Minister went back to his office and consulted with Vice-Minister Dong.

'Who have got that could go to Britain to bring back that foreigner?'

'There's me.'

'Far too valuable! And too high level and never been there before.'

'So you want somebody not valuable, low level and who's been there before.'

'Exactly. And more subtle.'

'I have a list of names of good officers. I don't know if they are subtle.'

'Never mind.'

'There is Officer Liu, Officer Gao, Officer Jia, Officer Chen - '

'Chen - been out before?'

'Yes.'

'Speak the lingo?'

'Yes.'

'Show me the photo.' Vice Minister Dong Bing handed over a file photo.

'Looks right,' said the Minister. 'Tidy?'

'Yes.'

'Bring me Officer Chen.'

Ten minutes later, Officer Chen came in to see the Minister of Religious Affairs who was smiling his most salt-of-the-earth grin, showing honest, nicotine-stained teeth, and brushing the bristles on the top of his head with his hand like a shy farmer.

'Thank you, Chen. Thank you for coming here.' He moved away from his boxy, energy-inefficient computer monitor and its filthy keyboard - both part of the deliberate disguise of a machine that had been RAM-enhanced many times and was vastly more capable than it seemed.

The Minister was skilled in computer programming and in internet cloud applications and careful to conceal it. He hid this savvy because he believed concealed strengths are useful when you need to take somebody by surprise. His view of computer and internet technology was that it doesn't require cleverness to operate successfully. He saw it as a series of steps and rules that need to be followed exactly regardless of whether the rules are understood. In this way, he thought, computers are like government.

He said to the dutifully waiting Officer Chen, 'Now, you can speak English, can't you?'

'Yes, Minister.'

'Dong tells me it says here in your file that you studied out there.'

'Two years as an overseas student.'
'And how old are you now - thirty?'
'Twenty-eight.'
'And what did you study?'
'Final year of a BA, and an MA in Cross Cultural Communication and English.'
'In two years?'
'Yes.'
'Clever.'
'It's the way it is there.'
'Interesting and efficient. Interesting, yes, because, as you probably know, what's wrong with all those old Western powers is that they're not efficient. Sit down, sit down. Let's talk.
'Efficiency is what makes China's success. That's why we have two results. One: the economy is growing faster than any other economy in the world. Two: the economy is growing faster than any economy has *ever* grown. The 21st Century will be ours. Even foreign experts say so, don't they?'
'Yes, sir.'
'And the 21st Century will be the start of a long beautiful era. I call it the platinum era. We had the silver age of Han and we had the golden age of Tang, so that's why I call modern times *platinum* - more beautiful, more useful and rarer. What's the foreign letter for platinum? Dong?'
'Pt.'
'Pt. Wonderful. Platinum: more precious than silver and gold; never rusts and resists corruption. The platinum era - that's my original thought. And the reason for all that is: scientific and efficient government. Look at India. The British knew what they were doing when they forced it to be democratic. Held them back a hundred years. Look at what they had in 1947 and look at what we had then - war, famine, invasion - and look at what we have now. Our people are happier, richer, fatter, longer-lived, better educated and part of a more powerful nation.

'I'm just an old relic but I know my history. Look at America. Democratic. Two parties. That means two monkeys on a stick. They fight. People back the winner. One monkey falls off the stick. The other one prances about. Starts a war, gets the Nobel peace prize. Only the monkeys change and there's no change to the *system*. Not for two hundred years. Two hundred years ago was the Qing Dynasty! The future is ours. Any questions?'

'No, Minister.'

'Good. That's settled. I like you. Tidy. Something about you reminds me of somebody close to me. Go there: England. Today. Last time you went over there for yourself. This time it's for China. Remember that. Find this man. Dong will give you his details. Invite him back to help us. Make sure he says yes. Don't rush anything but bring him back very quick. And do it for China. Use whatever means necessary. I mean - use *all* your powers. You understand me?'

'I think so.'

'Good. Now - listen to me.'

'Yes, Minister.'

'Don't talk to anyone. When you're there. Don't talk to anyone. You know what I mean?'

'Yes, Minister.'

Officer Chen and Dong exited leaving the Minister alone and he said, 'Now what the fuck do I do?'

CHAPTER 18
Day 1, 4 pm

It was just as Nelson said: somebody saw something. This was discovered in the early afternoon when Dong Bing sent out some of his best officials to investigate the area near the snowy field where the dead bodies lay. In this so-called *rural* district there were, it is true, some other snowed-over farming fields in quarter acre plots, though there were also many dense clusters of square concrete buildings. Some had offices above and workshops below, but they were mostly houses of farming families who had mastered the logistics of food sales to markets in the big city and additionally generated short-term wealth by selling portions of the land that had brought them the surplus crops, and invested profits in showy homes. The homes had steel rods protruding from flat unfinished roofs, pointing to the sky, ready anytime for future generations to build on the concrete achievements of the present and reach higher and higher. Each building was a statement of optimistic ambition based on a misunderstanding of future conditions.

In the middle of this landscape was the field. It was an overcast, cold day with grey light. All those within a one kilometre radius were arrested.

The third old man to be interviewed said, 'Well, maybe I was out last night and I saw some strangers but I never went nowhere near Old Woman Wang's chicken shed!'

'What were you doing outside?'

'I was feeding my pig when - '

'Feeding your pig? At that time of the night?'

'It was a cold, wild night. She was unsettled.'

'A pig?'

'I see, officer, that you don't know pigs. The palms of your hands are so beautiful.'

Other officers laughed.

'Shut up. Go on.'

'I heard a commotion. Tramping feet. A lot of people. Bright lights and bangs in the sky. I thought it was a festival.'

'Fireworks?'

'I saw them.'

'The people or the fireworks?'

'Yes. That's right. From a distance of course. It was dark, too. Many people walking slowly. Strangers.'

'What did you do?'

'I gave her some corn husks and patted her back.'

For the Minister of Religious Affairs, working in his office, the old man's story was one part of the puzzling investigation that was keeping him from being able to rest and relax. He was irritated and confounded.

He said, 'How is it nobody knows what's going on? How come nobody knew these little religious rabbits were gathering together? There must be somebody in one of our offices on the computers monitoring the chat and blogs. One hundred and forty-seven of these cultists making plans and none known by us - it's hard to believe. What is going on?'

Vice Minister Dong said, 'We are using the firework thing as a cover - do you think the two things are linked?'

This was not what the Minister wanted to hear.

He said, 'How linked?'

'It's a remarkable coincidence - '

'It's a remarkable coincidence. What are you - a TV news reporter?'

'That the two things happened together. Perhaps it's part of a campaign of attack on the Religious Affairs Ministry and the government.'

'Imagination is something you should keep to yourself,' said the Minister. 'We need answers. How come the army of people we've got monitoring the Internet didn't see anything? How come they're not following these religious fuckwits? Haven't we got a whole nation of wastrel wankers using and abusing computers all the hours of the day? Can't somebody virus somebody's computer? Can't somebody *find something?* A bunch of fucking culprits - that's what we want!'

'Of course, Minister. But it's not so simple. I think we should arrest certain staff in the Ministry.'

'Sure. Like who?'

'We don't know who they are.'

'That's the problem! Have the Shanghai people been there? Done their tests?'

'They have,' said Dong. 'There are already on the plane back to Shanghai.'

'Should have kept them here. Don't want news spreading around the whole fucking country. What did they say?'

'They said the tests results take time. Analysis needs to be done.'

'And the bodies are still lying there in full public view?'

'Covered over with snow and large plastic sheets, as you ordered.'

'Ugh! Scorpion shit! Now the weather's changed. Have to do something about that. Have to do everything myself. Where's the Party man?'

At that moment the Communist Party Secretary of the Religious Affairs Ministry knocked lightly on the office door and entered the room.

He said, 'What are you discussing now?'

'Dead Bodies,' said the Minister.

'Lying in the open daylight,' said the Party man.

'We're getting nowhere,' said the Minister. 'Nobody can do their proper job. People are getting upset.'

The investigations meant the Ministry's bureaucrats and Party officials had to cancel all other engagements for the day at short notice. They used false excuses given that the real reason was a secret, and thus lost income for consultancy work, attendance at meetings or functions where the presence of Ministry official added weight to the position of their sponsors. This was the kind of work that brought most income, official salaries being modest, and the well-paid work suffered whenever something unexpected happened.

Most officials had the foresight to talk with their colleagues about what lie they would tell their financial sponsors. If word got around that all the Ministry of Religious Affairs bureaucrats failed to appear on the same day, and all of them offering wildly different excuses, it would look suspicious and, more importantly, it would look careless and show a lack of respect for the sponsors. Missing a day's work was acceptable but damaging such a relationship was not. The lie they agreed on was: *emergency last minute preparations for the opening ceremony of a newly renovated temple.*

Meanwhile, at levels above and beyond the Religious Affairs Minister and Religious Affairs Ministry Party Secretary, the government and the Party wanted an answer to be found, with or without mass arrests, and fast. The four days' grace was now three. Under this pressure the Ministry hid all information related to the Shining Light of Truth, the deaths and the investigation, while it searched for a plausible source of blame. This was the clear target of all endeavours: a cause and a culprit.

CHAPTER 19

Day 2, 1:00 am (5 pm previous day, UK time)

In about the ninth hour of the plane flight from Beijing to London, Officer Chen looked out of the thick window and down to Europe, in particular that tiny part called Estonia, and was filled with the thought 'I'm coming back.' Chen reminisced about the two years spent in Estonia studying English and International Communication, in fact becoming nostalgic partly because since returning to China and starting a busy, demanding and responsible career as a government officer there had been no time to savour the memory of the experiences there. Officer Chen was from a poor rural family, and at school and college had been an undemonstrative, diligent, well-behaved student with perfect attendance and an entirely unblemished record. This quietude, determination and perfection was a result of poverty and the knowledge of who provided the money for this privileged education, and how. Officer Chen's studies were supported by the physical work of family members, mainly an older sister. A very heavy obligation. Estonia, Chen now thought, had meant release and isolation. Release from the proximity of the three rings of self-definition and pressure, that is to say: family, school and society. In China these three rings had also brought comfort, companionship and identity. With them gone, in Estonia, there was the ache of loneliness and loss of confidence. Chen had begun to fear the natives, the language, the climate and the food. In fact, many of the most important parts of life. Yet Chen was strong, and had self and social belief, and struggled on through the difficulties of unclear purpose, eventually becoming stronger still and glad of the whole experience. Stronger and glad, that was what remained of Estonia in Chen's heart.

England was a new part of Europe for Chen. At Heathrow Airport, there was a long queue at the immigration barrier for 'others', of whom Chen was one. With passport, ticket and other papers long ready, and having waited behind the yellow line, approaching only when gestured at, Chen reached the high counter, and was nervous at facing a fellow government officer.

The British customs man looked at Chen and said, 'Sowiluh, fingluns clauzd.'

Chen said, 'I beg your pardon.'

'Ingluns clauzd.'

'Closed?'

'Yair - arf dei.'

'I beg your pardon. I have my passport, visa and address of local residence. The British Embassy in Beijing - ' Chen looked around left to right.

'Orai, orai.' The customs officer took the passport and scanned it saying, 'Jusu jauk. Jusu jauk.'

Handing back the passport to Chen he observed, 'No sensuv yuuma,' explaining the phenomenon to himself with the words 'Mizrubbul chinkibitch'.

To reach the place of the man she sought, Chen deliberately took a public transport journey by bus via Victoria to observe London's romantic shabby streets bustling with the city's varied native groups, existing in a lingering atmosphere of the age of Oliver Twist and Jane Eyre and protected by public security officers on horses like clay figures of Western barbarian invaders from the Han Dynasty. She saw the ancient monuments and the statuary - half-man half fabulous beast - that were arcane symbols of mythologies and war. She saw stone temples that, she knew, were filled with images of blood and sacrifice. She caught a fleeting sense of a decayed empire that arose from a society developed in geographic and historic isolation.

Chen changed buses inside a central bus station, which felt familiar, like something in a provincial city in China, with yellowish lighting in general gloom, lack of clarity in signs and announcements, milling people travelling cheaply, obscure shouting, and bad tempered drivers.

When Chen got on her bus she said 'Portsmouth?' and the driver said 'No,' and took Chen's ticket.

The driver said, 'Munaims jackarfurellis, no' poetsmuf', tearing off part of Chen's ticket, handing the remainder back and saying, 'Duzen costennyfin tubby pulai'.

Sitting in the first passenger seat was a middle-aged woman wearing a loose headscarf and Chen asked her, 'Portsmouth?'

'Yes, yes, yes. Portsmouth.'

Chen sat next to her. 'Thank you.'

'You are welcome.'

'You are going to Portsmouth?'

'Yes. We are going together,' said the woman.

'Thank you. You are living there?'

'No, no, no. I visit my son. He is working there.'

'Ah, your son.'

'Are you Chinese?' said the woman.

'Yes. Are you British?'

'No, no, no. I am Egyptian.'

In Portsmouth, Officer Chen found the address where her information said Marcas Ghosh was living. She checked in to the nearby Ibis Hotel, and after that she went back to the street of Ghosh. She went everywhere by taxi and was delighted with the simple service: telephone a number, say where you are, and wait ten minutes. The taxis were clean and drivers charged what was displayed on the meter. They drove slowly and they stopped to allow pedestrians to cross the road. Chen wondered whether these were signs of civilization or idleness, and did not fail to recognize that she was paying for the time for local people to cross the street in front of her taxi.

The house where Ghosh lived was a big one - though he only lived in part of it. It was old and ill proportioned. The amount and variety of rubbish lying outside the house would suggest, at home in China, waste and wealth, but Chen knew that here, in Europe, this was a sign of want. Chen remembered the Minister's advice to go gently and quietly. So she waited and watched the house. It was evening but she was not sleepy, partly because of the time difference and because of the mildness of the temperature compared with Beijing winter. She was wearing a warm down jacket. She stood opposite Ghosh's house on the pavement in a residential street between a tree and a concrete post with a brick wall behind her that she sometimes leant on.

The street was quiet and Chen paid close attention to the few people she saw. There came an old lady in slippers and overcoat. She had tiny glittering eyes and said, 'Hello'.

Chen said, 'Hello'.

The old woman said 'I've got my lottery ticket. Wish me luck.'

Later, two girls and one boy walked past. They were aged about twenty, she thought. They boy was thin and wearing sports clothes. The girls were fat and wearing little. 'The butter they eat protects them from cold,' thought Chen. 'And their various types of lard.'

One of the girls looked at Chen and said, with an unfriendly smile, without stopping and with no intention of communicating anything other than contempt, 'Nee how'. The two girls both shrieked with fake laughter. The boy smiled. Chen did nothing.

'CHING BANG BONG!' shouted the second girl. More shrieking. Chen observed them.

'Wotcha fucken luckenatt!' said the second girl. She pushed Chen's shoulder. The first girl slapped Chen's face and the second girl kicked her ankle. Chen considered the blows. They had weight with no control. Of course, she had been hit plenty of times before though not by complete strangers. It was shocking. She considered retaliating and dismissed the idea as irrational. Complete strangers, an assignment for the Chinese government, first day, necessity of a low profile. She looked at the boy's large nose and imagined breaking it.

Later, other people came by and they ignored her, unless they were drunk.

There was excrement on the pavement. 'Whose is it?' Chen wondered. Her usual certainties were disappearing.

A black car pulled up and a man and a woman got out. They were Chinese. The man was big and muscular and wore a black suit that seemed comfortable on him - it looked like he'd slept in it for the last six months. The woman was scrawny and wearing a flimsy white dress and high-heeled sandals. The man had a grip on the woman's arm and was half walking her half dragging her to another black car. The woman wriggled and caught sight of Chen and her faced looked shocked.

The wriggling woman said 'Dàjiě!' meaning, in Chinese, *big sister.* The woman resisted the man and forced him to stop. She stood in front of Chen.

'Dàjiě! Dàjiě! Qiúmìng! Qiúmìng!' the woman said. *Big sister! Big sister! Save my life! Save my life!*

Chen saw that the woman's eyes were tired and the skin under them was grey. She remembered what the Minister had told her: 'Don't speak to anybody.'

The woman's face screwed up and she said 'Bié wàngjìle wǒ! Wǒ rènshi nǐ. Wǒmen shì péngyou!' *Don't forget me! I know you. We are friends!*

'Péngyou!' the woman said. *Friends!* 'Péngyou!' The final *ou* sound was drawn out in a long *oohhhhhhhhhh*.

Chen didn't say anything.

The woman said: 'Shuō a!' *Speak!*

On the spur of the moment Chen said: 'Cheo-um-bwep-kess-sum-ni-da. Annyeonghaseyo. Saehae bok manhi bonaeseyo!'

It was all she could remember from her first year university classes in elementary Korean.

The woman's eyes turned downwards, her frame went soft and resistance left her body. She said quietly, 'Wei shenme?' *Why?*

The man dragged her to another parked car from which came strong arms to hold and pull her in. The car drove away. The man in the black suit had already reached his car and that drove away too.

Chen felt a bellyful of doubt. The woman knew her - or seemed to know her. Who was she and what was she doing?

What was Chen herself doing? How would she ever get the foreigner back to Beijing? A man she'd never met, who'd never seen her. Who'd been arrested, held overnight, thrown out of China, been back in his own home not much more than four hours. Here at home, a big, young, foreign man, at home among his people in a big house, that Chen had never entered.

She looked at her cell phone. It was nearly 8 am in Beijing. All her tiredness came together. She was reminded of other times of tiredness, throughout her life. High school was the worst, preparing for the *gāokǎo*, the entrance exam to a university, the name of which could decide the rest of her life. University had been tough too, though she kept moving along the rails of the plans set on the sleepers of family expectations.

She looked at Ghosh's picture again. He had not come out and Chen had not seen him. The picture was an enlargement of a black and white copy of a scan of his passport photo. Tones were bleached and his features were flattened. She was gradually becoming dizzy and tired. She felt the pressure of time passing after waiting in the street for hours and hours.

She knocked on his door. It was opened by a messy, paunchy, curly haired white man of about thirty years old - definitely not the man in the photo. His brother? Cousin? Friend? Neighbour?

This man led her through a dark narrow, carpeted corridor saying, 'Marcas, nothing connected between you and China will ever surprise me. A Chinese woman on the doorstep at midnight is just perfect.'

The man led her into a kitchen. She went in. He was there, sitting at a table, still jet-lagged, a fresh bruise under his left eye. He was wearing a white T-shirt and a black sleeveless down jacket. In the brightness and moist warmth of the kitchen the moment was like slow time, or déjà vu. Chen thought she caught a whiff of familiar homely smells - star anise and chicken blood. She saw too many details and had too much focus. She saw his fingers, the colour of his skin, golden hairs on his forearm, the dimple at his elbow, and the silky luxury of his eyebrows. She didn't need to ask anything when she saw him.

She told him, 'It's an official invitation: come back to China.'

And Ghosh said: 'Yes'.

CHAPTER 20
Day 2, 1:59 am

The Party provides immortality to its members by severely restricting its membership, controlling the present, being the only authoritative witness of history, and maintaining social and political stability over time. The actions of its minority elite membership are of utmost significance among all actions in the present, are recorded as history, and remembered for a very long time, possibly, if stability and continuity persist, forever. This is a kind of immortality.

Through religion people can establish a relationship with the immortal spirit of the cosmos that is by definition unchanging and timeless. This relationship is a route for those seeking life beyond life but who are not members of the Party. In this way, the meaning of life can come to all, directly, and from the mere fact of individual existence. This realization is in itself a threat to Party authority. The individual, direct communication with God connects the believer to everlasting life, and the ideas communicated, the prayers prayed, the hopes, dreams, fears, wishes, and the *soul* of the believer exist forever in the mind of God. This is the reason the believers can be fearless of death; this is the reason the followers of the Shining Light of Truth can be brave beyond any expectation. They are connected to the ultimate force.

The large, loose, leaderless SLT provides connections between on-line participants. The shifting, undefined set of Sayings allows faith to fill in the gaps of explanation according to the spiritual needs of the participant. The existence of the believers provides mutual assistance, spiritual support, and encouragement. The desire to copy, input and forward, and re-form the Sayings, and read the constant reformations provides regular collective activities.

The Seven Sayings of the SLT make a self-help list that is easy to remember, mutable, suggestive, and creative of yearning. The Shining Light of Truth provides a sense of meaning and belonging to people who are unhappy, un-respected, isolated, lonely, sad, frustrated, or impotent.

For Honglan, Nelson's mother, her only power had been her beauty, meaning her relative sexual desirability to adult men. She wanted a power source of her own choice and control and she got it in the Shining Light of Truth.

Believers in the SLT looked for certainty in easy and everyday places, such as numbers. They lived with the thin, expectant sound of *qī*, seven. The sound of *qī* is the sound of breath being expelled from a guarded mouth, through teeth held rigid, not fully open. The sound of *qī* is a sound of a people waiting. They are waiting for the satisfied, complete, open exhalation of *bā*, eight, the number that fulfils, and the number that is coming.

CHAPTER 21
Day 2, 2 am

'You lose, I win', said the Minister. 'Time to strip!'

He was in his room with the five young women. They were sitting in a circle playing an old drinking game with new ruls of the Minister's devising. Players had to say, in unison, certain phrases and accompany them with fixed gestures, all fast. It was called *bees and honey*. It went like this: players said *bee bee* (thumbs and forefingers together), *fly fly* (elbows at sides, forearms flapping), *high high* (arms straight up, fingers wiggling), *low low* (arms straight down, fingers wiggling), *flower flower* (both palms outstretched at sides of face), *bee bee* (thumbs and forefinger), *honey honey* (thumbs, forefingers and middle fingers pinched together), *fly fly* (elbows in, forearms flapping). All together: *bee bee, fly fly, high high, low low, flower flower, bee bee, honey honey, fly fly*; and in Chinese: *fēngfēng, fēifēi, gāogāo, dīdī, huāhuā, fēngfēng, mìmì, fēifēi.*

It was easy to say these words slowly but tricky fast and it got more difficult the more alcohol players drank. The Minister was good at the game. The way to win was not to lose. Losers got progressively worse.

As well as losers being obliged to drink - *gānbēi!* - there was also a forfeit, normally, when the Minister played, '*Take off clothes!*' And item-by-item the losing women had done that. Now two women were totally naked and had reached the next level of forfeits.

The women were hired on a time basis. This was an expensive form of employment for the Minister and he chose it because he wanted them there, ready, always waiting.

The game was played again. His favourite said *fly fly* instead of *honey honey*. She was already naked so she had to kiss the Minister. She walked around the circle and kissed him and afterwards she sighed, slightly.

The Minister said, 'I am a very bad old man.'

The Minister was born in 1942 and came through a rough and tumble and loving upbringing by a mother in a rocky village in the hills of Fujian, hills made of granite and marble with a natural radiation that seeped into well water and nurtured cancers in those that lived long enough. The peaks above his village always hid a gang of clouds ready to roil, and the skies there could change faster than the mood of a snake and strike with enough venom and speed to knock even experienced mountain men from the sides of crags. Part hunters, part herbalists and part holy men, those who used the mountain tops reeked of independence, illegality and magic. The boy loved to watch the mountain men and like them he studied the weather carefully.

He was the second child of eight and the first-born male. He was mainly raised by his mother and elder sister, who wanted him to be tougher than other kids, and had shown him a hitting, pushing, barging kind of love, though a love subtle enough to know the purpose behind every shove and scold. And, gradually, he too came to understand what his mother and sister were doing.

His father had been one of a group of local men with rifles who might be described as either mountain bandits or peasant leaders and when the future Minister was aged four, his father was shot during a minor battle with uniformed soldiers. Fortunately, as things later turned out, these soldiers were part of the army of the *Guómíndǎng*, the Nationalist Party, who were at the time the government of China, the chief enemy of the Communists, and their adversary in the civil war that eventually led to Communist Party victory and the *Liberation* of 1949. This enabled the band of mountain gunmen to claim, once they saw who would win the civil war, affiliation with the Communist army. The bullet wound in his back permanently immobilised the future Minister's father, and kept him in bed, fertile, hard-muscled and irritable; fathering children, spitting at them and hitting them with the back of his hand, if they came near enough.

It was when his father died that the future Minister applied to join the Communist Party. His father had hated the Communists and continued to hate them while they paid him a hero's pension and eventually moved his family, at his request, down from the hills to a roomy apartment seized from a merchant in the port city of Quanzhou. His family name was *Wang*, which as well as being a name also means *king* and was the name of everybody in his home village and the most common name in China.

When invalid father Wang died, the future Minister's mother and elder sister encouraged his application to the Party because they knew it was the road to power and the eldest son/brother was their vehicle. The application was processed more quickly because of his late father's revolutionary war hero credentials that, being dead, he had no chance to challenge. By that time, both mother and big sister had stopped punching and fist fighting their eldest son or brother, and came to dominate him in other ways.

When he joined the Party in 1960 it had already been the national government for eleven years. It was no longer a revolutionary movement and Mao Zedong was temporarily sidelined from day-to-day management of the nation. The Chairman of the People's Republic was an able administrator and by some accounts a good man, President Liu.

Young Wang was sent to Fuzhou University to study Marxist-Leninism and Chinese Literature, and on graduation became a government official in the provincial bureaucracy, rising quickly because of merit and because of having a model political background as the educated son of a revolutionary hero peasant - symbolic of the Party itself. He was a new, fast moving star and had seven lucky years.

When the practical economist President Liu was defeated in a political battle with the poetical theorist Mao Zedong and *purged*, the future Minister, who was too closely associated with the ex-President's faction, was also knocked from his post. In the spring of 1967 he was *sent down* to the countryside to be re-educated, or punished for being educated and a bureaucrat, by working on a farm, tending pigs. It was in this period that his mother and sister's rough love upbringing proved particularly useful because the re-educational exile seemed to him like being back in his childhood village except the weather in his place of re-educational exile was worse - muddier in summer and colder in winter - and though there was less punching there was also less love.

Conditions were tough and it was a fight to survive. In a short space of time a tumult of shocking things happened, bad and good, and both types the source of guilty dreams for decades to follow.

One January day in 1969, at the isolated commune, future Minister Wang grabbed sex with a woman, another student of re-education. He remembered the woman but didn't know her name or history.

He was brought back to the city in 1972, aged 30, partly because of his (long dead) father's credentials and partly because the country needed competent officials. By circumstance and inclination he moved away from politics and towards administration, management and practicalities. He was first in the Fujian provincial capital, Fuzhou, where he showed some worth - and also married there - later called to Beijing and assigned to the Ministry of Religious Affairs, the smallest of the twenty-nine government ministries. He stuck there and rose because he was competent, clever, liked, and powerful in mind and body. He was already a lover of eating, drinking and tasting the flesh of women - no different in this from many others, only more so, and he feasted.

Now there were five attractive women in his bedroom, his belly was grand and replete, but he had the biggest political problem of his career.

They played another round of *bees and honey*. The Minister lost and took off his shirt. All stared at his stomach.

'Urgh. This? As a minister I'm entitled to wear a pistol for self defence,' he said. They had never seen him wear it before. A leather strap went up over his shoulder across his chest down to a smooth brown holster that was resting at the side of his gut. The holster outlined and exaggerated the size of the pistol underneath, and the end of the shiny pistol - with an evil little hole - was poking out from the holster, just enough, like a hint.

And at that moment the Minister's phone rang. His important cell phone, the one with China's national anthem as its ring tone. Few people had that number. He had to answer it, and he took it to the bathroom.

'He's a very bad old man and this is a disgusting old game,' said one of the women.

In the bathroom, the Minister was listening to his cell phone. It was the Party Secretary calling. It was the second day of the four-day limit to solve the crisis.

The Party man said: 'Can we talk now?'

'Sure,' said the Minister, 'any time is equally bad. Big potato been scorching your ears?'

It was a good guess. A minute ago a man with access to the Politburo, a member of a *Leading Group*, and the Party Secretary's highest connection, his *golden thread*, had insisted softy, breathily and with enormous pressure, for the Party Secretary to start getting a grip, fixing the mess, shaking down, and slapping some sense into the jumped up desk huggers of the little, left-over, long-due-for-closure departmental-section-level-outfit with the boastfully deceptive name of *Ministry* of Religious Affairs. It was a threat of demotion.

The Party Secretary said to the Minister, 'Let's speak directly: Dong Bing's taking control of the investigations. Is this with your approval?'

'No. And he's talking about my age.'

'You don't understand how serious this crisis is.'

'Understand it much more than you guess.'

'That may be. What concerns me is that Dong Bing's methods are powerful but not necessarily successful. There are many contradictions in this case and in our resources, including personal resources. We need to maintain our authority and we need to manage the problem of the religious believers, and the former is dependent on the latter. Now, does Dong Bing have anything on you?'

'What do you mean?' said the Minister.

'Information about you he could use to his advantage.'

'How about you?'

'I try to make it a rule never to underestimate the information others might hold.'

'Hah!' said the Minister. 'Are we nearer to finding an answer?'

'No.'

The Party Secretary and the Minister finished their call by reviewing the day's events and found there was little good to talk about. There were parallel searches going on, one for the perpetrator of fireworks and of the one for the cause of the deaths in the snowy field. One search was public and the important one was not. In a distracting show of openness - and partly because bangs had been heard and flashes been seen in the district surrounding the Ministry building - the Minister had briefed the local press about the search for the illegal fireworks starter. He had repeated parts of his morning speech to Ministry staff and had said: 'I say clearly . . . anti-social unauthorized and illicit use of prescribed explosives . . . *danger* and *criminality* . . . I tell you four things: One, I will not rest until I find the perpetrator. Two: I will find the perpetrator. Three: I will punish them. And four: I promise you all this.'

And indeed somebody was arrested at 4:30 that afternoon: a Ministry employee, a rubbish collector and deliverer to apartments of large canisters of cooking gas; a man who had a bad reputation and was a hot-tempered wife and child beater, a hard-liquor-drinking kicker of other people's pets who put up a suitably lawless resistance to arrest, knocking out teeth from one officer and breaking the nose of another before being knocked out and somewhat broken himself. Satisfactory as this was, nothing useful was found on the bigger, hidden search. The SLT was blamed but there were no details. There was a rumour among Ministry staff that SLT believers had injected the security personnel with tiny poison-filled syringes before using the poison on themselves. Although the Minister knew the rumour wasn't true he did not contradict it. He had nothing else to take its place.

The Minister's phone rang again - the important one.

It was Dong Bing: 'Minister. How are you feeling?'

'What are you calling for?'

'Can we meet?'

'Why?'

'I traced the midnight caller. The one who gave me the coordinates of the field. Where - '

'Come up here.'

'Your private apartment? Is that convenient?'

'We'll be alone.'

'I understand. I'll be there.'

And in five minutes he was, for the first time ever. The Minister took Vice Minister Dong to an office room with a desk and a couple of chairs. A room the Minister never used and he wasn't even sure where the ashtrays were though he knew where the bugging device was hidden. He found an ashtray and lit a cigarette.

'Want one?' he said.

'I don't,' said Dong Bing, the Deputy Minister.

'Of course.'

'How are you feeling now, Minister?'

'Ugh?'

'Your health?'

'Fuck my health.' The Minister was still lacking sleep and felt a general discomfort from his enlarged prostate. And he was pained at Dong being considerate. The Minister asserted some authority and told Dong what to do: 'Tell me again. I sent you back to the field. Tell me what you saw.'

Dong told about finding the dead bodies and said only two were alive, briefly, and gasping to breathe. Before she died the woman - the leader - had said, 'He did not come.' Captain Ma had said, 'Not what I wished for.' And he died. Both had eyes rolled back in their heads and blood coming from their ears. The woman had touched her heart. Over her heart was the pocket. In the pocket was the paper with the list.

The Minister said, 'How come only these two were alive?'

Vice Minister Dong said, 'I don't know. The woman was in the middle of the field and - from his footsteps - it looked like Captain Ma had walked towards her.'

'This Captain Ma. Brave leader type. Ex-27th Army Division was he?'

'Yes. Perhaps they died last because they were in the middle.'

'How does that make sense?'

'I don't know.'

'Maybe they were the strongest,' said the Minister.

'They were two of the oldest!' said Dong Bing. 'You know, scientifically speaking, younger people are stronger than older ones.'

'Some get stronger the older they are.'

'Up to a point.'

'And what next? You photographed the bodies?'

'Yes,' said Dong Bing. 'And that could be so useful.'

'Ugh.'

'Especially after you changed your mind about leaving the bodies buried in the snow and had them brought back here to better preserve them.'

'It's observation I care about, not preservation. Leave them in the snow and somebody is bound to see them. Better have them safe and sound where we can look at them any time.'

'Yes, where are they exactly?'

'In secure storage. And what happened this afternoon when you went back? You arrested the pig farmer.'

'Yes, though nothing he saw seems useful at the moment,' said Dong Bing.

'He said he saw the fireworks.'

'No, he said *bright lights and bangs in the sky.*'

'And the gas and rubbish man we arrested for fireworks: can we get the charge to stick?'

'Yes, though that's not the real problem.'

'What's the *real* problem, in your opinion, Vice Minister?'

'If this news gets out - '

'*When* it gets out.'

'Yes - *when* - because the illegal gathering was planned. There's chat about it on message sites. They were expecting someone. And not everyone who knew about it was there. There are people still out there - '

'You know who they are?'

'It's not easy. There are identities created by unreal identities. Chat sites; blogs. And there are memes, pinging around, not belonging to anybody.'

'We've got people specialized up to their necks in this shit.'

'I think we should arrest somebody *here*,' said the Vice Minister, spreading his arms wide in the office room.

'Here?'

'In the Ministry. Do I have your approval?'

'You might as well arrest yourself.'

'We've got to start somewhere.'

'Start? And who next? Me?'

'The most suspicious thing is the telephone call that came to me giving the coordinates of the field.'

'Have we got proof it really came?'

'Yes, it's recorded on my phone.'

'Ugh. Good. And you traced it?'

'Yes, it came from Beijing.'

'Big place.'

'But one private number. I say we start eliminating people. And keep monitoring that caller's number.'

'You're - *we're* - monitoring?'

'Yes.'

'And?'

'I'll keep you informed.'

After leaving the Minister's apartment Dong Bing did not rest. He continued monitoring and directing investigations through the night and, as he had through the day, he acted in a quicker and more rational way than either the Minister or the Party Secretary.

He was hurrying because he knew that the more time passed the more likely it was news of the deaths in the field would become public, and he knew that if news leaked before a good explanation for the events had been found it threatened the power of the whole Ministry. The Ministry needed to control information and find an explanation. If things went badly, Dong would be a loser. If things went well, and especially if he was instrumental in a positive outcome, he would have more influence and authority, and he would soon succeed the Minister in reality if not in title - though ideally in both.

Dong assumed that the Minister's and Party Secretary's lack of pace and clarity was partly due to age and lack of familiarity with digital media, and also to a common government reluctance to act, based on the belief that doing something may be wrong while doing nothing postpones all action and is therefore neither right nor wrong. Of course, the Minister and the Party Secretary had each their own reasons for being less than forthright in pushing ahead with investigations, reasons Dong did not know about, and Dong was mistakenly associating events and causes.

Many other associations and conjectures were being made by staff in the Ministry, and Dong was informed of most of them. Seeding rumours was the notion that the Shining Light of Truth was now a powerful force. A clerk who thought himself clever, recited a list of religious rebellions throughout history that had threatened the state. That the SLT was another such militant, government-threatening, pseudo-religious movement was an implication too provocative to be spoken, though easily understood. In Vice Minister Dong's view, the whispering of such dangerous nonsense was a sign of the awful consequences of not finding an answer and of not keeping the events and the investigations secret until that answer was found. To avoid these consequences required energetic and efficient action.

Among the several actions Vice Minister Dong was eager to carry out as soon as possible was bringing together Nelson and Ghosh. Despite hating his phone call experience with the eccentric Nelson and knowing that Ghosh was an idiot foreigner, he judged them to be somehow useful; Nelson because of his careless severity and Ghosh because his presence discomposed both the Minister and the Party man, and this was a minor weakness worth exploiting. And after all, Ghosh was Dong's item; it was the Vice Minister who found him, lost and dubious, close in space and time to the deaths in the snow.

While Dong went to his office to work through the night, the Minister retreated to his large and dark bathroom, and stood with his hands on a marble counter in front of a long wall mirror, apparently looking at his own reflection though actually not seeing anything. After some time the amount of which he found difficult to estimate, there was a gentle knocking on the bathroom door. He knew who it was and said: 'Come'.

She came in and said, 'Can I do something for you?' It was his favourite.

He said, 'Ugh. Something.'

'Tell me.'

'I'm a bit - ' He had wanted to say *tired* and stopped himself from expressing weakness. He sighed and his sigh said what his words omitted. In a way, this was the first time he had relaxed in front of one of his women; it was the first time he had showed himself tired, and was tired, and the first time he showed weakness, and was weak.

She said, 'Canada? I'll make Canada.'

'No,' he said, 'don't. Make some . . . make some tea.'

She went away and when she came back she was carrying a small ceramic tea tray with small cups and pots, and also the Minister's holster and gun.

The Minister said, 'I see you cleaned the room - since the fireworks, I mean.'

She said, 'Yes, I tidied it carefully.'

'It's good to be tidy.'

'I'm a tidy person. From a tidy family,' she said. 'I brought this; it's dangerous to leave around.' She handed him the holster and gun.

'Not so dangerous,' he said, taking the gun from the holster, 'without a dangerous person.'

'True.'

The Minister squinted at the pistol, close up.

She offered him a small cup of tea: 'Drink.'

He put the gun in his trouser pocket, took the tea and said, 'Here,' handing her the empty holster, 'you have this.'

'Me? Too dangerous.'

'You don't look dangerous. And this gun-holder looks dangerous but it isn't.'

She felt that merely having in her possession the holster of a high government official would be incriminating while refusing the Minister had its own risks too. He too was taking a risk in giving her the holster as a keepsake - she could cause him trouble - and she recognized that.

'Thank you. I'll keep it,' she said. 'Are you checking the weather? What's the forecast?'

The Minister had been checking a weather website on an iPhone.

He said, 'You won't notice any spring. Unsettled for days. No big storms like the other night. Not for a long time. Maybe never.'

He drank the tea. It was strong and bitter.

He said, 'I like this. This tea and the way of making it.'

'Not many do.'

'No, especially in my home province. They like that light tea with the pretty smell.'

'Not your taste.'

'You know me well.'

'You notice?'

'I have many things to notice,' he said.

She said, 'Why were you leaning on this counter? You looked worried.'

'Ugh? This? This rock? It's where I'm from. Hills of my home village. Marble from Fujian goes round the world. Japanese love it for the gravestones of their ancestors. Westerners put it in hotels. Arabs in their mosques. Beautiful.'

'It is.'

Minister Wang drank tea. 'Beautiful,' he said again, looking at her.

She looked steadily back at him.

CHAPTER 22
Day 2, 10 am

On the morning of the second day of investigations into snowy field deaths and midnight fireworks, all senior officials at the Ministry attended the opening of a Buddhist temple. It was reported in the media and Vice-Minister Dong Bing was interviewed by television stations, saying the renovation of the ancient temple was a sign of, firstly, the government's commitment to supporting the traditional faiths of the people, and, secondly, its support of religious diversity, and, thirdly, its support of the public expression of belief. Some of the nation's finest craftsmen had been employed, said the Vice-Minister, to restore the faded holy relics and dilapidated architecture to a pristine state befitting a modern, developed city. The government-led restoration of this site of national cultural importance would attract both believers and interested visitors from all over the world, thus enriching the cultural life of the city and bringing concomitant economic benefits.

On the day of the official opening the temple was brand new: this was not a renovation, it was a total reconstruction. There was a smell of acrylic-based paints and in some insufficiently ventilated areas the plaster was still damp. The main colours were lime green, red, white, glossy black and an almost fluorescent yellow that was attractive to certain insects.

Some areas of the temple were carefully painted with great attention to detail. The building as a whole was large and weak. Inferior concrete had been used and the foundations were not deep. This was the result of the money that had been thrown at the project missing the public target and hitting instead the private pockets of related officials and contractors. There was a large shop, not yet stocked except for soft drinks and packaged snacks. Each deep breath brought the smell of paint and the overall atmosphere lacked any reverence.

To create an impression of liveliness, popularity and enjoyment of the newly opened temple, all available Ministry staff were bussed to the site. Available staff included six off-duty deputy chefs and, as they were all playing basketball at the time of being rounded up, Bill was also taken with them to the temple, to add quantity to the crowd. He was used to spontaneous activities of this kind and on arrival he did not enter the temple, instead standing outside the main entrance by the rotary approach road and waited there patiently for the bus to be driven back. He wore a Russian style fur hat, thick gloves, and a great military coat that went down to his ankles and had the fur-lined collar turned up to his ears. His basketball tracksuit was underneath. Though his breath showed cloudy he did not feel the cold and he was absorbed in his own thoughts.

The Party Secretary had arrived earlier in a black Ministry Mercedes Benz and was walking at the head of four rows of self-applauding officials who were being filmed and photographed by back-stepping news journalists. The officials marched forward in steady formation producing a rich wave of handclapping; camera men and women edged away from them, maintaining the distance, somewhat disorderly, pushing camera buttons and triggering artificial optional clicking sounds in a spluttering pulse.

The Party man did not know Bill was at the temple until he caught a sideways glimpse of him through the open entrance gateway. Something in Bill's expression caught his attention. The Party Secretary lead his group into a turn and back past the entrance one more time, getting another sideways view of the solitary, great-coated figure, and he brought the marching to a conclusion. When he could detach himself from handshakes and chat, he went outside the gate. At a distance of five metres from Bill, not looking at him, and meanwhile keenly regretting that he did not smoke and could not use that excuse for standing alone outside a temple entrance gate, he said,

'Why are you outside?'

'It's not a place I can enter.'

The Party man was of course aware of Bill's religious objection to dragons and the places of dragons and other symbols his particular school of Christianity associated with devils and devilry. He said nothing.

Bill said, 'I'm going back.'

'Wait for the bus and go back with everybody.'

'There's no bus to go back there.'

The Party man knew what Bill meant and said,

'Why? Why now? After all these years?'

'Health and danger.' Bill coughed.

The Party Secretary said, 'I have the key to every door.'

'There are other keys and other key holders.'

'Wait.'

Bill walked away and got in a taxi. The Party Secretary had no way of hearing what Bill said to the taxi driver so he guessed Bill was pointing at a spot on his bilingual map of Beijing and saying, '*hǎo*?' - good? The driver was saying, '*hǎo hǎo*'. They were going to an airline ticket office. And Bill was going to buy a single ticket to America. There was a sound of leather shoe soles on fine gravel. The Party Secretary turned.

Dong Bing was beside him and smiling despite an obvious lack of levity and an absence of humour. He said, 'Where's that old foreigner going?'

'Who? I have no idea,' said the Party man. 'That file on Liu Wei, the Ministry assistant with the suspect Buddhist nun sister - '

'Yes,' said Dong Bing. 'Tomorrow morning, you said. Though I offered it earlier.'

'Let me have it this afternoon.' In this way, the Party Secretary was switching pressure to the other man. He walked back inside the temple.

Once back at the Ministry, the Party Secretary visited the Minister's office. They were spending much more time in each other's company than was usual. It was symptomatic of their crisis.

The Minister said, 'Just between you and me, I need to sell some of my buildings this week. I've no time to talk to buyers.'

'Don't expect sympathy for your property portfolio.'

'Oh, yeah. Maybe I'm not the only one with long-term investments slipping away.'

The Party Secretary had nothing to say to that.

Vice Minister Dong Bing knocked on the Minister's office door and walked in. The Minister looked to see if he was smiling. He wasn't. There were no greetings.

Dong said, 'Minister, there is something I want to ask you in confidence. Perhaps in order to protect me - though I don't need protecting - at the same time I appreciate the consideration - I feel - '

'Out with it.'

'I feel there may be some information you are holding back from me.'

'Is that right?' said the Minister. 'Is that how you feel?'

'It is.'

'We are in dangerous times.'

'We are.'

'When officials do not trust their leaders.'

'Ah. I don't know that - '

'Your ignorance will be your protection.'

The two men, the Minister and his most powerful Vice-Minister, looked at each other, partly in defiance, partly to understand the other. They already knew enough. Or so they thought.

The woman in the countryside in 1969 that the future Minister once slept with was Dong Bing's mother. The woman's absent husband was not Dong Bing's father. It was future Minister Wang. His would-be usurper, the Vice Minister, was his own son. This was knowledge that would be useful to either the Minister or Dong Bing and there was nobody alive able to give it to them.

The Minister, as he often said, had been formed by the punishment of being sent to the countryside as a young man. It changed him and made him bolder. Faced with a risk he would say to himself: *what's the worst that could happen?* I fail, get attacked, punished, and sent to the countryside - back to the kind of place I came from in the first place. Not so terrible. Sometimes I like it. Nothing to be afraid of. If I play the game carefully I stay where I am. If I gamble and win, I get more power and more interesting games to play. Though recently he'd lost the playful feeling. He was getting tired.

Dong Bing was getting ever more excited by the game. First thing in the morning he noticed nausea in his stomach caused by undigested fear and thrill. Like the Minister he also felt that, ultimately, he had nothing to lose except, perhaps, missed opportunity. *What's the worst that could happen?* I go back to where I came from. There's nothing to be afraid of.

Dong Bing was brought up in an elite orphanage for children whose parents were killed in revolutionary struggles. It was a privileged, pressured, protected and harsh place. His mother died, it was said, in an accident when a squad of deeply *red* Party members were engaged in a symbolic campaign to connect the Party to the countryside and the People. In this particular mass action the squad were engaged with wet sticky earth. While digging an irrigation ditch, Dong's malnourished mother found herself exhausted by the unfamiliar physical effort and when her spade stuck in the heavy clay, she tumbled into the ditch and drowned, unprotected by her ultra-left wing intoxication. Dong Bing was four months old.

His mother's young widower, equally *red*, through and through, was shot by soldiers of the Union of Soviet Socialist Republics in a 'border skirmish', or a display of ultra machismo and ultra nationalist aggression that became more important than life itself, for a few instants at least, quite long enough for somebody to die. Dong Bing was seven months old. He had no other close relatives.

He was intensely schooled and rarely allowed to play unsupervised. He was asked to remember an awful lot of information and as he grew through his second decade this information increasingly related to subject areas considered the best combination of untainted political thinking and progressive modernity, such as hydraulic engineering and ballistic physics. From the age of sixteen he also learned English words and grammar to the extent, by his own estimation, of eight thousand items of vocabulary.

'Syringes,' the Minister said. 'That's what they're whispering. Some of our Ministry officials.'

'I know. And now they're saying - because it was so cold - syringes made of ice.'

'Ice?'

'Inject, melt, leave no evidence.'

'Clever, imaginative, and no doubt totally mistaken.'

One way or another, Minister Wang and Vice-Minister Dong had to work together to solve, to their own individual satisfaction, the crisis the Ministry now faced. The Minister had noticed that his Ministry investigators were tainted with an unexpressed awe towards the Shining Light of Truth. For many of his officials, trust in some kind of inexplicable spirit, power, or *qi*, nestled like an ember in their hearts, and was kindled to flame by the wind of any mystery or fear.

The Minister went to the window and said, 'You know what's happening? Our staff, the longer this thing goes on, the more they believe.'

'Believe we will solve it?'

'No,' said the Minister. 'Believe the Shining Light of Truth. Are you any closer?'

'No. The fact that we don't know why the cultists died does not have any connection to the validity of their stupid ideology. Nelson said the fact they are dead and our security personnel are dead doesn't mean they knew what they were doing. Their thoughts are evil but thoughts and power are two different things.'

'There's a connection between you and Nelson.'

'Nelson and all that kind of people make me sick,' said Dong, while thinking: *But I can learn from anybody.*

CHAPTER 23
Day 2, 2 pm

Estimating that Bill would be back from buying his air ticket, the Party Secretary went to see him, first entering a locked empty room and then walking into a closet and finding inside it a hidden door to which he held the key. The hidden door led to a short, unlit corridor ending at a door opening to another closet, this time in Bill's room. Bill was there, resting on his bed, a ticket to Seattle on his bedside stand. Bill had been in China for forty years but his rooms had always been temporary. He'd been a foreign guest professor at universities and colleges, staying in accommodation provided by each institution, thus getting the use of oversized wardrobes, bulky and uncomfortable beds, and mirrored dressing tables that sufficed as awkward work desks. Five years ago the Party Secretary had sighed a breath that moved a thread that pulled a string that caused Bill to be given a post at the Ministry of Religious Affairs, and be housed in a lower level guest suite, the kind of rooms that might otherwise be used for the interpreter of a faith-based delegation from Somalia. Bill lay there now, napping on a dark, unwieldy bed with its frame marked with anonymous scratches, stab points and cigarette burns, the bed surrounded by chalky white walls scuffed black by the kicks and bumps of unknown previous occupants. Not for the first time, the Party Secretary felt pity for his exiled guest friend, sleeping on public furniture in a lonely public room.

The Party man didn't want Bill to leave for Seattle but didn't want to argue the point directly for fear of strengthening the elder man's resolve. He understood that Bill's wanting to leave was partly because he was sensitive to the Party Man's weak points and saw their relationship - or public knowledge of it - as the weakest point of all. The Party Secretary hoped to use his own weakness as a persuasive weapon.

Bill stirred and woke.

He said, 'You've come for your massage.'

Bill got out of the bed and uncovered the sheets on the side he had not been sleeping. The Party Secretary lay down there after taking off his jacket, tie and shirt.

As Bill massaged shoulders, spine, biceps and lower back, he thought again of the idea that the Party Secretary was losing his touch as a leader, a politician and a controller. The Party Secretary was thinking the same thing: when his plan to keep Ghosh out of China backfired, was that a one-off mistake or was it a sign of a shift and loss in judgement and authority? He took his thoughts from himself and moved them outside, to Bill, an old man returning to his birthplace.

He said to Bill, 'I should be massaging you.'

Bill said, 'That's my job. Massage isn't your strength.'

'You are leaving because you see my weakness.'

'Yes. And wanting me to stay is another sign of your weakness. You are losing the winner's edge. Getting sentimental.'

'You are leaving me now when I need you most in this crisis.'

'For me, the crisis is us. And I am causing the crisis.'

'I need your support.'

'We need each other, I think. And we need each other strong. You know how to play. You know how to win. For years you've amazed me. Arranged everything. Don't falter. You know why I'm leaving. Being here is weakening you. A point of danger. Gives a point of attack. For Dongy.'

'Vice Minister Dong Bing?'

'He's a good official and he is chasing the Minister and he's after you, too, because you are the same generation and the same level. Don't give him a point of attack. Don't give him *me*.'

'You're suggesting the Minister and I should protect each other.'

'You are associates in power. If Dongy can stick a scandal on you, it associates with the Minister.'

'That is his plan.'

'From Dongy's point of view this whole crisis is a golden opportunity and he's been quick to take it. From what you tell me he's been at the centre of it from the start, so much so that it is almost suspicious. He received the phone call, he was at the field so soon - '

'Not soon enough to be one of the dead,' said the Party Secretary.

'So: perfect timing. And it was he who picked up - or produced - this foreigner.'

'The Pakistan guy?'

'The one he put in *our* room,' said Bill.

'To see us both.'

'Perfect timing, or what?'

'And he's been working like a devil ever since without failing to notice any detail.'

'Such as me,' said Bill.

'This crisis is getting too close to failure - '

'And too near to us,' said Bill.

'This may be a passing,' said the Party Secretary.

'Time to move on.'

'To Dong Bing's generation?'

'You don't like him, do you?' said Bill.

'No. And you do.'

'Yes.'

'Why?'

'Well let me see. He's athletic and he takes care of his body. He's educated; has good manners. He's clean and well presented. Hardworking, steady. Speaks good English. Hygenic. His breath doesn't smell of garlic. He doesn't spit. He doesn't eat uncivilized food. He doesn't smoke. He doesn't have mistresses or use prostitutes. He doesn't gamble or bet, doesn't drink, except banquet toasts. He keeps up with the latest from America. Doesn't make vulgar body noises. Clothes are worn properly. He's not really corrupt - sure, I know he has various consultancies and gets money like every other official. But in his case it's more or less legitimate consultancy and advice. He likes rules and follows them. He hates superstition. He could be the future leadership of China.'

'On that last point, Teacher Bill, I may agree with you.'

'On that point.'

'Oh, how long have we known each other, and how deeply. And yet you can still allow me to see things in a completely different way, Teacher Bill.'

'The more you say *Teacher Bill* the more I know you don't agree with my opinions.'

'Everything you said about the Vice Minister is true.'

'And you still don't like him?'

'No. He has, as the saying goes, no sympathy; no subtlety; no sensitivity; and no spirituality. Following rules is good for controlling chaos but the civilized way is to follow wise judgements.'

'Philosophical.'

'Well, yes, so let's be practical. If he knew about you - about us - he would see it as a social evil, and from his point of view a weapon, and he'd use it on me, to destroy me, and he'd feel good doing it.'

'That's just what I said. You need to get something on him. You need to play this game.'

'Bill: don't go.'

'I've been massaging you for years. I know what's good for you. My going is good.'

CHAPTER 24
Day 3, 11:10 am

The Minister, Dong Bing and six armed guards sat in a parked white van on a runway at Beijing International Airport waiting for Ghosh and Chen to arrive on Air China passenger flight CA0938. The Minister's presence was a sign he wanted to control events though he pretended he didn't by saying nothing and spending the time checking on-line weather charts via his iPhone.

Dong said to the guards: 'Remember, Officer Chen has captured a highly dangerous foreign terrorism suspect. Officer Chen is likely to be handcuffed to him, or the suspect may be handcuffed. Officer Chen has probably enlisted the assistance of on-board security officers. In any case, although the suspect may appear trapped and subdued, he is, as I said at first, *highly dangerous*. He will stop at nothing. Extreme vigilance, fast movement, instant reactions - '

'There she is,' said the Minister as Chen came down the aircraft steps. Ghosh followed, carrying what was obviously Chen's pink and purple cabin baggage. 'I see them,' said the Minister, seizing up their situation exactly.

When Chen and Ghosh reached the bottom of the steps, Ghosh put the luggage down and unfolded the handle while Chen waited for him. She seemed to ask him which way to go. Ghosh pointed to a bus. Ghosh had arrived in China four times, Chen had only flown back once before. To Ghosh, the smell of the airport was also familiar - the dust of coke briquettes and something else that is not, though smells similar to, urine. He always noticed the smell, he never expected it, and he always became unaware of it after two minutes. With other passengers, they ambled toward their bus.

'Quick!' shouted Dong Bing. 'Get them before they escape!'

The van drove at speed towards the passengers. Only Chen and Ghosh didn't run away. The van stopped.

The Minister said 'Me first,' and jumped out with an enormous smiling yell, 'Welcome! Welcome! Welcome back to China! You must be very tired. We have a car for your convenience. Please, please. Please get in. Come, come. I'll take it.'

He put his hand on the handle of Chen's bag.

Chen and Ghosh were surrounded by the six security personnel, beefy men in black uniforms including baggy multi-pocketed trousers tucked into steel-toe ankle boots. They carried machine guns.

'No more luggage?' said the Minister. He guided Chen and Ghosh to the van. With one small movement of a finger he instructed an armed guard to pick up Chen's bag and put it in the van.

'Good, good.' Said the Minister. 'Everybody must rest. Please relax.'

To Ghosh: 'Thank you for returning to our China.'

To Chen: 'Thank you for accompanying our foreign guest. Well done. Fast work.'

To both: 'You need to rest after your long journey and busy time.'

To Chen: 'Your mummy and daddy will be very worried about their daughter. Take official leave from today and convey my greetings to them and thank them for providing me with such a satisfactory worker.'

'That's not necessary.'

'It's decided. I insist. Bring me back a bag of pickled turnip. I love eating it.'

Pickled turnip was the characteristic product of the area of Chen's village; in the process of preparing it her grandmothers make their homes stink for months. How did the Minister know?

'I'm not tired,' said Chen.

'It's an order,' said the Minister. 'Dong, give her the money for a soft seat rail ticket.'

The van drove from the airport to the central rail station. Ghosh and Chen did not want to reveal their hopes, fears or desires to the listeners in the van. It would not help them or their dignity. So Chen and Ghosh looked at each other, eye to eye. Chen did not express her horror: *what have I done to him?* Ghosh did not express his horror: *what will they do to me?* There was no point Chen or Ghosh saying, 'Don't worry,' or, 'Whatever happens, I'll be there for you.' The first was empty and callous; the second was a lie; and neither she nor he could predict what would happen. The world is a big and solid engine; two soft specks are of small consequence in its incomprehensible movement.

Chen got out at the railway station. Ghosh was driven back to the Ministry in silence. In the Ministry compound detention centre he was locked in a small room with no windows.

CHPATER 25

Day 3, 12:33 pm

It's not religion the Chinese Communist Party is afraid of, it's groups. As Minister of Religious Affairs Wang has often said, privately, *nobody gives a monkey's snot about religion.* There is fear of a group organizing without the government's approval because an organized group is a rival.

The first Shining Light of Truth gathering, in Xiamen, a city far to the south of Beijing, was already troubling to the government because, first, the gatherers were religious, meaning conflicted loyalty, and second, they came from outside Xiamen, showing wider group organization. The second gathering - in Shenyang, Liaoning Province, six hundred kilometres northeast of Beijing - was also troubling and by the time of the third gathering, which the Public Security Bureau searched for carefully and unsuccessfully, there was fear.

Faced with the phenomenon of multiple, nationwide, sudden, unpredictable, devoutly attended meetings of SLT believers, the government, with the Ministry of Religious Affairs as its executive, started acting like a furious father. SLT believers were caught and put in unlisted, unofficial, unacknowledged, hidden and therefore *black* prisons. SLT believers kept gathering, but to be safer they did so at night.

Via the Ministry, the government countered the SLT Seven Sayings with a four-word slogan: *Superstitious Subversive Criminal Traitors.* And the explanatory breakdown was: *Superstitious - irrational, unscientific and unnatural; Subversive - trying to destroy our China; Criminal - breaking our laws; Traitors - disloyal to China.* There were broad hints at links with hostile foreign forces.

In denouncing the SLT, the government publicized it nationally and made enemy traitors out of tens of thousands of ordinary people all over China, an enemy that if it does not die immediately cannot help becoming increasingly hostile. People who had no idea to challenge authority became one of the authorities' biggest challenges.

Among the many and varied actions taken to find an answer to the big questions about the dead bodies in the snowy field, arrests were made of under-employed graduates living in the low-rent rooms in the village nearest to the snowy field where all the corpses had lain. Two of these low-rent *ants* were accused by their fellow arrestees of being SLT believers, which they were.

The pair was questioned, first relatively peacefully, and they were just about to tell everything they knew - and they knew plenty - when the public security station chief came in and threatened them with violence. They refused to cooperate.

They had been sat in front of a plain wooden desk while the station chief's deputy drank tea from a cup with no handles and asked them quietly, 'Are you going to deny what everybody says about you being members of a cult?'

The man said, 'We believe in the Shining Light of Truth. That's what you mean.' The man was a poor physical specimen with a big head. He was aged twenty-five.

On the top of his desk the policeman slid one piece of paper from under another and said to the woman, 'You too?'

She said, 'Yes.' She was thin as sticks and with her long hair she looked like a kid's doll. She was also twenty-five.

The policeman was reminded of his fishing trips to the wide river at night at the moment that he felt the presence of a big catch.

He said, 'Do you know of any so-called *SLT* activity in this area?'

The man said, 'Two days ago there was a gathering.'

'Was there really?'

'Definitely.'

'Did you go?'

'We didn't.'

'Why not?'

'We were working. And there were enough believers ready to go.'

And the woman said, 'We can go to the next one.'

'When is the next one?'

'I don't know yet.'

The policeman looked at the woman and said, 'About this gathering you say there was - where did they go after it finished?'

'Wherever they wanted to go.'

'You admit you knew there was going to be gathering of an anti-social cult. Why didn't you tell the police?'

It was at this point that the station chief came in the room. He heard his deputy's question and he heard the replies.

The man said, 'Nothing harmful was happening. There was no reason to tell the police.'

The woman said, 'The police might stop the gathering.'

The chief said, 'You've admitted withholding information on an illegal gathering.'

The deputy said, 'And she threatened that they will gather again.'

'Again!' said the chief. 'When?'

'I don't know,' said the man. 'We just know there will be.'

'You give me threats?' said the chief. 'I don't want threats. I'll give you threats. I want the truth. And if I don't get it quick I'll stomp on your girlfriend's face.' The chief had a large and muscular body.

'I won't respond to violence,' said the man.

'Is that so?' said the chief. He smashed his fist into the man's nose. The man toppled backwards, still sitting in a wooden chair. His head hit the floor and thick blood seeped from his nose. The woman screamed. The chief slapped her across the face. He said, 'Now we are going to learn something.'

The man said, 'Don't do that.'

The chief slapped the woman again. She did not scream.

The man said, 'Unless you are peaceful we will not cooperate.'

The chief shouted, 'Hey! Get in here!' Four policeman came in the room.

The chief said, 'Pick him up. Take him out and break his resistance.'

One of the policemen said, 'And her?'

The chief said, 'She's mine.'

The woman said, 'Oh, Mr Policeman, you're not going to learn anything.' She did not seem to be frightened. There was something spooky about her. The chief hesitated for a moment.

The woman said, 'You are a lonely little boy.'

The four policemen and his deputy were looking at him.

The chief screamed, 'Take him out!' The men moved. He grabbed hold of the woman's collar and pulled her out of the chair. He had an impulse to rape her and in fear and anger he threw her at the wall with so much force that the bang to her skull killed her. The man who was taken outside to the public security station courtyard was beaten and kicked until he died. He did not say anything.

When, twelve hours later, the Minister heard about the interrogation killing of the two SLT believers he said, 'The fucking idiots!' He was angry. He threw everything off his desk. He kicked over a pedestal. He pulled the curtains off the windows. He picked up a chair and threw it at a wall. He stopped, breathing hard and thinking *this is the way I die*. In his mind was the next monthly meeting of the State Council, four days away.

Still panting, he said, 'Get me that fucker on the phone.'

When he was connected to the village police chief the Minister said to him, 'URRRRRGGHHHHHHHH! URRRRRGH-HHHHHHHH! URRRRRGGHHHHHHHH! You know what this means! You know what this means!'

The police station chief said, 'I'm sorry! I'm sorry! Minister, please!'

'No! You are fucking dead! Understand?!' And he threw the phone at the wall where it broke.

CHAPTER 26
Day 3, 12:34 pm

When the door of his cell was locked behind him, Ghosh's mind and body melted into sleepiness. The moment Ghosh fell asleep he was awakened and brought out for interrogation. He was pushed into the Minister's office - his second visit.

The Minister's manner contrasted with the calm he showed at the airport: 'What's all this about numbers, urgh? You and Nelson! What do you know? Speak!'

'Now,' said the Party Secretary, 'I suggest we proceed in a meticulous manner more likely to produce a desirable outcome by uncovering apparently minor though actually significant details that the interviewee himself cannot fabricate into an inauthentic coherence - should he ever wish to.'

'You're a cold-hearted bastard,' said the Minister.

Ghosh said, 'Why am I here? Have I been arrested? What is the crime?'

The Party man said, 'And may I remind everybody that this is an *interview*.'

'Oh yes, a voluntary interview,' said the Minister.

'Exactly,' said the Party Secretary.

'And everyone is free to go whenever he wants,' said the Minister.

'That's correct,' said the Party man.

'Just as long as the Party dis-invites them from attending. And we give prisoner man the key,' said the Minister.

'At the time of your arrest,' said the Party man, 'in the year 201_ on the 4th February at 2:37 am, what, exactly, were you wearing?'

The Minister said 'Urgh.'

Ghosh looked Party Secretary: 'I know you. And I saw your friend.'

And the Minister said, 'He's insane.'

A door opened, and in a loud whisper Vice-Minister Dong Bing said: 'Nelson is ready.' Dong Bing gave a phone to the

Minister who began talking to Nelson while the Party man spoke to Ghosh, quietly, saying: 'It may be difficult for you to understand that many innocent people are dead and many more are grieving for them. You were nearby. I believe you didn't cause the deaths or know anything about the conspiracy to cause them and, if you help our investigation, I am prepared to say so publicly. However, you were near. As well as helping us, you can help the people who died and their families. I think you may know something useful, even if you don't realize it yourself.'

'How many people died?' said Ghosh.

'One hundred and forty-seven members of the public and one hundred and fifty public servants.'

'Oh. I heard those numbers in the car. I thought it was a basketball game.'

'Basketball?'

'Something to do with basketball. Scores.'

Meanwhile the conversation between the Minister and Nelson went like this: 'Nelson.'

Nelson said, 'Uncle.'

'I'm not your uncle.'

'We will never know for sure. And before I help you to know what you want to know, I want to talk conditions.'

'How much?'

'Not money. Any fool can get that. I'll solve your mystery for information.'

'What info?'

'Something I don't know about the Japanese navy. Something useful.'

'Nelson, you can't - '

'Goodbye.'

'No, wait. Good. Urghhhh.' There was a long pause.

The Minister said, 'See what I can do. And payment on delivery.'

'Of course. Now let me talk to the foreigner.'

Ghosh was given the phone.

Nelson said, 'Hello. We are going to chat. I like to talk around and sideways. They say you're Indian.'

'I'm British.'

'They say you don't look it.'

'What do they know? Have they ever been to England?'

'They've seen pictures.'

'Yeah - Winston Churchill and Princess Diana.'

'The beautiful and the great. Churchill was beautiful. How could a few people from a small island country like England win so many battles and take over the world?'

'Certain economic conditions allowed it.'

'Ah! Do you believe that answer?'

'Yeah.'

'That's the reason those days are over and England is weak now and China is strong.'

'Economic conditions.'

'No. Because of the fact that you believe that *economic conditions* caused England to be great. Shows lack of confidence.'

'It's true.'

'Don't you like stories?'

'Everyone likes stories.'

'Truth is the least interesting story of all,' said Nelson.

'So why are you in Tokyo?' said Ghosh.

Nelson said:

'You ask me why I live in the Jade Mountains

I smile, unanswering; my heart is calm.

That's the old poem. I'm making up my own story.'

'Aren't there any stories in China?' said Ghosh.

'Too many. I'm exhausted with hearing them or making them. It's too much for one person.'

'So you live in Japan. Doing what?'

'Shopping.'

'You've got a lot of money?'

'Listen. Tokyo is the best place for shopping in the world. I have shopped and now there's no *thing* I want. You can have all my things. The only thing I want is my pink lampshade.'

'That's your story.'

'This Mao Zedong map they found - is that a story?'

'I don't know. It's Mao's story, told in a certain way.'
'The things in the list - do you know them?' said Nelson.
'Yes, I think so.'
'Tell me.'
Ghosh said to the room he was in, 'Give me the paper you found on the dead people.'
The Minister and the Party Secretary looked at each other, unable to reach a decision. Vice Minister Dong Bing, meanwhile, took an enlarged copy of the *Map* from a folder and handed it to Ghosh.

Chairman Mao's Positive and Negative Map of a Four-Sided Building

Beaten by Father
Lose mother
Learn violence
Lose wife
Make Zhou mine
Defeat Jiang
Lose son
Stung by 7,000 insects
Start Cultural Revolution
Betrayed by Lin
Plant seed of truth

Ghosh said to Nelson, 'First, Mao Zedong was born - in 1893, Year of the Snake. That's a story everybody in China knows. It's said he hated his father and loved his mother.'
'A story I understand,' said Nelson. 'Go on.'
Ghosh told how the boy Mao Zedong ran away from school and was beaten by his father and made to submit. How he became a rebel, a bitter opponent of authority, and was still loved by his mother until she died and left him, still growing up to be a half-educated Marxist revolutionary, finding failure and defeat until he learned the power of violence and the right way to use it. Ghosh told how violence was used against him by his enemies the

government when they executed his wife - because she was his wife - and of all his wives the only one he really loved, the story goes. How he had his ups and downs in fighting political and military battles, gaining, through bullying and treacherous blackmail, a right-hand man, Zhou Enlai, his ally and servant for forty-four years. How Mao by hook, crook, luck and skill won the war against his enemies to become the leader of China, and how the very next year his favourite son, the sane, healthy, capable son of the favourite wife, was bombed to death by Americans in the Korean War. How bureaucrats of the government he created gradually edged him from power until the day seven thousand officials gathered in Beijing to sting him with faint praise and hive him off to a pedestal set apart from authority. They called it *retirement*. How he spent his retirement cooking up revenge on these *insects* and served it with venom in the Cultural Revolution that manipulated the masses into squashing them. How in this triumph he set up a successor, a surrogate son, named Lin Biao, who let the anointment go to his head and tried to get rid of the old man ahead of time. How Lin failed and was killed to leave Mao facing the fear that death would mean the end of it all and final victory for the bureaucrats, the pragmatists, the *insects*.

Ghosh said, 'By 1976 he must have known he would never escape from his illnesses and that he was without sons, heirs, or allies of any worth.'

Nelson said, 'This list is a puzzle, and for any puzzle the best thing to do is think of numbers. Do you know the date of each event?'

'Yes. Except the last one: *Plant the seed of truth*.' Ghosh told Nelson the year of each event, and guessed the last.

Nelson memorised the numbers and combined them by adding, subtracting, multiplying and dividing.

He said, 'Wrong set of numbers.'

Ghosh said, 'How about the traditional Chinese calendar?' Traditional years?'

'I'll try them but it doesn't make sense. Too imperial. Especially when the list is focussed on new Emperor Mao.'

'How about Mao's age? His own age.'

'Time starts with Mao? Yes, good thinking. I'll try those numbers, too,' said Nelson. 'Now, you tell the Minister and the Party Secretary this: the sentences are coded numbers. Dates, ages, years - something. The numbers will add up and point somewhere. Who knows where? And if we do know, we may not like it. It may be a clue or it may be a distraction. Call me back in an hour. I need to calculate.'

CHAPTER 27
Day 3, 1:30 pm

Nelson was twenty-six. He saw numbers like others saw people - clear and real - and he saw them everywhere: times, dates, prices, quantities, repeated actions, countable gestures, and character strokes. For example, when he first saw any written characters he immediately saw the number of strokes needed to write them. Take 密码 *mìmǎ*, secret code. A total number of nineteen strokes, eleven for the first character and eight for the second; and the first character is made of a three-stroke radical and an eight-stroke phonetic. The second is five and three. Of course, for such everyday words as *secret code* Nelson knew the numbers by heart, and didn't need to look anymore. As a child he soon found numbers everywhere and started to use them.

When he was a boy his clothes were made by a tailor, an elderly man of skin, bone and delicate fingers, and who still existed in the fear of the Great Proletarian Cultural Revolution. The man four-folded every piece of paper he was given into tiny packages – just like the coded list of Mao dates was folded. The tailor and kept the papers folded until the first chance he had to burn them in a fire, at which point he unfolded them because folded papers are difficult to burn and may leave incriminating evidence. In this way the tailor carefully burned messages and sketches from Nelson's mother regarding trouser width and collar shapes, messages with numbers on them and other code-like symbols. If Nelson read the numbers he always had them in his head. He would shock the tailor by looking at a garment and listing its dimensions. The tailor thought Nelson had a measuring eye; what he really had were numbers, though it often amounts to the same thing.

The tailor worked in a shed in the street, a space about a metre square, with three walls of plywood and the fourth wall being that of the building the shed leaned against. Coke briquettes glowed in a clay-made brazier on the floor of the shed almost any time of year – handy for burning written things. Once, Nelson's mother sent the boy Nelson with a note demanding the earlier completion of a suit being made for his attendance at some family ceremony. The tailor burned the note, padlocked his shed and took Nelson to his apartment where the half cut and tacked suit was hanging on a string line in a grey room. While the tailor had him wear the suit and made adjustments, Nelson noticed a squat safe hidden under a rag in the corner of the room and wondered if the money inside it was folded up, like the notes. In fact, the tailor kept his money unfolded; under his pillow when he was asleep and in a secret pocket sewn into his trousers while he was awake. The safe was a sham.

Around that time, when Nelson was a boy of six or seven, he idolised the Monkey King, the favourite hero of Chinese boys for hundreds of years. The tailor made him a Monkey King costume and Boy Nelson thought he was the secret child who would grow up to be the Monkey King. In the old story, the Monkey King is obliged to protect the weak, pure and obsessed priest who is travelling through treacherous landscapes to find the holy words of eternal truth and bring them back to China. Monkey King is miraculously talented but needs discipline to accomplish anything. He doesn't want the priest protection job and doesn't like the job, and knowing this, the gods in heaven bind him to the priest through pain and the threat of pain in the form of a gold band around his head that tightens inexorably when he is bad and neglects his task. Monkey King can sometimes bear the pain of the tightening metal band - for short periods of escape - but as the band shrinks and the pain persists and intensifies he always surrenders and is bound back to the side of the priest. Nelson, like the Monkey King, is also prodigiously talented and fabulously undisciplined. For Nelson, the rings around his head were the rings of family, school and society. The bands had been attached to him several sizes too small and at a certain point Nelson's brain burst through. And now he has to construct and fit his own band. Otherwise his brains will spill and rot. This is his own torment.

CHAPTER 28
Day 3, 1:31pm

Locked in his prison cell, Ghosh's tired body was still and his tired mind was busy. He thought of many things and first among them was buddleia. Buddleia - is that two syllables or three? If *fear* is one, is *leia* more? For Ghosh, thoughts of buddleia meant thoughts of home and of the space and time of summer; calm summers on the quiet streets of Southsea, with the sun like kindness on the hanging heads of fuchsia in the tended gardens and on the heavier heads of buddleia in the untended. The flowers of buddleia bushes are curly cone shapes in purple or violet, attractive to butterflies, though treated as a weed. Buddleia grows everywhere in his hometown: along unloved railway sidings, from cracks in neglected walls, and in the charmless back yards of rented accommodation. Buddleia is from China where its names is *zuìyúcǎo*, drunken fish plant.

Buddleia was not in bloom when Chen had been there with him in England. It was not summer nor was it the ideal England of his dreaming recollections. The light was off for winter. When Chen had asked her question about returning to China and Ghosh said *yes*, Chen had immediately texted someone to hold two seats for them on the next Air China Air flight to Beijing. Ghosh and his friend and flatmate, Liam, stared at her in silence.

Then Chen said: 'I'm looking for a prostitute.'

Neither Ghosh nor Liam made a spoken response.

Chen frowned. 'Where do prostitutes live?'

'I'm not sure. Is this serious? Who for?'

'It's serious. It's for me. Somebody needs help. My help. A woman from my home province. When I met her a few hours ago I couldn't help.'

'OK.' Ghosh looked at his flatmate.

Liam shrugged and said, 'Internet and taxi drivers. And there's a flyer somewhere.' He opened a slim drawer in the kitchen table and pulled out a bunch of flyers. He selected one and gave it to Chen. It was black and white and showed a long-haired Filipina-looking woman in her underpants glaring over her shoulder at the camera. The main text was, 'Japanese massage'.

Chen said, 'She's not Japanese.'

'Yeah,' said Ghosh. 'It's marketing. Several prejudices are operating here.'

They called a number. Liam found more numbers and they called two more places. Chen and Ghosh went out walking at half past midnight through the streets of late Victorian red brick houses, some large, once family homes, and now shells, altered inside and used for different purposes. They found the street they wanted and Chen stopped outside a building and said, 'Yes. This looks like the kind of place.' It had a dirty yellow coat, not recently painted, with shut and locked windows, closed curtains, a certain mood of no love, and the name holding false promises. Chen read the sign: *Primrose Rest Home.*

She said, 'Primrose is a flower. Is that true?'

'Yes. Yellow flower.'

'Flower girls?'

'No. This is an old people's home.'

'It looks like a prison.'

The place they wanted was three houses away.

Ghosh pressed a buzzer.

'Yeah?' came a voice.

'I called earlier. Name's John.'

'John.' The door was buzzed open; Ghosh pushed through and Chen stayed outside. He was in a scuffed white hallway, facing stairs. He went up. In a scuffed white landing area, a middle aged Chinese woman was behind a counter, sitting high up, probably on a stool. Without looking directly at him, she said, 'Mr John?'

'Yeah.'

'What girl?'

'Er . . .'

On the counter top was a small plastic cat in gold and white; a cat god with left paw raised to welcome guests' money. On the wall behind the counter was a calendar printed for Wuzhou Precision Metallics Inc. Ghosh had a desire to speak Chinese, to reveal himself, to be a good person in the eyes of this woman. He knew that was not what Chen wanted, and resisted his desire.

The woman said, 'Girl. You girl.'

'Yeah. I'm new here. I don't know.'

'First time.'

'Yeah.'

'AH MEI MIMI XIAO LI!!!' shouted the woman. There was a deep silence.

After about thirty seconds, and more or less simultaneously, three white doors opened and three silent women came out. Here was a difficult choice.

One wasn't thin, and two were too thin. They all wore fresh make-up but their eyes were stale and their movements showed tiredness at this the start of their working day.

Chen had said long arms and curly hair.

'Only three girls in the house?' asked Ghosh.

'How many do you want? Only three now. How many do you want?'

'I want to go to the toilet,' said Ghosh.

'Toilet!' The woman behind the counter pointed at the nearest of the three younger women and shouted, 'Toilet!' The younger woman turned back into her room and Ghosh followed her. She gestured to a door. It was a scruffy toilet. Ghosh closed the door and telephoned Chen. He whispered, 'They don't have curly hair.'

Chen said, 'Wrong women. Wrong house. Come out.'

Ghosh came out of the toilet and the woman in the room said, 'You don't use toilet.'

Ghosh said, 'Sorry,' and gave her the money he had prepared. £50. She hid it in an instant and followed him out to the reception area. Ghosh went towards the exit and had trouble opening the door. The middle-aged woman quickly came out from behind the counter and manipulated the locks and handles, using the time to shout in Ghosh's ear. 'Toilet! Toilet! Fuck you! Fuck you! Never come back!'

Ghosh and Chen walked to another special house. This time the arrangement was different. There was a buzzer but no stairs inside - the first room was the reception and the other rooms were either upstairs or downstairs. Again, there was a middle aged woman behind a counter, and this room was dark despite being lit with many small lights set in the walls and ceiling, and the counter was like a bar, in glossy black marble-effect laminate, and there were masses of plastic flowers arranged in a vase.

'Hiya,' said the woman. 'Mr John, first time?'

'Er, yeah.'

'How can we help you?'

'Do you have, er, ladies?'

'Ladies? Yes, beautiful ladies.'

'Can I, er . . . '

'Certainly. Just a moment. Sit down. Relax. Don't look nervous.' She pressed a buzzer under the counter. Bells rang in other rooms. 'Just wait,' she said. 'Be relaxed. Can I get you a drink?'

'A drink?'

'Whiskeybourbonbacardivodkabeers.'

'Oh. Oh, no thanks.' Ghosh coughed.

'You coughed,' said the woman.

'Yes,' said Ghosh, 'I did.'

The woman smiled at him with a smile meaning *you're an imbecile.*

Two women appeared, one from stairs below and one from above. They weren't young exactly – it was hard to say. Ghosh looked at them carefully. He looked at the madam behind the shining bar.

She said, 'Yes?'

'Could I use the toilet, please?'

'Toilet?'

'Yeah, sorry.'

She uncurled and extended an index finger to reveal a long and intricately decorated nail pointing at a door. The door was in the wall of the room, six inches from the floor, and after pulling the door open Ghosh had to step up to enter a space so small he only just avoided hitting his shins on the toilet bowl. It was a platform cubicle for an embarrassing performance. He pulled the door closed behind him. He heard mumbled conversation, possibly laughter. He got out his phone and doing so hit his elbow on a tiny shelf of two spare toilet rolls. The shelf rattled and seemed likely to fall. Chen answered his call.

'Two women,' said Ghosh.

'Thin?' said Chen.

'Yes, both thin.'

'Curly hair?'

'Yes, permed.'

'Both?'

'Both of them.'

'What do they look like?'

'Well, it's difficult,' he said.

Chen kept silent.

Ghosh closed his eyes. 'Hey, I'm tired.' That was his first thought. He said to Chen: 'One looks like a neglected pet and one looks like she's been stood out in the cold most of her life.'

'That's the one.'

Ghosh came out of the toilet.

The madam said, 'Please flush toilet.'

'Oh yes, sorry. Sorry.'

'OK.'

Ghosh did as he was asked. He looked at the stood-out-in-the-cold-most-of-her-life woman and said, 'Can I go to this lady's room, please?'

'This lady' smiled with her mouth.

'This lady?' said the woman behind the counter. 'Lovely. Britney, please take the gentleman.'

Ghosh moved to follow Britney upstairs.

'Deposit please,' said the madam.

'Deposit?' said Ghosh.

'That's our policy. Especially first time.'

Ghosh paid £50.

In the room, he asked the *lady*, Britney, 'Can you speak English?'

She said, 'Yinglish?'

Ghosh had already got his phone out and reached Chen, who said, 'Yes?' Ghosh said, 'It's another world. These places: all Chinese women and Chinese ornaments. It's China in England.'

'It's not China. Business; market; customers. A responsible person says: this is England.'

Marcas thought about this for three seconds: first whether this was something he agreed with, second whether to communicate his view, and third, in what words.

He said: 'This is England,' and gave the phone to Britney.

First, she listened with her face blank. Next, her face came alive and her voice started talking fast and loud. She quickly checked herself, and spoke quietly and urgently. It wasn't Standard Chinese and Ghosh understood nothing.

The woman passed the phone back to Ghosh. Chen said: 'Wait twenty minutes then leave. Go the main door and hold it open. She will run out with you.'

'She knows that?'

'Yes. And speak to her in Chinese. She can't understand English.'

'What – nothing?'

'Some swearing and sex words.' Chen ended the call.

Ghosh looked around Britney's room. The bed was the centre with its head against the wall furthest from the door. Against the other three walls were: a canvas wardrobe on a cheap pine frame, a set of white laminate drawers, and a black office chair, gas lift, on five casters. Sleep deprivation, jet lag, drinking red wine with Liam, and the fear and nervousness of the deception and escape he was now involved in, felt like a heavy burden. Ghosh was thirsty. He said to the woman slowly in standard Chinese, 'Have you got water I can drink?'

'I have.' She opened a door to a shower cubicle and turned on the shower. She picked a cup from the floor and held it under the shower to fill it with water. She wiped the bottom of the wet cup with a hand towel and handed it to Ghosh. He drank. It was a cheap mug with a faulty glaze and some rough china around the rim and was decorated with a red and green motif and the words *Merry Xmas!*

The woman motioned him to sit on the bed. As he sat he noticed the mattress was still wrapped in plastic but it was not new. It was too soft in the middle. He lay on top of the bed with the empty cup in his hands, the posture of an effigy on an unattractive tomb. All his muscles ached.

'Who are you?' said the woman.

'I'm tired,' said Ghosh.

There was a pause.

'Me too,' said the woman, quietly.

There was a longer pause. The woman said, 'Is it twenty minutes?' She had no watch, clock or phone. She didn't know what time it was. Ghosh looked at his phone. He had been in the room only seven minutes.

'What the hell,' he said, 'Let's go now.' As it turned out this was a fortunate piece of impatience. He called Chen: 'We're coming out now.'

'Good,' she said.

Ghosh stood up and stretched, letting out an involuntary sound that was a mixture of sigh and scream.

'Are you ready?' said Britney.

'I'm ready. You?'

She didn't answer.

They went out of the room together.

While Ghosh and Britney had been in the room together, the smart-looking woman behind the counter, the house madam, had felt suspicious of toilet-user Ghosh. She had phoned a heavy associate: 'Just wander over,' she said to him. 'Maybe nothing.' He started wandering.

Reaching the bottom of the stairs, Ghosh went straight and guilty to the house main door. The door was weighty. He wrenched it open. Britney rushed towards the open space. Just at that moment, the house madam's heavy associate arrived in the doorway. He was a man like a box packed in a black suit. Ghosh stopped, gawping, holding the door open.

Britney flung out her arm to strike the heavy man. The guy stepped back to avoid the hit and slipped in his genuine leather-soled shoes, his skull meeting paving stones as he bit his tongue and got concussed. Britney's straight-arm clenched-fist swipe swung on and thumped Ghosh in the eye.

Ghosh said 'Ow!' Britney grabbed his elbow and they stepped over the well-dressed enforcer prone on the threshold and were in the street. Chen was there.

Ghosh said, 'Pity we haven't got a car.'

Chen said, 'I called a taxi.' Sure enough, an Aqua Cars silvery-painted Skoda pulled up and they got in.

'Miss Chen?' said the driver.

'Yes.'

'Where to?'

'Ibis Hotel. Please.'

Back at the hotel in Chen's room Ghosh felt a rush of released energy and paced across the room. 'Wow. That was awesome. We rescued somebody,' he said.

'That was the easy part,' said Chen. 'This woman has no money, no phone and no passport. Now it gets difficult. In five minutes she could be back where she was.'

CHAPTER 29

Day 3, 1:45 pm

Vice Minister Dong Bing was relaxing by making notes once again on his project to list Chinese inventions - his spare moment hobby.

'An Authoritative List of Chinese Inventions

8. Tea
9. Chess
10. Checkers
11. Banks
12. Money
13. Rice
14. Golf
15. Government
16. Domesticated dogs
17. Civil service examinations
18. Zoos
19. Democracy
20. State-sponsored execution
21. Weaving
22. Dumplings
23. Agriculture
24. Pottery
25. Irrigation canals
26. Promotions by merit
27. Noodles (including Italian)
28. Still life painting
29. Landscape painting
30. State-sponsored exploration
31. Poetry
32. Philosophy
33. Sausages
34. Geology
35. Ploughs
36. Civilization
37. Football
38. Organized medicine

39. Ceramics
40. Cuisine
41. Maoist thought
42. Newspapers
43. Kites
44. Astronomy'.

CHAPTER 30
Day 3, 2 pm

Ghosh lay on the boards of the mattress-less bed in his cell and fell asleep. Thirty seconds later Ghosh's cell door was opened and a bowl of rice gruel was handed towards him. It had thin slices of pickled cabbage sparsely distributed over its surface and under its surface at the edge of the bowl was the guard's thumb. Ghosh took the bowl. There was no spoon or chopsticks. The food wasn't warm. Ghosh ate what he could. A minute later the guard took the bowl away and Ghosh was taken out of his cell to a latrine block. He had already peed in the corner of his relatively clean cell and the stink of long used, long unwashed open concrete trenches was one that, in Ghosh, induced constipation. He stood by the holes looking uncomfortable. The guard beside him was stocky and his shaved head had such dense black hair against the pale scalp that it looked blue, particularly in folds around the back of his neck.

The guard said 'Oh well, it's like that,' and lead Ghosh back again. On the way from latrine to cell, Ghosh saw a small rat.

'Oh! A rat!' he said.

'Silence!' shouted the guard. The guard opened Ghosh's cell door, shoved Ghosh inside and, for the first time, came in after Ghosh. The guard shut the cell door and looking grim and dark blue said, 'Do you like rats?'

'Oh yes.'

'Very intelligent. Good memory.'

'Very affectionate.'

'And good at learning.'

'And loyal.'

The guard opened the door, stepped outside, put his key in the lock and said, 'It understands people, too.' He pulled the door closed, locked it and left Ghosh alone inside.

Before sleeping once more, Ghosh thought of the rat and wondered where it was now and how much it *understands people*. He thought about the need of prisoners for friends within the system. And he thought of some of the other people who have been prisoners in China during his own lifetime, making a list to occupy his worrying mind.

He thought of the electrician who created the *5th Modernization* - democracy, wrote it on a poster and was sent to prison for nineteen years. He thought of the man from Hong Kong who was arrested for carrying a sweater to a political prisoner in Guangzhou, and he thought of the man who stayed in prison for fourteen years and never got the sweater. And at the end of the list he put himself.

CHAPTER 31
Day 3, 3 pm

Ghosh fell deeply asleep in his cell, and in his sleep he saw summer in England; a summer day in the northern part of the earth, a day so long it distorted time; summer with a pale clean blue sky and distant white clouds touching the horizon, the kind of huge clouds that transform at a speed slower than that of real life. He saw a white cloud, flat underneath and piled up above like the massive brain of a pig, a colossal pig with an IQ of 10,000, a being magnificent and lovely and God, and inspiring fear in people.

Ghosh was woken up and a phone struck his ear.

He heard Nelson's voice say, 'What are we going to chat about now?' Guards took his arms and he was dragged to the Minister's office, still with the phone pressed to his ear, and grumpy at being woken, too soon to be afraid.

Ghosh reached the office. He was panting from the sudden awakening and the exertion.

He said, 'I'm in this prison, I don't know where I am, I don't know what for, I don't know what time it is, I - '

'I understand. And we are all in some kind of prison.'

'Easy to say.'

'It is,' said Nelson. 'I won't say it again. Your situation is difficult. To change it, we need to talk about the *Map*. We need to solve their problem.'

'*We* need? Tell me what's the point of me solving anything? And what's in this for you?'

'I'm in it. It's a family affair. The frozen stiff that was holding this *Map* - that's my mother. My dead mother.'

'I didn't know that,' said Ghosh.

'As for you,' said Nelson, 'You're in it somehow. I don't know what way. I do know that if you help them - if you help *me* - I'll help you. I'll get you out, my friend.'

'OK.'

'And so now: numbers.'

'Numbers?'

'So far we've got numbers. Next we need to know what those numbers are the names of.'

'Names?' said Ghosh.

'Numbers show the pattern. Names show the object.'

'Why's your name Nelson?'

'A hero,' said Nelson. 'A fighter who only wanted to win and didn't care about being popular.'

'Admiral Nelson?'

'Who?'

'English sea general. Sailor fighting Napoleon. The ships, the sea, the war.'

'No, not that kind of fighting. And a modern person.'

'Oh, I see . . . Nelson.'

'Yes.'

'Why him?' said Ghosh.

'I wanted to be like him: to win every game and not care about being liked. And I love speed and I love to keep moving.'

'Why's that?'

'To distract the evil spirits in my brain. You know Buddhism, you know *The Dream of Red Chambers*? This life is not the only one. This life of mine now is just a short season, a season in hell. And I move around quickly to dodge the pain.'

'You sound like Rimbaud.'

'Rambo?'

'Yeah, Rimbaud.'

'I love Rambo! *Bang-bang, bang-bang, bang-bang, bang!* He's a model hero.'

'I think that's a different Rimbaud,' said Ghosh. 'Rimbaud is 兰波 lánbō, and Rambo is 兰博 lánbó.'

'Two names. What's the difference?'

'Ah . . .'

'Rambo is a human being and pure at the same time', said Nelson. 'That's his real strength. Of course he's lonely and doesn't have any friends but he still influences people, people still think of him. It was a long time ago.'

'Ah, yes, it's a different Rimbaud,' said Ghosh. 'My Rimbaud was also a long time ago, in France, and he did different things.'

'What was your Rambo doing when he was my age?'

'What age?'

'Twenty-six.'

'He was . . . he was in Africa, trading. Coffee and Guns,' said Ghosh.

'Sounds like my Rambo. Sounds like my dream. What was Mao Zedong doing when he was twenty-six?'

'It was the year his mother died. He was alone in cold Beijing.'

'And how old was he when he hated his father?'

'That was when he ran away from school, he was nine, his tenth year.'

'Did you ever run away from school?' said Nelson.

'No,' said Ghosh. 'I liked school.'

'That's why you know all these little details about our Chairman Mao.'

'And you don't?'

'Knowing that isn't worth ten years of my life reading books in a classroom.'

'Did you run away?'

'I didn't run away. I stayed away. How about you - were you running away when you were arrested?'

'I was drunk. Kind of running away.'

'And what happened?'

'I was in car first and next in an office - '

'Yeah, and the numbers the Minister was talking about?'

'Oh, they were ignoring me, thinking I couldn't understand anything and they were talking about this map, I guess. I hadn't seen it yet. They were talking about *seven thousand* and they didn't know what it was and I said 1962 and they told me to shut up and put me in an empty room. Well, not really empty, as it turned out. That's a story in itself. And Room 62, too, by coincidence.'

'There are no coincidences. A room, a number, a date. That's it! Tell the Minister and the Party Secretary that the numbers name *rooms*. Rooms in the Ministry. That's why it's a *map*. But it's not finished. There's one more thing. We still need to know the meaning of the rooms. We will speak again. For now that's *it*.'

CHAPTER 32
Day 3, 5 pm

Ghosh was taken back to his cell with an escort that was rougher than need be.

Ghosh shouted, 'I can walk!'

They didn't let him. They dragged him. He squirmed. A guard hit him in the stomach.

'Where are you from?' the guard said.

Ghosh was dropped and locked in his cell. He was angry, exhausted, upset and afraid. Eventually he slept. He woke up feeling exhausted, his heart racing, desperately needing to sleep and not being able to sleep. Some irritating phrases were singing clearly in his head:

Mocky TROMblay
Je reGRET
LorROPpo zonshun
Para PETS.

This was what his Dad used to chant at bath times to the shivering boy Marcas while he was being towelled dry on the white cotton bath mat in their big cold house. *Mocky TROMblay, Je reGRET, LorROPpo zonshun, Para PETS.* The familiar rhythm of it was a comfort to a five year old, and could drive an adult insane:

da-da DA-da
da-da-DA
da-DA-da da-da
da-da-DA.

Mocky TROMblay, Je reGRET, LorROPpo zonshun, Para PETS.

Ghosh didn't know it was Rimbaud's *The Drunken Boat,* originally: *Moi qui tremblais, . . . Je regrette l'Europe aux anciens parapets!*

The sounds of the guard had woken him; boots on the concrete floor and the scraping of the metal door. The guard said,

'You. You know what you are? A snail in a beehive. Everyone is buzzing around wanting to know about you.

Some are interested and all the rest want to know what's so interesting. Some like you; some hate you - they've all got an opinion.'

He handed Ghosh a bowl of lukewarm noodles in an oily broth. Ghosh sat up on the wooden bed that had no mattress or blankets. He was still wearing his puffed down coat. He put the bowl on the bed beside him.

The guard said, 'The other guards don't like you because you're dirty.'

'Dirty?'

'Pissing in your cell.'

Ghosh decided it was better not to say there was no choice; that he had banged on his door and shouted for a toilet. It was the guards' prerogative to decide right and wrong and dirty.

The guard had stepped into the cell and shut the door.

He said, 'I have your rat.'

Slowly and carefully the guard put his cupped hand into his jacket pocket and when he took it out there was a bright-eyed rat standing on the palm.

'Who's interested in me?' said Ghosh.

'Oh well. There's the Minister and some people in the Ministry and some people privately and there's the Party. And Nelson's your friend.'

Ghosh frowned.

'Don't think about it,' said the guard. 'Nobody knows what it means. Certainly not you.'

Ghosh sighed. He looked at the rat.

The guard said, 'Let's see if he likes you. Hold out your fist. Open the fist.'

The rat walked from the guard's palm to Ghosh's.

'He agrees with me,' said the guard. 'He trusts you.'

The rat was standing still and moving its head.

'Rats are curious and explore every nook and cranny of new places,' said the guard.

'I know,' said Ghosh. 'I love rats.'

The tiny feet of the rat on his palm felt gentle and light, and Ghosh felt the awful vulnerability of a living being that was at that moment dependent on his goodwill. The eyes of the rat were black, watery and mobile.

Ghosh said, 'Rats can't see well.'

'Right,' said the guard. 'They just know dark and light. They have good noses and feel hot and cold. They like warm hands.'

'Rats usually clean themselves after being on people's hands. Even people they like. And still some people say rats are dirty.'

'Dirty? No, it's the conditions they have to live in. They don't build the prisons.'

'Is this the one I saw?' said Ghosh.

'I think it is,' said the guard. 'He's a good one. Look, he's relaxing. He likes being stroked.'

Ghosh was running his left thumb and index finger carefully along the rat's spine.

'Can you hear him sing?' said the guard.

'No, I can't. You?'

'Me neither. My kids can. My ears aren't good. Too many cigarettes.'

'Smoking?'

'Bad for the hearing.'

'Really?'

'Huh!' shouted the guard. 'What! What are you fucking saying?' He snatched up the uneaten bowl of noodles, exited the cell and slammed the door. He shouted, 'Don't understand! Not a fucking word! Shut your face!'

As the door was being locked from the outside, Ghosh heard the footsteps of another guard walk past. The guards greeted each other and the other guard walked on. He heard the first guard cough. And the cough was to Ghosh and meant: *you know why I did that, don't you?*

CHAPTER 33
Day 3, 8 pm

Ghosh sat down and thought back to England and to what had happened there when he and Chen had got the woman, Britney, into Chen's hotel room where they faced the problem of what to do with her. She had no money, no phone and no passport.

Chen said, 'We've helped you get out of that house, now what do you want to do?'

Britney was looking at the floor and said, 'At that moment, when I first saw you standing like a heroine statue in the street, that was all I wanted: to get out of that house. I never want to be there again; I never want to do that again. Enough!'

'And now what?'

'I'm not asking for your help any more. You did what I asked.'

'You can't stay in this hotel room the rest of your life.'

'I could if I died now.'

'Is that what you want? Is that what we helped you for?'

'No, no. I'm sorry. Thank you for helping me. Big sister; little brother. Thank you both. I'm feeling weak. I'm tired. I don't want to die.' Britney clutched at Chen's arm and said, 'I can't go back to China. There's a debt like the mountains. My family want me to work. They don't know what I have to do. Going back to China is a failure if I'm not bringing money back. That's useless.'

'What can you do?'

'Maybe work in London - in a restaurant. I've heard about it.'

'No passport. Illegally?'

'I won't be the only one. I don't have a passport now and I'm working.'

'Isn't there a chance of them finding you?'

'A big chance. The Company will know where to look.'

'Will they look?'

'They'll keep their eyes open. If they don't catch me they lose money and they'll be embarrassed.'

'That's important?' said Ghosh. 'Being embarrassed?'

'The most important,' said Britney. 'If somebody runs away it means anybody could run away and nobody is afraid. They need the fear. To keep us.'

'Are you afraid?' said Chen.

'Of course. But I want to try. I can change my name; change my hair - a little.'

'Without a passport you can't leave.'

'Yes. That's a big problem. It comes back to the first problem: money. With money I can buy my passport. Either my real passport or another one.'

'Did you have a real passport?'

'I think it was real. It passed every border check on the way to England. But it wasn't me in the photograph.'

'How much is it worth?'

'As much as I am willing to pay for it.'

'We need to negotiate.' Chen called the customer number of the house where Britney worked. The madam answered and Chen said in Standard Chinese, 'We have Britney.'

The madam said, 'What do you want?'

'Passport,' said Chen.

There was a rustling sound. A man said, 'You've had your fun. Bring our woman back now.' He was the heavy who landed on the pavement.

'Passport,' said Chen.

'Fuck you,' said the man.

Chen said, 'If - '

'No fucking way. She's our property.'

'But - '

'Fuck your mother's cunt.'

Chen said nothing and the man said nothing.

Chen said, 'We've got money.' She ended the call.

The man she'd been talking to was kicking furniture and was cursing the madam for her negligence, her stupidity, her carelessness, her incompetence, her age, her ugliness, and for being a whore. He kicked a chair and broke it and knocked the madam to the ground with his fist.

And he called the last number on his phone: Chen.

'Twenty thousand,' he said.

Chen said, 'Is this two peasants haggling over gizzards in the meat market? No. A business proposition. She can earn you £50 per customer and with nine customers a night - if you're lucky - that's £450 a day and for six days a week - at the lucky rate - that's £2,7000 a week and £10,800 a month before any of your expenses - about a third - and your professional obligations - another third. So the real price is £10,000. The same as three month's profit. That's what we'll give you. Upfront. Benefit of cash now. No loss of value.'

'We could use her for two years.'

'Huh! She's going to die of something first.'

'She's not the type.'

'She'd do it to spite you. So take the money. Now, this night. You. Straight to you. Tell us where to find you.' The call ended.

Britney said, 'What makes you think we get a day off every week? He must be laughing at you. Anyway it's a trick. He's not the real owner. He's the minder. He could sell you the passport and he'd still want me. He'd give you the passport, take your money and take me too. I belong to the Company - same as him. He could explain selling a passport but never be able to explain losing a woman. He'd never give you the passport without taking me first. And the Company would only accept money for me if it totally pays off my debt. And they'd want to punish me for running away. And fine me for breaking the contract.'

Chen called the minder again: 'Call your people. We want the woman.'

The minder said, 'I called them already. It's £50,000 - plus a fine. No negotiation.'

'Hopeless,' whispered Britney.

Chen said, 'We'll give you £8,000 immediately and in cash. Give us the passport.'

'It's not that kind of deal. You're not buying the passport. You're buying the woman and all her debts to us. The passport is security. We give it you when you've paid for the woman.'

'OK,' said Chen. 'We'll call back when we've got the cash.' The call ended and Chen said, 'No passport.'

Chen and Ghosh decided to send Britney to a cheap hotel in London. They would send her by taxi.

Britney said, 'How can I contact anybody?'

Ghosh said to Chen, 'Give her your phone.'

'Yes,' she said.

Then Chen checked herself. Though she wanted to help this woman her duty was with Ghosh - or rather with the Ministry and her target was Ghosh. Ghosh was important and the flower woman was extra.

She said, 'No.'

'What?'

'Not my phone. Definitely not. Give her your phone.'

'My phone? Do you know what you're asking? That concussed heavy guy is no joke. What if he gets the number? And the number of people on there.'

'Him? He won't. They have to catch Britney first.'

Ghosh shrugged his eyebrows.

Chen said, 'OK. You're right. Sorry. But without a phone she'll have no contact. It's not perfect.'

'I'll say,' said Ghosh.

They gave Britney the phone number of hotel she was going to in London.

'It's not perfect,' said Chen again, this time in Chinese.

Britney said, 'How can I contact anybody? How can I call my mother? I can't go out and haven't got a passport. Is this freedom? I'm a fool. I was feeling really bad and then I saw you. I thought I knew you. It was a mistake.'

'It was,' said Chen. 'In a way. An understandable mistake.'

'That's my life: three bad fates to choose. Go back home with nothing except debt and disgrace and the memories of what I did and what was done to me in this country. Or stay like I was in those houses. Or like now, run away to emptiness and fear.'

'It's a risk,' said Chen.

Britney said, 'I have no hope.' And she started to cry.

In the end they had to leave her. They gave her money and instructions written down. They called a taxi. They went outside to see her off. After the taxi left and they stood in the night shadows, they saw a man walk towards the hotel entrance from a parked car. It was the minder they'd seen at Britney's house, the one who had fallen in the street, the same one Chen had talked to on the phone. Ghosh and Chen walked away from the hotel, without the minder seeing them.

Chen said, 'This is a wild town.'

Ghosh said,' I've lived here all my life and never seen it. Have you got stuff in the hotel room?'

'Just clothes. Nothing I need. Things I can buy again.'

They walked around in the early dark morning. It was 3:15 am. They were matched in sleeplessness.

Chen said, 'I couldn't sleep on the plane.'

'You probably slept the night before.'

'Yes.'

'I'd had a bad night. We'll both sleep tonight.'

'We will', said Chen.

CHAPTER 34
Day 3, 8:30 pm

In a spare moment, Vice Minister of Religious Affairs, Dong Bing, added to his list.

'An Authoritative List of China's Inventions Compiled for the Education of the People.

45. Lathes
46. Chisels
47. Planes
48. Spectacles
49. Fireworks
50. Schools
51. Circuses
52. Universities
53. Kindergartens
54. Prisons
55. Lawyers
56. Lacquer
57. Playing cards and card games
58. Police
59. Many delicious dishes
60. Acupuncture
61. Crossbows
62. Codified law
63. Wrought iron
64. Segmental arch bridges
65. Suspension bridges
66. Steel
67. Toilet paper
68. Many kinds of rudder
69. Umbrellas
70. Kung fu
71. Abacuses
72. Silk
73. Wheelbarrows
74. Elements of mathematics including negative numbers'.

An invention is more than the first manufacture of a product, it is the way it is used and becomes part of society and culture. And Dong Bing anguished over whether to include the cell phone in the authoritative list of Chinese inventions. He had a physical repulsion to using desk phones, and to him they were fat, ancient and backward, reminding him unwillingly of elephantiasis, bloated legs, pathological obesity, imbecility and immobility. He relished the clean, cordless, unattached, light, crisp and free feeling of cell phones. Cell phones were modern, part of the future and had no past, dirt or contamination. Yes, he thought - cell phones are Chinese.

'75. Cell phones'.

CHAPTER 35
Day 3, 9 pm

The reason Britney's minder knew to come to the Ibis Hotel in Portsmouth and to find Chen's room was because he called one of the night shift supervisors at Aqua Taxis. The cab company phone operator took the call and she transferred it to the supervisor, saying, 'It's Bob the Chinese.'

Gary the supervisor took the call, 'Alright, Bob.'

'How are you, Gary? Business good?'

'Midweek. Bit quiet. How's things with you?'

'To be honest with you, Gary, one of our girls gone missing. And a customer. He took her in a taxi. It's OK but we're worried about her. Where the taxi took them?'

'Hang on,' said Gary. He consulted with the operator. It so happened that the driver, Matt, was just then in the crowded office.

Gary came back to the phone, 'Two girls, was it?'

'No. One girl from us and another woman was with him already. You don't know some funny bent blokes. He wasn't English.'

'Yeah, Matt says looked a bit Muslim. Two birds, eh? Dirty sod.'

'Dirty, you are right. Where did they go?'

'Ibis, it was.'

'Thank you, Gary.'

And about thirty minutes later, after going to the Ibis Hotel and finding Chen's room empty and hearing that another taxi had been seen leaving with a Chinese woman, Bob the minder called Aqua again. He said, 'Hello. Gary. I want to speak to Gary. This is Bob. Chinese Bob.'

The man who answered was a driver and not the phone operator, who was at that moment *powdering her nose*, her euphemism for eating a pack of chocolate brownies in the toilet. The driver put the phone down on the tabletop and picked it up again. He said, 'Gary's out. Is this about the Chinese girl?'

'Yeah. Where did they go?'

'Yes. I know where they went. The cab took them to Cambridge.'

'Cambridge?'

'Cambridge,' said the driver.

'Ah! *Jiànqiáo*. She will be farming there.'

'Leeks is it?'

'Maybe killing chickens. Cheers for information.'

In fact Britney was on her way to London, as planned. When the taxi reached the cheap hotel in Earls Court the driver said, 'Awlie dahrin, daz chew under fifty paan.'

Britney passed over the money Chen had prepared and got out without saying a word and without looking at the driver.

'Sillichinkibitch, nosensovuuma.'

CHAPTER 36
Day 3, 9:30 pm

At 9:30 pm the prison guard kicked the heel of his boot on Ghosh's cell door, waking Ghosh from a brief sleep.

'Lights out!' shouted the guard, and kicked the metal door again.

'Sleep! Be quiet!' said the guard, kicking again with a loud clang. The light in Ghosh's cell went out, switched from the outside, by the guard.

'It's you again,' said Ghosh, quietly. Equally quietly, the guard said, 'It will always be me.'

The guard came silently into the cell carrying the rat in the crook of his elbow. He shut the door. He put the rat on the palm of his hand and the two men looked at the rat. The guard brought two hands together and the rat stood protected in the cradle of his warm red palms.

As for Ghosh, his protection had been ordered by the Religious Affairs Ministerial Branch Party Secretary. Ghosh's knowledge was dangerous to the Party Secretary and could also be dangerous to the Minister. The Party Secretary calculated that whoever controlled Ghosh controlled the timing and location of that danger and so had selected his own most reliable guards for the task.

Ghosh and the guard talked about the rat. On its front feet the rat had four pink toes and the nub of a thumb, and on each back foot he had five toes; all of the toes looked delicate.

'This is a man-rat,' said the guard.

'I know,' said Ghosh. 'Women-rats are more active and have softer fur.'

'Men-rats like to be petted more.'

Ghosh used the back of his index finger to stroke the rat's back.

He said, 'I've got an idea. Let me show you something.'

He took off his belt. In the cell, the only furniture was a bed and the bed was a wooden box, with no mattress, wider at the top than at the bottom. When the bed was pushed against the walls in a corner it formed an 'L'-shaped tunnel at floor level - a rat-sized a tunnel. Ghosh rolled his belt into a circle and wedged it at one end of the tunnel, between wall and bed. It was the short arm of the 'L'. The belt formed a circular entrance or exit. He took one niblet of sweetcorn from his pocket.

'Where did you get that?' said the guard. 'Your meal was pig bones and white cabbage on rice.'

'There were two corn niblets stuck to the underside of the cabbage leaf.'

Ghosh broke the sweetcorn niblet in two and said, 'That should release the smell.'

He put the two broken halves on top of the rolled up belt.

'Oh,' said the guard, guessing what would happen.

'An experiment,' said Ghosh.

'Yes,' said the guard. The guard put the rat down on the floor just inside the entrance to the bed-wall tunnel - the long arm of the 'L'. The guard covered that entrance with the large sole of his boot. The rat was confused, a bit afraid and tried to exit but found no gap between boot sole and wall or bed. He sniffed again. He turned around, his tiny feet making a tiny sound on the dusty ground. He moved ahead cautiously. Air was still far away. He began to run. He reached the corner of the 'L'. He paused briefly. Behind him was a boot sole and ahead was air. He turned the corner and ran faster and faster, and as he reached the end of the tunnel he smelled sweetcorn and instead of exiting the obvious way through the looped belt circle, he jumped up onto the top of the belt and took the sweetcorn in his mouth. As he jumped down Ghosh caught him in his hands. The guard came around from his boot-sole-sentry position.

'Did he eat?' said the guard.

Ghosh handed the rat from his hands to the guard's. The rat's mouth was chewing.

'Ho, ho!' said the guard.

'I have one more,' said Ghosh, showing a sweetcorn niblet.

'Let me see this time,' said the guard.

Ghosh split the niblet and put it on the top of the looped belt, as before. The guard set the rat down at the far end of the tunnel and Ghosh put his foot there to block the rat. The guard moved to the other exit of the tunnel. This time the rat was quicker. He sniffed the sole of Ghosh's shoe once. He turned and began to run toward the air. He ran to the corner, turned, reached the end of the short 'L', jumped on the rolled up belt, took the sweetcorn and jumped down again. The guard caught him.

The guard said, 'Saw him! Saw him!' He stroked the rat. 'Oh yes, yes, yes. A clever rat! Interesting! That's nice!'

The guard looked at Ghosh: 'After eating the rat has to sleep now. You, too.' He moved to exit the cell.

Ghosh said, 'Rats and people are a bit different. Rats don't sleep all night long. They sleep many short sleeps, day and night.'

The guard stopped and said, 'They call me *Xiǎo Dí,*' - Young Di.

'*Xiǎo Dí.*'

'And my friends call me an English name, *Eddie*.'

Ghosh said, 'I have a Chinese name: *Guō Mǎkā*.'

'*Guō Mǎkā,*' said the guard. 'Made from the sound of your foreign name?'

'Yes.'

'But which characters?'

'*Wall, horse, coffee.*'

'That's a strange name,' said the guard. 'A bit strong, a bit bitter and surrounded by a wall. Maybe it suits you.'

The guard exited and Ghosh was locked up again. The night was eight hours long.

CHAPTER 37
Day 3, 11 pm

In his cell at the headquarters of the Ministry of Religious Affairs in Beijing, Ghosh recalled the questions he asked when he and Chen had been walking back to his house in Portsmouth from the Ibis Hotel and their goodbyes to Britney.

He had said, 'You know how she called you *sister* and *friend*. Did you ask her about that?'

Chen said, 'The time she saw me in the street she spoke my local dialect and most the important thing is she called me by a name few people know.'

'Your name?'

'Not my name. My sister's name.'

'Sister?'

'Twin sister.'

'Twin sister?'

'Stop repeating me. We can talk about this later.'

'Of course. And what did Britney say?'

'She denied using those names.'

'Weird.'

'Maybe. She said she hadn't taken a good look at me. She made a mistake. It was dark. She was distressed.'

'So she *did* call you *friend*?'

'Maybe she did and maybe she didn't. It was dark and I was distressed, too. Maybe I was hoping somebody would call me *friend* or *sister*.'

'So why did you want to help her?'

'She needed help. And there was something between us that I can't explain. Part of it is just because she's from the same province in China as me. The sound of her voice was familiar. And I also thought: *that could be me*.'

'What do you mean?'

'Same age, from the same place, in this foreign country - but for different reasons. Following orders.'

'How did she come here?'

'I don't know. Somebody loaned her a huge amount of money that she has to pay back with cruel interest. She's an undocumented worker from a north eastern province, a poor village, not my own village, one similar, and nearby. She did what she thought best to get on and improve her life and her family's life and she ended up here. In some ways it could have been me; she could have been my sister.'

They walked into Ghosh's house and sat at the kitchen table.

'Another thing I wanted to ask - you could have taken a bus directly from Heathrow to Portsmouth.'

'I wanted to see the old empire's capital. You know, I've heard about it for years and studied English for so long and that is the place the langauge came from originally.'

'Won't your bosses be upset at tourist trips?'

'It takes exactly the same time. I checked that first.'

'And how was London?'

'Magnificent and lonely.'

Marcas Ghosh and Chen Ying did not sleep. They were bonded by the intensity of their few hours of adventure and adrenalin together. They spent the morning talking, quickly, for hours, and when they stopped talking for three breaths they kissed. Neither could say who made the first move. They clutched each other and each pair of lips exposed itself to the exploration of another. They had gambled and were winners of each other and filled with elation big enough to need no talking about. They were held in a heightened moment that included the taxi trip to the airport and lasted until they were on the plane to bring them both back to China. By the middle of the flight, high in the sky, Ghosh and Chen had each recognized this: they shared an instant affinity and a lasting connection. And at the airport in Beijing they were split by the Minister.

CHAPTER 38
Day 3, 11:55 pm

Chen was back in her home village and, apart from brief family reunions at Spring Festival, it was her first visit for years to this poor, slow, quiet place. She had her excusing stories to tell, of course, the reasons for this unannounced, unexpected, out of season arrival, but the stories were hard to tell and hard to hear and there was strain for everyone. She had a frown on her face, a hidden frown. After her dinner had been prepared, served, eaten and cleared away, Chen's mother said: 'What's troubling you?'

'I'm thinking of someone.'

'Twin?'

She was thinking of Marcas Ghosh. She should have been thinking of her twin. She said to her mother: 'I often think of twin sister.'

She thought of the atmosphere around Ghosh, an atmosphere that awakened the memory of the smell of things from long ago in history, her own history. She thought of the hairs resting softly on his forearm. She thought of his eyes, gentle like an animal, ruthless like an animal, and altogether like reality. She thought how she'd led him, willing and blind, into a trap. She thought how he was in a black prison. She worried about how they were treating him, how was he reacting to the treatment, and how he was bearing it. And most of all she came back to the thought that Ghosh would now hate her because she was the agent who caused him to be a prisoner.

She had been employed to catch him, as now she knew, and in the process he had also caught her. She wondered how much he knew that. She asked herself: 'What are these thoughts? Why do they bother me? Why do I think them? Why can't I stop thinking them and of him?'

She had been used: tricked into bringing an innocent person into the path of harm. Without willing it to happen, old faith in her superiors and career had been pulled from her like a tooth. As if to soothe the aching gap a new care had developed: care for Marcas Ghosh.

Her mother said, 'Your twin sends a letter every week.'

'And money?'

'Always money. Only money. No news.'

Chen's mother continued to work, sewing decorative flags of many countries, used for computer store openings, employment fairs and other less than joyous celebrations. The house was full of cloth threading towards the sewing machine in the centre of the main room, the engine of the house. That week the flags were all the same, a lonely blue sky with a thin moon and one star, from a country Chen did not recognize.

Chen said, 'Where does she live?'

'Don't you know?'

'I don't.'

'You write to each other.'

'I think we are the last two people in China who write letters to each other.'

'Many people in the village write letters. Educated people.'

'Good. I mean people in cities, our generation.'

'You both write a good hand.'

'I went to the address on her letters.'

'Her house.'

'The address. She doesn't live there.'

'She's moved.'

'It's not like that. It's not anybody's real address.'

'She picks up our letters there.'

'She never goes there.'

'Her friend picks up the letters there,' said the mother.

'Somebody - not her. I waited to see,' said the daughter.

'Her friend.'

'She's hiding.'

'No. How many times did you wait - just the once?'

'Three times.'

'She's ill.'

'Nothing about illness in the letters every week. And the times I went to wait - that was over three months.'

'She's got a serious illness.'

'Maybe. I don't think so. I don't feel it. It's something else.'

'A man? What can we do? She has her reasons. You've made a mistake.'

The more her mother spoke the less convincing it was for either of them. Silence came back between them. Chen went outside and stood in the cold. There was no wind and the cold fell gently on her face. It was about seven in the early evening. Crowds of stars were out. From a pocket Chen took the letter from her twin. The part that interested her was this: 'Sometimes I look at pictures in magazines and want Western dining chairs and a dining table with many forks and spoons and glasses to drink out of and a white dress for a wedding not a funeral and chandeliers and wallpaper decorated beautifully and flowers standing on the table instead of food - ah, but all this strangeness that you see in magazines is not happiness or a family.'

Chen didn't understand what her sister intended by these words and picked up a sense of introspective sadness, a feeling her twin had never expressed before, either in letters or in speaking. Her sister was called elder and she was the younger, on account of a minute or two separating their emergence from the womb. *Jiějie* and *Mèimei*: Big Sister and Little Sister. They had always thought of themselves as partners in life. From the age of fifteen, the elder had worked and the younger had studied, and the money from the work supported the studies. The decision that Little Sister be the student and Big Sister the money-maker was based on who got the higher marks in middle school examinations. The fact that these were the wrong marks, that teachers had confused the identical twins, was known only by Big Sister, and she kept it to herself, believing it takes more brains to make money than to study.

So Chen - Little Sister - went to high school and from there to university and to post-graduate study and overseas study and finally got a job as a government official and was posted to the Ministry of Religious Affairs and went to work in the big city.

Big Sister also went to work in the big city, a full ten years earlier, and earned money for Little Sister's high school and university. Though they were near each other they met rarely, being busy in their own ways, and both always assuming there would be more time in the future, when in fact there was less. And now they hadn't seen each other for five years. They lived in each other's lives as loved and absent ideals.

As a student, Little Sister Chen had also worked, when she could, in part-time jobs and at private tutoring; living frugally and saving money. These were habits she had not lost since becoming a successful person, an officer in a ministry. She had not learned the habit of carefree spending. She had not relaxed. She treated her clothes with great tenderness and cooked dinner with leftovers for next day's lunch to save money on eating out.

And it had become time for Little Sister to pay back money to Big Sister. She had the money now. The younger Chen had mentioned it repeatedly in letters and the elder Chen had refused. Younger Chen had sent money and elder Chen had sent it back. Younger Chen asked to meet and elder Chen wrote back saying, 'Yes!' And at the last moment there were always excuses. That's when Little Sister started looking for Big Sister's address and, finding it wasn't her home, waiting for her there to pick up her letters. The elder sister was resisting a face-to-face meeting. The younger sister knew that and she didn't know the reason. She didn't know that Big Sister believed her face would show changes caused by her work and her life, a work and life that she didn't want her younger twin sister to know about. Refusing to be seen was a short-term answer to the problem and the elder sister hadn't found a long-term answer so she held on to the hope of a better future.

Younger sister Chen, now exiled to her own birthplace, could not go back to work. From the highest place in the Ministry had come an order to 'rest and relax' - for two months. The Ministry had tricked her, not for the first time. In her home she found a gap between herself and her parents. They had sacrificed themselves for the sake of opportunities for their younger daughter. The daughter had taken the opportunities and had become a person with different experience, education, and expectations from her parents, a person, in short, from a different social class. Her parents' sacrifice and her own efforts had created this gap, a gap at the heart of their family.

Chen's being home was inconvenient and uncomfortable for her parents and no refuge for her. And other things had changed, too. Up until this point in her life her actions had been regular and the immediate future predictable. Now she didn't know the future. Her trip to England had disturbed her calm, meeting Ghosh, especially, and also the unexpected and disturbing meeting with Britney. Chen didn't know her twin as she once had, and instead she knew Ghosh. The path of her life was blocked or forked. Chen had to get out of this situation. She had to get the frown off her inner brow.

Chen had her resources. She was practical, intelligent unafraid, deep and strong; she was good at managing everything; her difficulty now was in opposing her official duty. Having drawn attention to the frown and asked questions, her mother had set her on her way. Chen knew what she had to do next. She had to get her sister from her hiding place. And most urgently, she had to get Ghosh out of black prison. Once she knew what she had to do, she started making plans.

She went back inside her parents' home. Her mother looked at her.

Chen said, 'Thanks, Ma. Thanks for everything. I'm leaving first thing tomorrow morning.'

CHAPTER 39
Day 4, 2 am

One day somebody, somewhere, using a Baidu.com portal for *seeking something*, communicated this message:

What I am posting is not a post, it is my loneliness

Replies came.

that is the truth
it is my loneliness, too
we share this truth: loneliness

A thread built up with replies tumbling together in a song of shared feeling from strangers.

your loneliness is mine
your loneliness is mine because my loneliness is yours
I am not lonely because I know you are lonely
now I am not lonely
not loneliness is the truth
loneliness was the way to truth
we are together because of truth
we see because of truth
truth is a light
we are seeing truth
truth is shining
the shining light of truth

A name was born, a name in a meme, an internet catchphrase, born from the anonymous loneliness of internet users. It went from the *seeking something* forum to instant messages, texts, mails, blogs, and social networking sites. In seven days, the link to the original post was opened and viewed 412,344 times. There were 17,877 replies, many just copying the key phrase in a kind of salute of recognition.

Net users changed their screen names to create a massive family of support for *shining light of truth*, which is written in Chinese with three characters as *Shining Light Truth*, and no need for *of*. The three characters were used to make a four-character net name for tens of thousands of anonymous message posters. The posters added an extra, signature character to form new identities such as: *ShiningLightTruthEast, ShiningLightTruthNow, ShiningLightTruthMe, ShiningLightTruthWoman, ShiningLightTruthFox, ShiningLightTruthVoice, ShiningLightTruthHundred, ShiningLightTruthRocket, ShiningLightTruthProtection, ShiningLightTruthForever, ShiningLightTruthSee, ShiningLightTruthPeace, ShiningLightTruthTruth, ShiningLightTruthUniverse.*

And thousands, and tens of thousands, more.

Although it was not the primary intention, the use of 'family' names made the supporters harder to trace.

Certain online posters altered the original meme slightly and anonymously, and the alterations were easily accepted because everyone was feeling the same, just a bit different, that tiny amount different, and then that tiny amount different again.

The Seven Sayings of the SLT were memes. Each of the Seven Sayings started life as an isolated meme and was formed by copying, repetition and alteration. None of the Seven Sayings was stable because they were subject to on-line editing.

Each of the Seven Sayings contained all that led up to it, and all that led up to it could be seen. Nothing was finished; the Saying of today lead up to the Saying of tomorrow and tomorrow's Saying will be richer and deeper because it will contain all that went before it, including today.

The same on-line technology of deliberate obscurity was used by the Party. The government decides which other organizations - state or private - can run Interconnecting Networks with direct access to the World Wide Web. The government controls who can make a website and which websites can be seen. Any individual IP address on any device, anywhere, can be blocked. A computer and a website can be blocked but a space for chat, posts or comments is a much looser, open place that can contain many things including the government's own messages.

There is an army of paid posters who receive five *máo*, half of one yuan, to enter a chat room, blog or similar and deposit a positive statement about the government. They are nicknamed the *wǔmáodǎng* the *Five Mao Party*, and their existence is sometimes denied and sometimes lauded as *a new pattern of public-opinion guidance.*

People with power can use secret untraceable networks or computers not linked to a network, they connect to a network outside China, hack into overseas servers, link from one server to another, or activate one device by the remote control of another. Ordinary users can do some of these things and the simplest thing is to go to an internet café and join a chat with a new name. If there are enough people chatting on the topic, it takes too much time for the government to monitor every single user. Users take a risk, a gamble, and each time someone gambles it encourages other gamblers.

In this pattern of behaviour: posting, monitoring, catching, shutting, and migrating, many are involved. One of those was Nelson's mother. She changed her name from Hónglán to Yǒnglán, *Everlasting Orchid*, and though Chinese names do not always mean simply what they appear to do, this one was intended to.

She was the one who had the idea that SLT believers could gather together. She posted using a proxy server, based in the US, that was later blocked. She was not a leader; her suggestion was read, taken up and copied. Actually there were many *Yonglans.* Yonglanone, Yonglantwo, Yonglanthree, Yonglanfive, Yonglansix, Yonglanseven, Yonglansevenseven, Yonglan7, Yonglan77, Yonglan777, and so on. They spread the message.

The original Yonglan's suggestion was for believers to physically manifest their presence in Xiamen, a prosperous deep ocean port on the south east coast, two thousand kilometres far from the capital, isolated by seas in front and mountains behind.

There was in the area a long history of adoring a sea-mother goddess, and a large Buddhist temple, a point of pilgrimage for the Chinese Diaspora all over South East Asia. The port was a former British trading territory, a former Japanese Imperial Army base, and since 1980, a *Special Economic Zone*. A scenic, comfortable city on a hilly island where tigers used to live, until the 1930s, when they vanished from the land as did the spirit of reverence.

And now the island is a pin cushion of buildings, bright, fresh and spiky with white apartment and office towers.

Even before the first gathering, Saying #5 had come into being: *hold hands and make connections*. Then Yonglan wrote about an actual meeting, when believers would hold hands and communicate, and that message was carried and copied, unchanged, for five weeks. Suddenly the date and time and place was decided, and added to the post. It was like the completion of a standard Chinese sentence which puts time, person and place before any action. The sentence was: *september third thursday in the afternoon at 5 o'clock, we believers, in Xiamen above the temple on the hillside path, all meet together to hold hands and make connections.*

They gathered on the hillside as the rocks cooled and the sun sank over the sea, in September, on a Thursday. Sixty-three of them. Above the famous temple, among boulders and hard trees stunted by sea wind and gritty soil. On the dry ground the sixty-three stood and spontaneously held hands, Nelson's mother, Yonglan, making the first move to do so.

The steepness of the narrow path, the size of the tumbled boulders, and branches of the rough claw-like trees prevented the whole sixty-three from standing together. They stood in nine groups of seven. Sixty-three is nine times seven, and one away from sixty-four which is eight times eight.

They looked down on the temple complex, its stone courtyards and clouds of incense smoke, ponds fat with turtles, and tour groups of trippers in matching baseball caps from overseas Chinese outposts in Malaysia, Indonesia and Thailand. They looked across the sea to the small island that is an anachronistic speck, un-joined to China, held by

Taiwan, an illogically separated body, within sight, within swimming distance, near but not touching the main body of the nation. The nine groups of seven held hands and looked at that island, waiting and expecting. After some quiet time, they disengaged and went their separate ways full of a memory of togetherness.

That was the first gathering. It was quick to form and disperse and nobody was arrested. There were gatherings all through the autumn and winter and by the fourth gathering the government could predict its happening and by the fifth, in Zhengzhou, Henan Province, they could arrest all the gatherers, another sixty-three. None of the arrested, questioned, beaten, imprisoned, isolated SLT believers could tell them when the next gathering would be. Nor could they tell who were the leaders of the SLT, what SLT rules were, and how many 'members' there were.

The gatherings continued and Yonglan was often present, though never in those the Public Security Bureau found, and so never arrested. And many other Yonglans posted about future gatherings, and messages, memes and sayings related to something shining brightly forever, and tens of thousands read the posts and copies of the posts.

The Public Security Bureau monitored the posts, deleted the posts, blocked the posts, and it blocked messages with references to *gatherings, SLT, shining, light,* and *truth.* It tried to control the society that lives on the internet. The PSB and the government could do this but it could do nothing to damage the happiness of the *virtual internet,* that is to say, people talking and others listening.

CHAPTER 40
Day 4, 5:30 am

Marcas Ghosh woke up in his cell in the dark early morning with a stupid phrase looping around his head: *boiled egg cutter offer*. He had slept enough; over five hours after being locked up by the guard, later waking and thinking of Chen and England, and sleeping again. He shifted on the hard boxy bed from his back to his side and immediately felt his sweat turning cold between the skin on his back and the compressed layers of his T-shirt, flannel shirt, fleece top and down jacket. He had a headache he was hardly conscious of except as a sense of irritation. The stupid phrase *boiled egg top cutter offer* went round in his head like a radio announcement. Was it a tool for cutting off? A boiled tool? A discount on egg cutters? The best offer on cutters? And why was it in his head?

Ghosh was frustrated by his immediate discomfort and by his imprisonment. He was angrier than before and more focussed on the cause of his anger. He wondered what time it was and looked for his phone - but of course that was the one thing that had been taken from him when he'd been put in this cell. He still had his passport because it wasn't as useful as a cell phone. He took out his passport but he couldn't see it and it couldn't tell him the time. It was so dark he couldn't tell the difference between opening his eyes and closing them.

Ghosh's dark world went white. A voice was shouting at him. As his eyes adjusted to the cell's fluorescent light tube being on, he saw an angry man standing over him, shouting, and he saw the guard at the door with a key.

The angry man was saying: 'Britain is cruel!'

This stranger had a cube-shaped head and bags under his eyes so full that their folds of flesh wobbled as he shouted. His breath had a stench of garlic that went straight to Ghosh's stomach and almost succeeded in turning it.

'Britain is cruel! You say you love animals. Liars! World's number one torturer of animals! Rats! Dogs! Monkeys! Lions!'

'Lions?'

'Pets of the British kings and queens! And rats! Rats are the most tortured. Every year three hundred and sixty ten-thousand animals cut open and poisoned with pills, perfume and lipstick.'

'Lipstick?'

'This is the chef,' said Xiao Di, the guard. 'He loves rats. I told him you love rats. But he found you are from England. He's been getting on the web.'

Ghosh started off conciliatory: 'What you say might be true . . .'

'*Might be*? What!' said the chef. 'You're denying it?'

Ghosh changed his mind: 'What has this go to do with me? Torture? Yes! Me! It's me being tortured! Screaming at me about something you saw on a computer!'

Ghosh started to shout: 'Why am I here? What have I done? Call the British embassy! While you're talking about rats, it's me that's not free. Being tortured! Screamed at in the middle of the night!'

Ghosh was still lying on his bed and he shifted from his side to his back and looked at the ceiling. It was dirty.

He said, 'Talk about England and animals? OK, let's talk about China!'

Ghosh shouted at resinous tar and nicotine stains on the ceiling, some of which had clumps of old cobwebs stuck to them. Other parts of the ceiling were black with mould.

'Judge a country by a website? Not me. Let's judge a country by what's happening now! Here! Now! Me! You!'

His voice picked up amplification from the hollow bed and noticing that, Ghosh screamed at the ceiling mould: 'HERE! NOW! ME! YOU!'

Sound waves of Ghosh's voice spread through the corridors outside and had anybody heard them and traced them to their source, they may have wondered what one of the Co-Chief Chefs of the Ministry of Religious Affairs was doing in a foreign prisoner's cell.

The chef looked at the guard.

The guard said, 'Ah, Xiao Guo,' addressing Ghosh by a respectful yet friendly title, 'Old Chef doesn't mean any harm.'

'I don't,' said the chef.

'He's upset because he loves rats.'

'I do.'

'He does,' said the guard.

'And lions,' said the chef.

'Lions?' said Ghosh.

'You're a little lion,' said the chef. 'Roaring like that.'

'It frightens the rat,' said the Xiao Di, making Ghosh turn his gaze from the ceiling to the guard's direction.

'You've got him here?' said Ghosh.

'We all love rats,' said the guard.

'I was just upset,' said the chef. 'I embarrass myself.'

'No,' said Ghosh. 'I completely understand.'

Anger had been met by anger; conciliation by conciliation.

Xiao Di said, 'I've got something.' He picked up a piece of pipe work. It was the waste pipe he had just pulled loose from the bottom of a sink in the corridor, the sink that was supposed to be used for washing by prisoners. There was no water connected and the waste pipe was clean, wide and straight. He set the pipe on the floor so that its mouth covered half of the exit of the rat-sized tunnel between cell wall and bed. He put a piece of sweet corn at the other end of the waste pipe. He moved to the other exit of the bed-wall tunnel and there put the rat down, covering the exit with the sole of his boot, as before, and obliging the rat to run in the space between bed and wall to escape. He hoped it would go in the pipe and run along it to the food.

The question was this: would the rat run for freedom as soon as possible or would it choose to run down the waste pipe and take the sweet corn? The tiny feet of the rat could be heard running down the tunnel between wall and bed, along one wall and then the other. The rat ran out at the earliest opportunity, avoiding the tunnel made by the waste pipe.

The guard said, 'Aya!' As he moved to pick up the rat, it jumped over his hand and kept running. The rat ran alongside – outside - the waste pipe to its end where it found the sweet corn and took it. At that point the guard could catch the rat.

'Freedom *and* food,' said the chef. 'This is one clever rat.'

'We could get more tubes,' said the guard. 'Lots more tunnels. Join them.'

'Make a maze,' said Ghosh.

'Yes, complicated, to test the rat.'

'To teach it.'

'Yes, train it to be cleverer.'

'Give it lots of decisions.'

'We've got the same kind of thinking. Hey! There are some pipes in the engine of the broken down truck in the yard behind the kitchen. We could use them. They twist and turn.'

'Make the choices less straight.'

'See if the rat always chooses the safe option.'

'Or the option with most food.'

'What kind of food?' said Ghosh.

'Ah, yes,' said the guard. 'We've got to give it more choices.'

'Let's not go too far,' said the chef. 'We can't pretend to be God. Not even the Communist Party.'

Ghosh said, 'Do you mean we can't pretend to be the Communist Party? Or do you mean the Communist Party can't pretend to be God?'

'You decide. I'll not discuss the Party.'

'Don't you like the Party?'

'I don't say anything about like or don't like. I'm a Chinese and I'm a communist. But as a chef, I dislike anyone who doesn't relish his food. The Party Secretary of this Ministry is that kind of man. He eats so that he doesn't die of starvation later in the week. He eats anything you put in front of him. It doesn't matter what it is. That's not human.'

The rat grunted as the guard was stroking it.

Ghosh said, 'Why not feed him rats? Not this rat, of course.'

'Food is food and we have to eat it and rats are too good for that Party man. I'd feel sorry for the rat and feel sorry for the poor rat's ancestors to be eaten by that Party bastard.'

The chef looked at the bruise below Ghosh's left eye and said, 'So they beat you?'

'No, no,' said Ghosh. 'An accident.' He'd forgotten he was marked by Britney's fist.

'Yeah, we know that kind of 'accident',' said the chef. He sniffed and said, 'It's a bit cold in here. Anything I can bring you?'

'Yeah, newspapers.'

'You going to read?'

'No, if I wrap myself up they would keep me warm,' said Ghosh.

'You want more comfort?' said the chef. 'You know, once you've settled into a routine you'll never escape.'

He said to the guard, 'Come on. We have to go.'

They left and locked Ghosh in. They took the rat with them. Ghosh thought *What's the difference between rats and mice? The name.*

Into the stillness, darkness and silence of the cell and of Ghosh's mind gradually came the stupid phrase *boiled egg top cutter offer.* He concentrated on not thinking *boiled egg top cutter offer.* It didn't work. The door opened. The guard's hand came in through the small opened gap. The hand cupped an egg. Ghosh took the egg. It was still warm. The door closed. It was a boiled egg. Ghosh cracked it and ate it.

CHAPTER 41
Day 4, 7:22 am

On the day following Ghosh's return, the on-line and print editions of the Beijing-based English-language newspaper, *Global Times,* had the following article.

Home>>MetroBeijing>>Update>>Society

Police seek missing Brit

Source: Global Times
[07:22 February 7]

A British national who disappeared in the early hours of February 4 is being sought by police.

The missing man surnamed Ghosh was last seen in a troubled and drunken state leaving an official reception held by the National Association of NGOs (NANGO) in Beijing.

Ghosh attended the dinner as a representative of the International Red Cross and was liberally provided with dishes and alcohol by the NANGO, according to police.

Beijing municipal police on February 5 received a report from Ghosh's concerned local colleagues when the UK passport holder failed to appear for work, did not answer phone, text or email messages, and was not found at his apartment.

Police in Beijing began making a thorough investigation to find the missing man.

They searched his apartment and found SIM cards, a laptop computer, and several empty bottles of alcohol.

Ghosh reportedly left the official dinner in an argumentative state and felt wronged by society, it is reported. He has mixed race parentage, is approximately 30 years old and said to be around 175 cm.

Despite Ghosh's obvious vulnerabilities China regards him as a guest and we will do all in our power to find him, police said.

After reading the news, junior diplomats at the British embassy in Beijing discussed the case.

'He's obviously a weirdo but the Chinese will be shitting themselves.'

'Probably dead drunk at the bottom of a sewerage pit somewhere.'

'From what I know of Chinese officialdom, they'll be in a blind panic trying to find him so they can avoid an international diplomatic incident,' said the official who graduated from Cambridge University and benefited from the renowned tutorial system.

'I can imagine them substituting other dead bodies to present to the world and save face.'

'All for some hopeless FUKACT.'

FUKACT, the acronym for *Failed UK And China Too*, is slang among British embassy and consulate staff in the China region and derives by analogy from the 19th Century acronym *FILTH – Failed In London Try Hong Kong*. It means China is not easy, and it is applied by the diplomatic staff to almost any of their fellow countrymen and, behind each other's backs, to colleagues.

CHAPTER 42
Day 4, 7:30 am

At 7:30 am day-shift guards came to the detention area that contained Ghosh's cell. Ghosh had eaten his boiled egg and had hidden the shell. He was awake and ready and afraid. Hearing the footsteps and voices of the new guards as they moved about, he began to shout. Shouting seemed unmannerly and hysterical. But if he spoke normally nobody outside his cell would hear him.

'Lawyer! I demand a lawyer! British Embassy! I demand the British Embassy! I am a foreign guest. I have my rights!'

Ghosh heard a group of guards stop in the corridor. They seemed to be talking about him and he heard the word *foreign* or *foreigner*. His cell door was opened and eight guards walked in quietly. A guard supervisor stood in front of him and looked at him. Ghosh expected him to say something. Meanwhile four guards had moved to his sides and two on each side took hold of his arms. Ghosh realised they were restraining him with plastic handcuffs and he started to shout again: 'Why?' His voice was cut off by the gag that two other guards had passed over his mouth and tied at the back of his head. Another guard had secured a plastic rope around his ankles to prevent running and kicking. The guards left the cell and locked the door.

After some time, Ghosh resigned himself to sitting on the edge of the cell bed, his hands tied behind his back, his legs tied together and most uncomfortable of all, a strip of cotton tied across his mouth. The cloth dried his mouth and tongue, cut the sides of his lips, and made it difficult to breathe because his nose was blocked and he couldn't blow it or wipe it. He felt the need to pee. He felt helpless. He began to doze.

More than an hour later he woke up as somebody was taking the handcuffs off and untying the gag. A white British man walked into his cell not having seen the gag or cuffs. He was saying, 'Sorry to wake you so early. Is everything OK?

Now the best thing to do is cooperate fully and hope for expulsion.'

Behind the British man were three Chinese officials, all smiling. One of the officials thrust at Ghosh three pomelos tied together with nylon string.

The official said, in English,'Yes, yes, yes. Take, take, take.'

Ghosh didn't say anything. First, he had just woken up and second, his mouth was dry from the gag and he couldn't yet speak. The visitor thought Ghosh was stupid. He had read the *Global Times* item headlined *Police Seek Missing Brit*.

He said, 'You know who I am, don't you?'

Ghosh shook his head.

'Well I'm jaimsteemackintire from the Embassy and I'm here to assess the situation and answer any questions that you might have, OK?'

'Get,' said Ghosh.

'Yes?' said Mr James T McIntyre.

Ghosh had to run his tongue around his mouth to produce saliva and continue his sentence: 'Me.'

The pauses and the tongue movements made Ghosh look like a low-budget-movie nutcase.

'So,' said McIntyre. 'We know all about you. You were completely, er, *tipsy*. You went missing. You were found. You are being held here pending.'

'Out of here,' said Ghosh, finishing his sentence.

'Now, Marcas, I don't want to be, you know, but this thing could go either way. So, speaking straight, as I've said, the best way forward is to cooperate fully and hope for an immediate expulsion. Not to mince words: eat humble pie; not to mince words. I'm sure you know what they're like. Face. High Power Distance. All that. Grovel a bit; be sincere. That's the hard thing: getting it just right. So I think they were freaking out before they got you back. It would look really bad if some random foreigner was found dead in a ditch, you know what I mean. Some people are saying they're dying to get rid of you.'

'Free me now.'

'It's not like that. Gone are the days. Ha, ha. So it's just a matter of time. And so you just play along, say *I was a naughty boy*, you know. By the way, that black eye of yours is suspicious. How did you come by it?' He looked at his mobile. On it, he noticed a song by Mumford & Sons was still playing and he could catch its tiny tinkling from the earphones in his pocket. It was a comfort.

Ghosh said, 'Oh, eye, my eye.' He felt it and it was sore. 'It was a woman,' he said, remembering Britney.

McIntyre made his face to mean *need I say more*, and said, 'So I won't keep you much longer.'

'What? Aren't you a lawyer? I want some legal advice. I want to get out of here. I haven't done anything. Aren't you going to help me?'

'Look mate, I *am* helping you. That's why I'm here, yes? And, no, I'm not a lawyer. Did I say that I was? I don't think so.'

'How can I get out of here? What help can you give?'

'So, er, Marcas. You've filled out the EXP 450? Is that the correct spelling of your name: M-A-R-C-A-S? These are your next-of-kin details? And we can contact you at this email address here? OK, that's fine. So is there anything else I can help you with today?'

'I'm in prison. I haven't got email access. What's the point of next-of-kin details?'

'Well, so what's the point of being arrested, hey? Ha, ha, ha!' McIntyre turned round laughing at the three officials behind him. The three officials also started laughing though none knew what was funny.

'These gentlemen seem very concerned about your welfare and I'm sure you're being treated extra well, being a foreigner and everything, you know what the Chinese are like with us *lǎowài*. Mr Wang here and Mr, er, Mr, he said his English name was Rock - or was it Lock! - spot on for a prison, ey? And Mr, er, and they seem very reasonable and up-to-date and so on. So . . . Ah yes, would you mind just signing this form they gave me? No, no. Don't bother reading it. Yes, it's all in Chinese. Just a formality. No need to worry.'

'What's going to happen to me? Where's my lawyer? What have I been charged with?'

'All in good time, I expect. These things, you know, it's China, don't need me to tell you. So, now if you could just sign the paper.'

'Have you read this?'

'No, mate, I haven't. Haven't got time, really.'

'Could be anything.'

'So, I'm sure it isn't. Now if you could just . . . .'

'Whose side are you on?'

'So I'm taking a deep breath and observing that you don't seem very grateful for what people have done.'

'What have you done?' said Ghosh.

'We have visited you. *I* have visited you. So what you don't seem to realize, Marcas, is that you are a very lucky man to be seen at all. It's only because I had a cancellation that I was able to come here today. So I didn't need to come here. I decided I would. I don't expect any thanks. We meet all sorts. And a lot of them seem to get into difficulties, like yourself.'

'What are you doing - helping me or telling me off?'

'And I'll ignore that remark. So it's the living in China that gets to a lot of people, we find. Seems to magnify any problem they already had. End up in trouble. Now if you could just sign these papers.'

'No.'

'Now there's nothing much I can do for you if you won't cooperate, Marcas. I'll be going now, I've already overstayed and these very gentlemen want a quick chat. '

'What about?'

'So, er, that's with me, actually, not you. Now then: cooperate and hope for expulsion. That's what I say. You'll be home sooner than you think.'

'Wait.'

'So, er, bye.'

CHAPTER 43
Day 4, 9:30 am

The Party Secretary was in the office of the Minister of Religious Affairs and said, 'It happened three days ago and we still have no answer. If we don't find something today everything will be out of our control.' With the palm of his hand he smoothed his already smooth hair.

The Minister's hair was a sticky mess; he didn't touch it.

He said, 'What have you been doing?'

'All morning I've been contacting people, asking questions, checking replies, and ordering more questions,' said the Party Secretary.

'And?'

'Ten thousand replies and not one answer because not one of the cultists admits to knowing anything useful.'

'You arrested some of them?'

'Of course. All over the nation.'

'We weren't doing that.'

'It's too late. Don't you understand?'

'What do they know?'

'Some of them say they knew about the gathering and some of them say they wanted to be there. Others say they didn't know and they wish they had known.'

'Are they resisting questions?' said the Minister.

'No, they talk too much and what they say is too much nonsense,' said the Party Secretary.

'Tactics? To confuse us?'

'That's hard to say. Certainly their replies are confusing because everything is explained in terms of their cult doctrine.'

'What?'

'Numbers, for example, seven, eight; and holding hands; and meeting 'number eight'; and the appointed time; and fulfilling potential. And they all claim to be sorry.'

'*Sorry*?'

'Sorry that our people were there; sorry that they were killed; sorry they weren't holding hands.'

'The Party has saved us a lot of effort.'

'And after all that effort we have got nowhere. What were those cultists really doing? Why did they kill themselves? Why did they kill the security personnel? Will it happen again? When? Where? How? What for?'

'A rare sight?'

'What?'

'Party Secretary Zhao losing his calm face.'

'I'll lose more than my calm by the end of today. And you will, too. We have, thus far, been extremely lucky but we will not be able to contain the news indefinitely. It's going to burst out.'

The Minister coughed and accurately spat yellowish and greenish phlegm into a waste-paper basket. The Party Secretary looked at him.

The Minister said, 'I don't understand why we got rid of spittoons.'

'Hygiene was the reason.'

'Hygiene? It's worse now. People still need to spit.' He coughed again, ominously. He didn't spit.

He said: 'We need someone to blame.'

'If we don't find one, we will be blamed,' said the Party Secretary. 'The logic will be: If we knew about the SLT gathering beforehand we were culpable, and if we didn't know beforehand we were incompetent, and if we still don't know what happened we are doubly incompetent, and we are finished.'

'Who is nearest to us? Who knows what we know? Who doesn't know what we also don't know?'

'Dong's always there at the right time.'

'It's suspicious. Might mean guilt.'

'It might mean he's always right,' said the Party Secretary. 'Where is he now?'

'Do you think he's overslept?' said the Minister.

'You hope so,' said the Party Secretary.

There was a light knocking on the door and Vice-Minister Dong walked in, carrying his shoes.

'Where are we now?' said the Minister. 'A temple?'

'Oh, excuse me, Minister. I know it's not proper. My feet got wet in the snow and I just took my shoes off on the way here. I'll put them back on.'

'No, no,' said the Minister. 'Don't want you catching your death of cold. There's some old newspaper on the table over there.'

'What snow were you standing in?' said the Party Secretary.

Dong Bing stuffed his damp shoes with the newspaper pages and said, 'In the field. The field where - '

'You went back there? Why?'

'Where they all died. I wanted to check again. Possibly we missed something. And I want to understand the place more. Something terrible and incomprehensible happened and I want to know more about it.'

'I'm surprised you didn't wear overshoes,' said the Party man.

'I did,' said the Vice-Minister. 'Somehow the wet got through.'

'Must have been there a long time,' said the Party man.

'It's worth a thorough investigation,' said Dong Bing.

'And did you find anything out there?' said the Party Secretary. 'In the snow.'

'There are six things.'

'Spit 'em out,' said the Minister.

'One: there have been no unauthorized attempts to breach the security cordon and enter the field area since the deaths. Two: there were no items left behind in the field. Three: twelve vehicles that were left abandoned nearby, apparently by the dead cultists, remain untouched. Four: no items or documents of interest were found in the vehicles. Five: no local resident has revealed anything of interest under questioning. And six: no unexpected visitors, including cultists, journalists, bloggers, or anyone of any suspicious type has been reported in the area since the morning of the 4th February.'

'Six negatives,' said the Party Secretary.

'Same as the medical report,' said the Minister.

'What? Have you read it already?' said Dong Bing.

'No. *Medical Report from Shanghai.* It's just come on my computer. Email. Attachment. Ugh! It's fifty pages long.'

'Open up and read,' said Dong.

'I'm doing that. It's taking time.'

'Why did you choose this Shanghai group? Why not somebody nearer?'

'Ugh, well, I know one of them and they don't know anybody here. Help keep things quiet,' said the Minister.

'For a while,' said the Party Secretary.

'Yeah! A while! Better than no while!'

'What does it say?'

'Don't know yet,' said the Minister. 'It's fifty pages long.'

'Oh, there's so little time,' said Dong Bing. 'And you're under so much pressure.'

'*Me*?' said the Minister.

'We. We are. We all are.'

'But?' said the Party Secretary.

'Well,' said Dong. 'As the one responsible for all those duties, and - '

'Having failed in those duties,' said the Minister.

'Well, ah, it might appear, to those without full knowledge that - '

'*It might appear*?' said the Minister, tapping his computer screen. 'One hundred and fifty soldiers killed! There's been nothing like it since the Civil War!'

'No.'

'OK,' said the Minister, looking at his computer. 'I got the main points of this medical report. Went to the conclusion. There are some equations or what-do-you-call-'em - '

'Data tables,' said Dong Bing.

'Right. They died of heart attacks.'

'What gave them heart attacks, all at once, all together?'

'They don't know.'

Dong Bing began reading from the computer screen: 'Toxic indicators: nil. Radiation in equivalent average annual exposure: 1.80 millisieverts.'

'Is that many?' said the Party Secretary.

'No, it's average. Low,' said the Vice-Minister. He continued reading: 'Surface wounds: none recent. Some minor burns.'

'Minor burns?'

'Internal bruising: none detected. Truama: none visible. Right and left ventricles: average, not obstructed. Major arteries coronary area: some evidence of spasm in some patients.'

'Is that the heart attack evidence?' asked the Party Secretary.

'Almost certainly,' said Vice-Minister Dong. 'Yes.'

He continued reading from the screen: 'Nasal cavity/ larynx/ oesophagus: not obstructed. Contents of stomach: varied; normal.'

'How can you read such small characters?' said the Minister.

'It's eight point,' said the Vice-Minister.

'My eyes, these days,' said the Minister.

'If you highlight and then roll the mouse wheel you can zoom - '

'You think I know that kind of shit?'

'Nervous system: intact, no abnormalities.'

'Fucking shut up with reading the list. We get the picture,' said the Minister.

Tension and pressure were building up everywhere.

CHAPTER 44
Day 4, 11 am

At eleven o'clock in the morning of his second day in a cell at the Ministry of Religious Affairs, Marcas Ghosh was taken to an interrogation room. High officials in the Ministry first came and looked at Ghosh from outside the interrogation room through a small glass panel in its door. The Minister and the Party Secretary then entered the room and a call was put through to Nelson's luxury suite in Tokyo. As far as Ghosh was concerned, the phone calls were the most important part of his day. To the officials with him in the room, the rambling conversations between the foreigner and the maverick in exile were a distraction that they tolerated because the longer that answers eluded them the more impatient they became, and the more likely to try risky indirect approaches, such as the Nelson-Ghosh discussions. This behaviour was at best a sign of a lack of confidence, and at worst panic.

A cell phone was passed to Ghosh.

'Hello again,' said Nelson. 'What time is it for you?'

'Phone time,' said Ghosh.

'It's just before my nightcap,' said Nelson. 'I take milk and honey, warm. Then I'll sleep my sleep, and wake up for a beautiful dinner to start my day.'

'*Day* when it is night.'

'The middle of the night, that's when all the interesting changes take place. The deaths that happened in the snowy field, they were all in the centre of the night when everything is darkest. I wonder if that was important.'

'Important for those that died,' said Ghosh. 'Security people and religious people both.'

Nelson said, 'Take a breath. Let's wander around the world with our words. Maybe we'll find something. Is that good? Now - do you think Mao Zedong was religious?'

'He was the leader of a popular peasant rebellion inspired by a foreign philosophy that promises a glorious future life.'

'Are you saying communism is a religion?'

'I guess Mao was more loyal to rebellion than the philosophy he used. Though he believed individual will has an enormous power. That's kind of spiritual.'

'Was he crazy?' said Nelson.

'I don't think he was,' said Ghosh. 'Because he used his belief on himself and on others - like a weapon.'

'He made it practical.'

'And successful.'

'He was a winner, like Nelson.'

'You, or your hero?'

'I am my own hero,' said Nelson. 'Did he have any other ideas?'

'Fixed opposites. You know the old idea of constant flow? Yin flowing into yang, hot things cooling, cold things warming, day becoming night, youth becoming age, age flowing to death and death to re-birth. Mao took that idea and stopped the flow. He used Marxism to do it.'

'Tried to stop time.'

'In practical terms, on an everyday scale, opposites *are* fixed. Women aren't constantly flowing into men. Opposites live together peacefully or they clash. Thesis, antithesis - clash. Mao was practical as well as mystical. He understood the mystical to manipulate the practical.'

'Are numbers involved?' said Nelson.

'No!' shouted the Minister, snatching the cell phone from Ghosh. 'No! This is all wrong! Less about numbers and more about deaths!'

The Party Secretary looked at the Minister.

The Minister said to him, 'They're getting nowhere. Why did it happen? Are they going to strike again? These two exiles are wasting our time!'

'Should we get rid of him?' said the Party man, inclining his eyebrows to Ghosh.

'Kill him?' said the Minister.

'I didn't suggest that.'

'Well maybe you did and maybe you didn't and maybe you're right.'

The Party Secretary said to the Minister, 'It was you who wanted to use Nelson despite his being unorthodox and his involvement being unorthodox.'

'Nothing's happening. Time's so short.'

'And it was you that requested to bring this foreigner back,' said the Party man.

'It was your idea,' said the Minister.

'This kind of squabbling isn't the best use of our time. Rather decide whether we do or do not want these exiles to continue their talking.'

'I can't listen. Got to go and do something.'

'Do what?'

'Sudden man's feelings. You wouldn't understand.'

The Party man made his face expressionless. The Minister threw the cell phone back to Ghosh and hurried out of the room.

Ghosh was a foreigner in China; Nelson was Chinese in Japan. And both of them were outside the group of officials desperate to find explanations for the deaths in the snowy field. Ghosh had no interest in finding an explanation and had no means of doing so. He was caught coincidentally in a crisis not connected to himself. He was imprisoned and in danger and he felt that only by talking to Nelson was there a rational way out of his predicament. Nelson had life-changing plans and the current situation was an opportunity that could provide him with the means to carry out his plans. For that reason he wanted to find the explanation, and speaking to Ghosh was helping him do that.

Nelson said, 'OK, so we already know the numbers show rooms - or one number shows one room. I don't know what the number is. Not yet. This fixed opposites idea makes me think every item in the *Map* is a positive or negative event, and they make positive and negative numbers that combine, cancel each other out, and leave one number remaining. The problem now is that the remaining number doesn't make sense.'

Ghosh said, 'How does that work?'

'For example, *Beat Jiang* and *Start Cultural Revolution* are positive and negative events.'

'In Mao Zedong's life?'

'Right. If we take his *age* as the number - he was fifty-five when he beat Jiang and seventy-two when he started the Cultural Revolution. Plus fifty-five. Minus seventy-two. Put them together and it makes minus seventeen. Do that for the whole *Map*.'

'Are those events just examples?' said Ghosh.

'Examples of what?'

'Of positive and negative things.'

'They're in the *Map*,' said Nelson. 'See?'

'Yes, and how do you know if they're negative or positive?'

'They are or they aren't.'

'Who decides?' said Ghosh.

'They're on the *Map*!' said Nelson. 'Whoever made the *Map* chose them.'

'Yes and who decides whether the events are negative?'

'It's all clear.'

'What about the Cultural Revolution?'

'Yeah, that's one of the negative events. What about it?'

'It's not negative.'

'Hey - Mr History Man! You know, the Big Proletarian Cultural Revolution. The nightmare that still makes us scared in the daytime. Afraid all the people we know will turn into monsters. No one trusts anyone and no one believes anything except that a Louis Vuitton handbag under 8,000 RMB is a fake.'

'Yes, I know.'

'And paying 8,000 RMB is no guarantee of not being ripped off. I wasn't even born in the Cultural Revolution and I'm still suffering from it. Are you saying it was good?'

'No, I'm not saying that.'

'Almost any Louis Vuitton bag is fake - whatever you paid for it.'

'Yes, I know. *I'm* not saying the Cultural Revolution was good. I'm saying Mao says it was. It's not my mind. In my mind I create Mao's mind.'

'But it's wrong - completely wrong.'

'What is?'

'The Cultural Revolution was bad, not good. Saying it was good is wrong. Superficial. There were people in that. My mother. My grandmother. Me.'

'You weren't born.'

'The people who made me were made in it. They made me. It made me. It was wrong.'

'That's a different issue.'

'Ah, now who's the cold-hearted bastard?' said Nelson. 'China for you is just a theory.'

'Maybe it was,' said Ghosh. 'Not now I'm in prison on the point of - '

'Death,' said Nelson. 'You're on the point of death. Make no mistake about it.'

'Now, who's the cold hearted - '

'Not me. I'll get you out. But - don't wait. If any chance comes - take it.'

Ghosh sighed and didn't say any words.

Nelson said, 'Hey. Wait. *Ts-ts-ts-ts.* I've seen the number. Added it your way. *Your* positive way.'

'Mao's way.'

'The same. Your way is right. Negative to positive. You can tell the Minister and his friends there that we've got it. Tell them the numbers combine to produce one number and that one number is the number of a room and that room holds the key to the mystery. *Why* it holds the key - I don't know.'

'And the number of the room is?'

'Can't you do simple mathematics?'

'I can.'

'So?'

'This isn't simple.'

'Add it up your way. The maths is simple. Maths is almost always simple. It's the effect and the consequence and the meaning of the maths that distracts people. And that makes everything easy for me.'

'Are you going to tell me the number?'

'First the Minister. Bye bye.'

CHAPTER 45
Day 4, 11:30 am

The Minister texted his favourite woman after he left his office, telling her to meet him in his bedroom. She was with the four other women in the Minister's living room, relaxing and ready, checking phones for messages. She didn't say to the other women why she was leaving the living room and none of them asked her, though they all noticed. When the Minister arrived he sat in a leather armchair and started taking off his shoes and socks. She sat on one of the wide arms of the chair and began unbuttoning his shirt. She was wearing a yellowish-beige dress of a light synthetic fabric. The dress was short and loose and when she sat down it had wafted up to show white underwear and the skin of her thighs and waist and stomach. She adjusted her position on the large arm of the chair and the dress wafted up again. The Minister appreciated the contrast of the soft limp cotton of her underwear and the firm warm skin. She started undoing the Minister's belt buckle. The light from a lamp caught her hair as it fell to the side of her head while she bowed to the task. The Minister said, 'Not as young as you were but still very beautiful.'

'That's right,' she said as she reached behind her to pick a cell phone from a purse decorated with a million golden sequins.

'I'll call my friend Lili. She's the most gorgeous seventeen-year-old you will ever see. Every man wants her, even priests, and she - there's so much she wants to learn from a powerful older man.' She was tapping numbers and saying, 'One-zero - '

'No, no, no,' said the Minister. He held her, his hands on her legs, just above the knee. He leant forward.

She continued tapping and said, 'So young, so fresh, so ripe, so obedient. When she comes here you'll never leave this room for weeks, I guarantee it.'

'Ugh. No, no, no,' said the Minister. 'You.'

'Oh good,' she said and began smiling. 'It's ringing.' She stood and took two steps away from the armchair. 'Hello. Lili? It's me. Yes, me. Me.'

The Minister stood up from the armchair, too.

She said to the phone, 'Yes, I know you're bored. I've some very good news for you.'

The Minister was on his knees and wrapped his arms around her legs. His grip caused her to shake but she did not fall. Her long hair shook from side to side.

She said to the phone, 'Just a moment.' She looked down at the Minister and maintained a distant smile. He was looking up to her. His view of her was cut in half by her dress. On one side he looked up along her thighs to the slight bulge at the front of her white underpants, and on the other side he looked up past her foreshortened body to her face held flat to his view. She waited, not for long.

He said, 'Yes, you.'

She pointed her thumb at the cell phone and said, 'This girl is so new and will do anything to make you feel comfortable. She can be here in - how long? Twenty minutes?'

She spoke to the phone, 'Twenty minutes?'

Even the Minister could hear the reply from the phone: 'No. Fifteen.'

She said, 'Fifteen minutes, seventeen years old, right here.' And she pointed to the floor, and also to the Minister's crotch - it was the same direction.

The Minister said, 'Ugh. No. No, no, no.' He stood up and took a step backwards. He sat in the black leather armchair.

He said, 'It's you.'

She still held the phone, still smiling, and she waited.

He pointed his chin at the phone, 'Not her.' He pointed his chin at the door that led to other rooms, 'Not those women there.' He pointed his eyes at her, 'You.'

She said: 'Us?'

'Us,' he said.

She stopped smiling, turned off the phone, and dropped it into her bag.

He said, 'Do I stink so bad?'

'Of garlic and cigarettes.'

'Only that much?'

'You know how much.'

'You can take me?'

'I can take you.'

Meiyuan sat on his lap, her legs together. He stroked Meiyuan's hair.

He said, 'Good.'

His phone began to ring, the private one.

She said, 'It's not good news. Don't answer it.'

'I won't,' he said.

He did. The caller said that he was Nelson. And that the answer to the map puzzle had been found. That the answer was the number of a room in the Ministry. That the room and the person who uses it held some key to the mystery of the Shining Light of Truth and their deaths in the snowy field. That the number was eight. Nelson said, 'I wanted to tell you personally. The room that has the secrets is room eight. You're the first person to know. And that is as it should be because eight, as you know, is the number of your room.'

On hearing Nelson use the phrase *your room* the Minister of Religious Affairs cut the call. He looked at Meiyuan and he began to stand up. She slipped from him like a comfort blanket. He stood in his bedroom and she sat in the armchair. He stood and she sat. After ten breaths he called Nelson and spoke to him standing up.

'That is the number?' he asked.

'It's a brute fact,' said Nelson.

'Just a number.'

'There's more to numbers than most people think. What's the retirement age for public officials?'

'Sixty-eight,' said the Minister.

'And you are?'

'Sixty-seven.'

Nelson laughed a high-pitched laugh. He knew the Minister was sixty-nine.

The Minister said, 'You think you know everything. You don't.'

'True. I don't know why she's dead.'

'Your mother?'

'You're the one that told me. Showed me.'

'Yeah, it's true I'm a bastard. Born one. Have been one and will be one. As you should know.'

'I was sad. I cried. My heart was squeezed in my chest. It hurt.'

'Now you want to hurt me.'

'You wanted an answer. I gave you a number. Tell me what you know.'

The Minister said, 'I know the Ministry is old, dating back to Old Mao. *The Villa*. The new building is a copy. I know that in the months before Mao died, when his body was weaker, he got more mystical. Left a lot of messages. In poems. I think he tried to set it up. Shining Light of Truth. The numbers. The waiting.'

'Why?'

'Maybe he made up a religion to beat the *pragmatists* - the bureaucrats, his enemies in the Party. I'm one of them. He thought that the second he died they were going to overthrow him and his ways. And we did. He thought religion could beat them. Us. He wanted to be the winner even after he was dead. Maybe he thought religion could keep him alive.'

Nelson said, 'He made the *Map*?'

The Minister told Nelson that Mao had made the *Map* - almost certainly. It was left among poems, sayings and warnings from the man who used violence while alive and the spirit while dead to try to prevent what he had created vanishing with his life. These papers were all hidden in Room Number 8 of the Ministry of Religious Affairs, and Minister Wang had the *Map* because Ministers always lived in Room 8. And the Minister had made the mistake of giving everything, including the puzzling *Map* to Honglan, the woman he'd loved most and longest.

Nelson said, 'Why?'

'Your mother was looking for the path to higher happiness. Fast.'

'And why didn't you just burn all those papers?'

'Minister of Religious Affairs. It's my duty to be interested in religion. And I am. Deeply.'

'Do you know why she died?'

'Strange question.'

'And that's no answer.'

'No.'

'What more do you know?'

'Nothing you need to know.'

'And what are you going to do with the English man?'

'English man? Ugh. Him. Has he told anybody else about this number? Have you?'

'Not yet. We will do. I'm going to send him this chart - made from the *Map*. He helped make it. I'm sending it to you now.'

Date	*+year*	*-year*	*Event*
1902		*10*	*Beaten by Father*
1919		*26*	*Lose mother*
1927	*34*		*Learn violence*
1930		*37*	*Lose wife*
1932	*39*		*Make Zhou mine*
1949	*56*		*Defeat Jiang*
1950		*57*	*Lose son*
1962		*69*	*Stung by 7,000 insects*
1966	*73*		*Start Cultural Revolution*
1971		*78*	*Betrayed by Lin*
1976	*83*		*Plant seed of truth*
+total	*285*		
-total		*277*	
Final	*8*		

Nelson said, 'If you want to kill the foreigner you'll have to think hard and do it carefully.'

'More mystery deaths?'

'No mystery to you, I think. And anybody who knows that number is in a dangerous place.'

'Now *I* know it,' said Minister Wang.

'You knew it already.'

'You're dreaming. Must be your bedtime. What time is it in Japan? Same as here? Behind?'

'Ahead. Japan is always ahead of China. Goodnight.'

'Bastard.'

'Family character, uncle.'

'Not your uncle.'

CHAPTER 46
Day 4, 2:30 pm

As officials got closer to the deadline for delivering an explanation of an irrational event, they were becoming less rational themselves.

The Party Secretary said to the Minister, 'We cannot underestimate the seriousness of the problem we would face if, by early morning tomorrow, we had made no further progress and discovered *no* answer to this case. Such a situation would be a threat to the integrity on the nation's laws, a threat to national security, a threat to social stability, and a deadly threat - '

'To your own scrawny neck.'

The Party Secretary looked steadily and coolly at the Minister.

The Minister said, 'Yeah, yeah - and my fat neck, too.'

'I am glad you are aware of the dangers - '

'Course I'm fucking aware. Now, listen - a foreigner. Could a foreigner be behind it?'

'Foreigner? What Foreigner?'

'Any old foreigner. Speaking of *national security* - as you were, you must be closer than me.'

'Closer to what?'

'Intelligence services. Spies. Secrets and lies stuff. Any rumours? Plots? Campaigns?'

'The convenience of that well-trodden avenue is attractive but it is deceptive and could easily lead us into dire straits. The Foreign Ministry, foreign powers, and, if it is all mistaken, the popular reaction would be negative.'

'Yeah, I know. Folk are sick of government blaming foreigners for little things while the big things are ignored.'

'The Japanese - ' began Vice Minister, Dong Bing.

'Yeah! Japanese! Right!' said the Minister, seized with energy and pointing his finger at the Party Secretary. He said to Dong Bing, 'What about them? Buddhist aren't they?'

'Yes, Minister,' said Vice Minister Dong. 'And, no. And more to the point, Minister, they had a religious cult in the early 1990s that killed people mysteriously.'

'Now you're talking,' said the Minister.

'The cult members carried the poisonous gas - *sarin* - in a liquid form, sealed in plastic bags and spiked the bags with sharpened umbrellas, releasing the vapour underground, on crowded passenger trains near the station for the headquarters of the central Japanese government.'

'What happened? Kill any government people?'

'No, they killed some subway passengers.'

'And themselves?'

'No, but nearly. One almost died before he injected himself with the antidote.'

'Now I remember. That's it! Got to be worth looking at. Insane religion. Sarin gas. Easy to make. Easy to carry around! Check that! And plastic bags!'

'Yes, Minister,' said Dong Bing.

'You knew all about this Japan thing?'

'Yes, Minister.'

'So why didn't you tell us before, you non-speaking turd?'

'I . . . I . . . '

'Ugh. Yeah. Waiting for me to come up with the brilliant idea about foreigners.'

'Er, yes, Minster.'

'While you're checking what I told you, check if there's any Pakistan connection.'

'Pakistan?'

'Yeah, we got this foreigner locked up. The one talking to Nelson. It's suspicious how he knows all this information.'

'He's not from Pakistan,' said the Party Secretary.

'Pakistan - connection with Tokyo, Japan. Coincidence?' said the Minister.

'He's not from Pakistan.'

'Hard to say where he's from. Bluff and double bluff, if you ask me. Dangerous game.'

'Dangerous for all of us,' said the Party Secretary.

'No kidding,' said the Minister. 'We need rid of him sometime.'

'Now?' said Dong Bing.

'Now,' said the Minister, 'we end this meeting. We'll come up with plans for what we are going to say tomorrow. You get on with this sarin thing. Tests. Science. Any Japan links.'

'And Pakistan?' said Dong Bing.

'Yeah, Pakistan, sure. You know what I think?'

'No,' said Dong Bing.

'Inside job,' said the Minister looking at Dong Bing, his junior rival. The next Minister, perhaps - or probably.

'Somebody inside the Ministry knows what's going on,' said the Minister.

'I have the same feeling,' said the Party man. 'Let's meet again at four.'

The officials separated to go about their various tasks, including making plans for tomorrow, the deadline day, the day when many things would be decided. If *this* happens - Plan A. If *that* happens - Plan B. If something else happens - heaven knows.

The Party Secretary went to his rooms and as he entered he thought, 'I'll tell Bill to eat lunch alone', but Bill was gone, away, to Seattle, and the Party man hated himself for making the mistake, and exposing to himself his own frailties. He left his rooms immediately and, without any lunch, began making a solitary tour of the Ministry building compound in order to *smell the mood.*

He walked softly through back passages and up and down fire escapes, unhurriedly and purposefully, thinking and listening, and looking from afar at anybody he saw, reading their faces and foreheads. He used special keys for doors that seemed to be closets but were not and which were connected to corridors leading to unexpected exits, emerging quickly at higher levels. For the Party Secretary, this internal perambulation had the effect of sharpening his senses and focussing his thoughts; it was the action he took when he wanted to think and to decide. If anybody ever saw him he called this solitary silent walk a *sanitary inspection.*

The focus of his thoughts at present were the investigation, his plans for its success, and his plans in case of its failure.

He was just about to exit from one basement closet when he heard his job title being cursed.

'Party Secretary! Party pervert! Unnatural! He's left his food again!' It was the cook, the one who loved rats - the Party Secretary's cook - and the Party leader recognized the big, rough, drinker's voice.

'He's got no sense for food. Can't respect a man like that. Not a man.' The cook was drunk and that was obvious, even without seeing him. During a pause in talking, the Party Secretary heard the sounds - exaggerated by clumsiness - of a bottle cap being unscrewed, a gulp being snatched and the expiration of breath that expressed tough satisfaction: *hehhhhh!*

'Trying my best,' said the cook. 'Work's not worth doing if it's not appreciated. Trying my best to cook something good for the top-knob big potatoes - at least the Minister eats proper. Old Wang the Minister! Knows good stuff when he puts it in his mouth! But I'm not assigned to him. Oh, no. I get the no-sense Party wax-work doll. Hate that Communist. No feeling for food; no feeling for women; no feeling at all. I'm a sensitive man. It hurts.'

The Party Secretary heard another man speak: 'Are you drinking that bottle or just holding it?'

'Hah?'

'Give it here.' The other man was Xiao Di, Eddie, the guard. The Party Secretary knew that, too. Xiao Di wasn't drunk and wasn't drinking. His intention was to put an end to the cook's binge. He took hold of the bottle but the cook didn't let go so that by pulling the bottle to himself, Xiao Di pulled the cook up close.

The cook whispered loudly in his ear, 'I tell you - what did that man eat today? Nothing. What does he eat most days? Freaking perverse. Cooling food when it's cold. Heating food when it's hot. Winter: a bit of chopped cucumber, a melon, braised marrow, a few pieces of *apple*. Summer: beef. *Fried beef!* And bits of potato.'

Actually, the diet that the cook was describing was Bill's, not the Party Secretary's. The Party man ate sparingly and carefully: plain rice, some vegetable, clear soup. He understood good taste but did not indulge and what he ate was not noticed by the cook or by the staff who carried food to his rooms and took away the leftovers. They didn't know Bill had been there.

'I'm a good cook. I'm the best cook in this place. And what do I get? A man that has no feelings. That's my fate. That's my life. My punishment. Give me that bottle!' The cook snatched at the bottle and tugged too hard. He fell back and bounced against the closed closet door. Xiao Di heard the thud of the cook's body against the door, and he also heard another sound - a gasp, apparently from behind the door. He looked sharply at the door. He noticed that it was worn but the keyhole looked fresh inside. As a guard, he had a particular interest in keyholes. He shouldered the door. Nothing happened and it was locked. He pulled the cook into a stumbling walk and dragged him away, heading towards the cook's room with its simple bed where he could sleep off the drink. And as Xiao Di led the cook away he looked back at the closet door, believing that there was someone behind it.

Just before three o'clock in the afternoon, the Party Secretary called for a meeting of all Ministry security staff apart from the absolute minimum who were required to stay on duty. Uniformed and un-uniformed, roused from sleep, from mere idling, and from various administrative duties, one hundred men and women gathered in Security Centre Reception Room Number 1. Xiao Di was there.

The Party Secretary spoke, deftly jigsawing together phrases from other, previous speeches; phrases with precise definitions and exactly chosen words, all made to fit perfectly in the smooth and practised voice of a senior Party official who had risen to power through merit, capability and attention to detail.

'In modern China,' he said, meaning since 2006, 'executions have been held in specifically designed areas indoors, mainly, with only authorised personnel present in keeping with the most up-to-date international standards. And conditions for prisoners are notably improved too, signifying a greater value placed on the quality of each and every citizen's life, even those who have been found to have broken its publicly accepted rules.

'This improvement continues', he said, 'and I am hereby announcing, now, with immediate effect, in this facility, and nowhere else, as a model and advanced front in the reform programme, an increase in the financial value of the monthly allowance earmarked for food expenditure for prisoners.'

The current food budget was RMB 180 per prisoner per month and of that amount RMB 18 was spent on food items and the guards kept the rest.

'The monthly per-prisoner expenditure will increase from RMB 180 by one hundred percent to RMB 360. It will double.'

There was a gasp of genuinely amazed approval: *Oohhhhh*. This was a significant increase in income for almost every worker and it could make a big difference to their lives.

'Naturally,' said the Party Secretary, 'in the difficult transition period of the implementation of these new measures we expect the continued support and cooperation of security personnel, the strict adherence to rules and regulations and the swift execution of new orders.'

The staff who heard this were all thinking that they would be prepared to cooperate a lot for that kind of money increase - for the first few months at least.

When this meeting was adjourned, one of the lesser Communist Party officials approached Xiao Di and informed him that he was required at the Party Secretary's office immediately. At the office door, Xiao Di knocked, heard the words *come in*, and entered. He saw the Party Secretary sitting at his desk as an official placed three A4 print outs separately before him to read. The Party Secretary moved his gaze from one paper to another, left to right, calmly taking in the key details and showing no expression on his face. After pausing for one second to consider and categorize the new information, he raised his head slowly to look at Xiao Di, who was still standing by the door. The Party man glanced at one of the three chairs in front of his desk and Xiao Di advanced to stand behind that chair and did not sit down and was not asked to do so. The Party Secretary coughed slightly and at that signal the two other officials in the room exited through a side door.

The Party Secretary was still looking at Xiao Di when he said, 'When you talk with your colleagues, at various posts inside the Ministry, formally or informally, working, eating or drinking, in groups, or just one to one, what will you tell them about this meeting?'

'Not sure, Party Secretary Zhao,' said Xiao Di.

'Tell them your good work has been noticed and you were thus commended and subsequently asked to lead a workshop on detailed safety procedure at the forthcoming security personnel staff training event. Is that understood?'

'Yes, Party Secretary.'

'Do you want to lead such a workshop?'

'Er.'

'Tell them you didn't want to lead the workshop and only agreed because you were pressured into it and there's no going back. When is the staff training event?'

'Is it May Day? Labour Day?'

'That is correct. Your workshop will be at three o'clock.'

'It's . . . thank you. It's . . .'

'An honour?'

'I'm much obliged.'

'Ah,' said the Party Secretary looking to his right towards a semi opaque window that had a view of nothing except vague grey light.

'So would you do me a favour?'

'Yes, Party Secretary.'

'You know our foreign guest in secure room 494?'

'Yes, Party Secretary Zhao,' said Xiao Di, the image of a rat in his head.

Even though the Party Secretary continued to look at the unfathomable grey light he sensed that Guard Di had now become more tense.

'Are you protecting him well?'

'I am.'

The Party Secretary waited for two seconds and turned to look at Xiao Di.

He said, 'I want you to redouble your efforts. Attend him day and night. Always know where he is. And whatever happens to this guest, by whoever's orders at whatever level of Ministerial authority, always know how to contact me immediately.' He opened a desk drawer, top left, took a piece of paper between thumb and index finger, rested his arm on the desk while still holding the paper, and without lifting his arm from the desk, rolled his hand slightly towards Xiao Di. Xiao Di leaned forward and took the paper. It was a cigarette paper, cut in half, with a phone number written on it in pencil, lightly.

'Can you do that?' said Party Secretary Zhao.

'I can.'

'Good. This service will be remembered. How is your family?'

'Very good.'

'Your hard-working wife?'

'Very good.'

'Your eight-year-old boy?'

'Very good.'

'Your elderly mother and father in their new apartment?'

'Very good. Thank you. Thank you.'

'That's good. Understood. I need to work.' The Party Secretary looked down at his desk; pressed a key on his laptop. Xiao Di turned and left and heard a slight cough as he did so.

The Party Secretary's intention was to control the movements of Marcas Ghosh. The small matter of Ghosh's existence and close presence represented danger and the

Party man wanted to control that danger. He also knew that the Minister was likely to want to have Ghosh killed or disappeared one way or another, and he estimated that the Minister's intentions were in themselves risky and likely to go wrong both from the Minister's point of view and his own. In order to forestall any risk he wanted to be able to locate, move, release or hold Ghosh at any moment, and he calculated that he could use the capable and discreet Xiao Di to help do that.

Party Secretary Zhao was an excellent judge of men and he was correct in his estimation of the capability and discretion of guard Xiao Di, but there was a complication to his calculations of which he was not aware. Not only did Guard Di fear the Party Secretary, as was to be expected, he also hated him. Xiao Di understood what the Party Secretary wanted and began planning to do the opposite. And for some reason, he also began thinking of ways to help his friend the cook escape from the Ministry and find some suitable and more rewarding employment elsewhere, fairly quickly.

Meanwhile, back at Xiao Di's work station, unknown to him, one of his colleagues, the one who had stayed back on duty while the others heard the Party man's speech, was receiving a private phone call. It was from Nelson, a person that guard did not know. None-the-less, he was listening intently as Nelson was telling him a story about fifty thousand Yuan in used notes that would appear at a particular time, tomorrow morning, in a particular branch of MacDonald's, at a particular table, in a brown paper bag of the type used for takeaways, and that if the guard happened to be there at that time and at that table, he could take the bag away and nobody would know anything about it. This was a story that seemed to fascinate the guard.

Of course, the guard had his suspicions: 'Who's it for, then, this takeaway?'

'It's for you.'

'And how much will it cost me, this takeaway?'

'At the moment - nothing. I just want you to take it. I hate to see waste.'

'And afterwards?'

'Afterwards there is a matter of forgetting things and remembering things.'

'Forgetting what things?'

'Locking things. In the middle of the night when everything is easy to forget.'

'Ah - another takeaway, is it?'

'You can say that.'

'And what kind of *hamburger* are we talking about?'

'One I've never seen but probably would recognize straight away.'

'How?'

'It's a special hamburger. Different. Imported goods.'

The guard thought for a moment and said, 'I think I know that hamburger. And what things do I need to remember?'

'Two things. First, if a woman comes, just before you forget something, well, the woman is from me and what she says is what I say. Remember that.'

'A woman.'

'A strong woman. '

'OK. And what's the second thing I should remember?'

'You should remember a certain time and a certain place and a certain table and a certain brown bag.'

'Oh, I remember that no problem. I look forward to the takeaway.'

'Please enjoy it. What's your name?'

'Call me *Zhang*.'

The line went dead and the guard starting imagining about early tomorrow morning and about how everything could be different then.

And at the same time, all over the Ministry of Religious Affairs, senior officials were making their plans for tonight, for tomorrow morning, and for the rest of their lives. The deadline was approaching.

CHAPTER 47
Day 4, 5:35 pm

For all the senior officials at the Ministry of Religious Affairs seeking a plausible, satisfactory or even a true answer to the mass deaths that occurred three full days and sixteen hours previously, time was tight and getting tighter. And yet, Vice Minister Dong Bing found a minute or two while alone in the Minister's office to extend his list of Chinese inventions. He pulled up the saved list on his notebook computer and started to type. First he wrote the introductory rationale which had so far only existed in his mind, and augmented it with a fourth reason.

'The list has four purposes: First, creating it was an activity that engaged and exercised the author's mind when it was otherwise less than fully occupied, thus increasing the mind's strength and stamina. Second, it fed and developed a sense of pride in our people, history and nation, thus bolstering the author's patriotism and, if broadcast publicly, that of all his compatriots. Third, the list has the power to educate and to improve the Chinese people's level of culture, thus enhancing the quality of civilization in our nation. And fourth, this list will educate foreigners and enable them to deepen their understanding of China's history, creativity and advanced civilization both for their own benefit and for the benefit of a more enlightened world, while simultaneously causing the respect given to China and her people to grow closer to that which is truly deserved.'

Dong Bing thought that the fourth point satisfactorily completed and *globalized* his itemization of purposes. He continued to expand the list.

'An Authoritative List of the Chinese People's Inventions throughout History, Intended for Publication and the Education of Peoples of the World.

76. Karaoke
77. Origami
78. Maneki neko

79. Sushi
80. Flower arranging
81. Bonsai
82. Surfing
83. Tea ceremonies
84. Japanese culture'.

The Vice Minister spent more time than he expected on typing, and was more absorbed in his task than he intended, thus allowing the Minister himself to sneak up and read his screen.

'What's the meaning of that!' said the Minister. 'There's no Japanese culture! Whatever they have - it's ours!'

He slammed the lid of Dong Bing's notebook and the machine went *beep-beep beep-beep beep-beep beep.*

CHAPTER 48
Day 4

Early in the morning of her second day of enforced absence from Beijing, Officer Chen bypassed the whole public transport system of buses and trains, and for the first time in her history of returning to or departing from her home village, made use of another time schedule and another geography: she took a private car, as soon as she could, directly from her family home to the exact place she wanted to go. A second cousin in her village knew someone who had a car for hire, and following a series of phone calls connecting one cousin to another, the car owner arrived in his vehicle at her parent's house. Chen's mother left off sewing the flags of an unknown nation, her father let his cigarette burn down un-smoked between his fingers, and on the threshold of their home they wished her *goodbye, safe journey, good health* and her mother said *talk to your twin* and *call us*.

Chen got in the car and asked to be driven to Beijing. As they drove Chen was amazed to think that nobody except herself was preventing her from ending her imposed exile and nobody was preventing her from entering Beijing. When the amazement passed, she felt a kind of shame, realizing how much she had lived the way others wanted, and after the shame she felt a kind of anger, and then power.

During the journey she texted her twin: *995*. The sound of the numbers, *jiǔjiǔwǔ*, is like *jiùjiùwǒ*, meaning *help help me.*

Her twin answered: *today can't.*

Chen replied: *time place?*

Very difficult.

Help help time place?

For thirty minutes there was no response.

Chen texted again: *need your help. This time my life. Time place?*

Wait, came the answer.

Hours later, when the car was approaching Beijing, Chen told the driver to head to a district in the city's north west, and as they came within a kilometre of the Ministry, she asked him to park at an eating place that served truck drivers. She told him to go and eat.

'You want anything?' he said.

'I'm not hungry. Bring me something small. You eat first.'

Five minutes later the driver was back. 'I've eaten,' he said.

'Good?'

'No. This is a big city. They have no heart.'

He gave her a card box containing eight *bāozi* - soft white steamed buns, warm and gentle all the way through to a centre of pork cooked with sugar and soy sauce.

'Good choice,' she said.

'Yes,' he said. 'The man who makes these is from our own county.'

Each *bāozi* was the size of the palm of her hand. Their damp skins stuck to the card box and tore away leaving scraps of their fluffy interior. She ate them all.

'Where are we going?' said the driver.

'Nowhere,' said Chen. 'We are waiting.'

An hour later Chen got a text. Her twin had written: 'Meet 30 mins l8r.' There was the address of a restaurant. Chen was astonished to see how close it was to the Ministry compound and wondered if her sister knew how to locate Chen's position from her texts.

She answered, 'Good.'

She woke the driver from his nap and it took them five minutes to reach the restaurant. She waited until the meeting time and she waited forty minutes after that.

Chen's sister arrived in a taxi. They saw each other at the same time, sitting in the back of two different hired cars. Chen's twin got out of her car and Chen got out of her car and they met halfway. They hadn't seen each other for five years.

Big Sister, *Dàjiě*, said, 'I couldn't get away.'

Little Sister said, 'Let's go inside.'

As of old, without wishing to or not wishing to, they each saw into the other, seeing every movement or slight alteration in the expression of the face as the symptom of a thought or a feeling, and they understood these thoughts and feelings, too, because they could not be hidden. And, also as of old, the instant after sensing into the other, each knew that the other was equally able to sense into herself. Each twin wondered whether they held any secrets, either knowingly or unknowingly.

They saw that Big Sister looked older and more beautiful, and stronger and more tired than Little Sister. They also saw that although Little Sister was the protected one, the one in whom hopes and cash had been invested, she had also aged and had also suffered and was also strong. Although Big Sister had sacrificed her life for the benefit of the other, her individual willingness to sacrifice had not given the other complete protection from the troubles of the world, and it was disappointing for Big Sister to see that.

A teenage waitress came to their table dressed in a cheap, fashionable red overcoat. Her hands were also red.

'What are you eating?' the waitress said.

'Fried noodles,' said Little Sister.

'What kind?' said the waitress.

'You decide,' said Big Sister, without looking at the waitress. They had no idea to eat anything.

They were still looking at each other. They could see that Big Sister did not work in a factory and neither was she the manager of a shoe shop, as her letters home had variously claimed.

'How long have you been doing the job you are doing now?' said the elder twin.

'Since we last met.'

'Five years ago. Your Master's graduation.'

'At that time, were you already doing the kind of work you are doing now?'

'I've been doing it, here and there, since we were seventeen,' said the elder.

The younger sister said, 'They way things are. Our lives. It wasn't me who chose it.'

'Nor me.'

'I didn't know the kind of work you were doing.'

'Same here.'

'And I didn't ask you to do it.'

'Nor me.'

'I started doing this job and now I can't easily get another one. Other jobs won't want me.'

'You sold yourself to something. And now you want to change.'

'I don't want. It is changed.'

The waitress in red brought teacups without handles, a teapot, two pairs of chopsticks, and two small plates. She laid them on the table, fussily, and started pouring the tea.

The elder sister said, 'Leave it. We'll do it.'

She said to her younger sister, 'We wanted you to have a stable job, a powerful job, a job everybody could respect. If you had that job we need never worry or fear.'

'I did what I thought was needed.'

'Best for you, for everybody in our family.'

'Did not think about it.'

'I tried not to think about it.'

'Couldn't imagine what you were doing.'

'Didn't want to imagine it.'

'It's true.'

'If not for you it wouldn't be worth it.'

'It was.'

'I did what I was asked.'

'I didn't think whether it was what I wanted to do.'

'Or whether it was good.'

'Often it was bad. I tricked a man so he could be put in prison. An innocent man.'

'I've seen so many shocking things it's difficult to be shocked anymore.'

Little Sister Chen started washing their cups, plates and chopsticks with the tea, swirling the tea to rinse each item deftly and with a minimum amount of wasted hot liquid.

Her sister said, 'We always do things differently.'

'No, we do different things but we do them the same way.'

The waitress brought steaming hot noodles. She started serving the noodles to one sister's plate.

'Leave it,' said Little Sister.

She said to her elder sister, 'You think I've had it easy.'

'You think that's what I've wanted to say for twelve years. You think you carried the burden.'

'You got money for me.'

'Everything else was what you did.'

'The money was needed'

'Yes, without the money - '

'And sacrifice.'

'And sacrifice. There would be nothing without sacrifice. It wasn't a matter of just spending money.'

The waitress came and picked up the teapot to pour tea and found the sisters had not drunk any and it was pointless. If the waitress didn't go to customers' tables she was sent by her boss who said, *it's not your job to stand still.* A new waitress afraid of bothering customers had been sacked ten days ago and it was now easy to seem busy because of both the fear and the extra work caused by her colleague's dismissal.

Big Sister said, 'What did you mean: *need your help*?'

'I've never asked for your help all these years.'

'You took it.'

'I obeyed you by taking it.'

'And now what?'

'The man I tricked so he could be put in prison.'

'He's trapped.'

'I want to free him.'

'Who is this man to you?'

'He's mine.'

'You've decided?'

'Yes.'

'I've also decided on a man.'

'Good. Tell me.'

'You first. What's his trouble? Tell me the story. Why is he in prison?'

'You're shocked.'

'I'm not shocked a man's in prison. I'm shocked you know a man in prison. What's he there for?'

'I don't know. He thinks he saw something he shouldn't have. Secrets of the higher ups at my work - the Ministry. Way high up.'

'Is he a trouble-maker?'

'No, it was an accident.'

'Unlucky.'

'Very unlucky. He's a foreigner.'

'Foreigner! How can it last?'

'It doesn't matter. It's now that is important.'

'What do you want to do?'

'I want to get him out.'

'And why are you talking to me?'

'Who else can I ask?'

'My man needs help, too.'

'What kind of help?'

'He needs to move - get away from Beijing. But without anyone knowing. Can you fix travel tickets for us for tomorrow?'

'Maybe. Where to?'

'Way down south. And a passport for me.'

'Why do you need a passport?'

'Why? The same reason you need to help a foreigner in prison. You tell me why.'

They talked about the best way to spring Ghosh from capture. And the younger twin thought of ways to arrange tickets for Big Sister and her man to go by plane deep down south the next day. And a passport for her sister in case the plans failed and she – and her man – had to fly.

Younger twin Chen said, 'Yes, yes. I can say mine is lost, get a new one immediately, and you can use that.'

She was shocked when she saw the name of the man who was getting the ticket, the man her older twin was taking with her.

'Maybe we should have talked earlier,' said Big Sister. 'What did you mean: *this time my life*?'

'My life is changing,' said Little Sister. I'm taking over. It's becoming my life. My life will be my life. It is my life now. I don't know how to describe it. It's too new.'

Big Sister did not say, 'Selfish!'

She did not say, 'Your *life* exists because of what I've done! What we've all done!' She could have said all that but she didn't because she didn't want to be responsible anymore. She wanted to live without carrying her sister's future. She wanted to live alone, apart, separate, and able to make her own connections.

And Little Sister did not say, 'I took all the hopes you had and it was my duty to make the hopes come true, whatever I was doing and no matter what I wanted.'

She said, 'Now we are in our twenty-ninth year. I will support you and I will support myself.'

'I say the same,' said her elder twin.

'Each duty is ended.'

'It's not necessary anymore.'

'Work for ourselves and what we want.'

'I say the same.'

'We'll do it.'

'Free the men - and be free ourselves.'

Big Sister gave Little Sister a pistol holster.

'It looks real,' said Little Sister.

'It is real. Only no gun in it.'

'Just a bluff.'

'It might work. Listen - I have to get back. You came asking me for help and now you've helped me more.'

'I don't think so. It's half and half. Equal.'

'Maybe it always is.'

'Thanks.'

Younger twin Chen spent the next few hours arranging tickets for her sister and her sister's man, and for herself. She used her own name, her job title, and contacts given to her by her superiors. In the same way, she reported her passport lost to an official she knew in the Ministry of

Public Security. She mentioned urgent missions and she used the Minister's name. Of course, she did not mention the Minister's suggestion that she stay in her home village. The official gave her the number of a contact in the passport issuing section.

This contact, after hearing Officer Chen's story, said, 'Wait a minute.' He checked some records on a secure computer.

He said, 'Ah, I know all about you, Officer Chen. It's all clear: you are a *special* officer with *special* travel requests.'

'I do what people need me to do.'

'Ha, ha, ha. Understood. Are you planning a short trip to Europe?'

'I'll tell you the truth: I am.'

'Ha, ha, ha. And is this trip for one or two?'

'For two, I hope.'

'Ha, ha, ha. You see - I know everything. Send a driver here in an hour. The passport will be ready. We have all the data, photo, everything.'

'Thank you very much.'

'It's nothing.'

'Can I do something for you?'

'Oh, no, no, no! You're on government business; I am just helping government business. This is our duty. Nothing for me.'

'Perhaps one of your superiors?'

'Ah, that's very respectful.'

'A little souvenir.'

'What part of Europe?'

'England.'

'England? Talisker single malt aged for ten years is good, and eighteen years is better. A case.'

Around 8 pm Officer Chen got a phone call from an unknown voice claiming to be called *Nelson*.

'Who are you?' she said.

'I just told you. I'm Nelson,' said Nelson, laughing.

'I'm not listening,' said Chen.

Before she had even finished saying it Nelson started quickly on Chen's full name: 'Chen Ying. Age twenty-nine. Junior Officer, fifth rank, Ministry level, Ministry of Religious Affairs. And Ghosh, Marcas, British. Ministry of Religious Affairs Detention Area One, cell 494. Are you listening now?'

Chen said nothing.

Nelson said, 'What do I want? I want our friend to be free. I am trying my way, and I want you to try your way. Nothing is guaranteed to work. If you want money or anything else, save my number and use it. Good luck.'

'Who are you?'

'We discussed that already.' The call ended.

For the next several hours Chen waited until carrying out the next part of the plan she had made with her elder twin. At exactly 2 am, Officer Chen went to the Ministry. It was the time when staff were fewest and there was the least possibility of anyone knowing about her being supposedly in exile. The fact had not been broadcast. There were too many other things to be done that day and there was no benefit to make it public news. Nobody among the night staff knew she had been sent away. Nobody was suspicious to see her or her ID. Chen was thrilled to feel that there was nothing stopping her entering the Ministry compound except her own obedience.

She made her way towards the detention area. She was wearing a pistol holster. To anyone she met she was bluff, seemed angry and offered no explanations. It was a manner of behaving she had often seen used by her superiors. Sometimes this manner came from being genuinely irritated, overburdened and afraid. Sometimes it did not. Doors were opened for her. She came to the office of the night-time supervising guard of the detention area. The office was about one metre square with a tiny desk, and the supervising guard was asleep with his head on the desk. His working day was long.

Chen slapped her official ID on the table. The guard woke slowly, then, seeing her, quickly.

Chen said, 'I am Officer Chen. Who are you?'

'Guard Zhang.'

'Anything to report?'

'Nothing. No, Officer.'

'Prisoner disturbance?'

'Prisoner disturbance? No, nothing. Quiet. Usual.'

The entire desk top was covered in a slab of clear glass, and under the glass were bits of paper including a chart showing a plan of the detention area and the position of the cells.

Officer Chen jabbed her right index finger at the chart. 'Where is the foreign prisoner?'

'Foreign criminal? He's here. That cell,' said the guard, pointing.

'I need to interrogate him.'

'Now?'

'Yes.'

The guard looked at Chen's holster. He said, 'Ah, that's difficult. I have the keys but I'm not allowed to leave here. Not unless there's an escape. That's the night shift rule. No doors opened and no movement. And the two guards in the corridor are not allowed to leave there - and cover me here - unless there's an escape.'

'Who's talking about escape?'

'No, nobody, just. . .'

'Interrogation.'

'Yes, but I can't leave - oh - I can phone for authority. Wake somebody. It's an urgent matter.' He reached for the desk phone.

'No, no', said Chen. 'I can wait. When does the night shift change?'

'Six. Just before.'

Chen took a piece of Ministry memo paper from her pocket and wrote an order and she signed it as the Minister. The guard saw that she signed as the Minister and made sure she couldn't notice that he saw it. The order was: *Release foreign guest Ghosh at six o'clock in the morning.*

CHAPTER 49
Day 4, 10 pm

While Officer Chen was busy contacting many people, and hours before her early morning return to the Ministry compound, Ghosh was spending his second evening alone in a cell with no notion of what Chen was doing. He thought about how Chen had lead him to capture; wondered if he should doubt her; felt entitled to do so; and he tried doubting though his heart wasn't in it. He had nothing to do except worry and had nobody to talk to until the window in the cell door was opened and a hand appeared there, holding a phone.

Ghosh took the phone and said, '*Wéi?*'

The phone voice said, 'It's me.' It was Nelson, having just finished a beautiful dinner in Tokyo.

Ghosh was suppressing his fear and one of the results of the suppression was that almost everything was a source of anxiety, and he began to hate every new incident.

Ghosh said, 'What there is to solve? We're finished.'

'Me and my life - that's what I need to solve.'

Ghosh breathed out angrily.

Nelson said, 'As Chairman Mao said, if you need to fart, then fart. You'll feel better for it.'

Ghosh tutted with irritation. 'I'm in prison. You're free.'

'My heart is with you. I've lost sleep for you. I'm helping you. Where will you go when you get out of the Ministry?'

'Back to England.'

'Yes, of course. My meaning is before that, in Beijing. You may need to hide.'

'It's not my city and I stand out everywhere.'

'Obstacles reveal the desire. What would you do if you were free?'

'I can't think about that. I can't think about anything. Once I get out I can start thinking what to do.'

'You should start now. Stop worrying about what's happening or not happening. Start thinking what to do to get out.'

'What are they saying - Minister - the officials - whoever?'

'Good - that's right. Start thinking. They say that because of what you know you may be dangerous. This makes it dangerous for you. You might be killed by the Minister. My uncle. Though he denies it.'

'Killing me?'

'No - being my uncle. He was always visiting my mother's sister when I was a kid. My aunt. And that aunt's kid looked nothing like her - or me. He's an odd one out. He's the boy my 'uncle' the Minister gave her. That's what I think.'

Nelson kept quiet for a while and said, 'It's like what Rambo says: You can't escape what you really are.'

Ghosh said, 'And you are *Nelson*.'

Nelson said, 'I admire Nelson and I use his name as a sign of respect. It shows anybody who understands.'

'I don't.'

'I admire Nelson Piquet because when I was old enough to look to the world and seek a hero, he was there. He was the leader, the best, and the winner. A natural, and he was always driving, everywhere, any kind of car, faster and faster, and not just to win the paid races. It wasn't a job. It wasn't for the money. And when he got money he was like me - he played with money, for fun. And he didn't care about what he said - words don't count - and he understood about cars and machines and systems and what they are, and about numbers. And the people who don't understand these things make rules to hold back people like Nelson and me, stop us going fast, stop us playing, because they think we should go the same speed as everybody else and not treat things as a game, and not win.'

'Nelson *Piquet*? Was he a Formula One driver that died?'

'He *is* a driver and he is not dead. That's important - he's not dead. He isn't a religious maniac like some of his rivals. He is wiser than that and braver - in the way I want to be brave. Why are you called Ghosh?'

'It's a family name. It's my father's name.'

'And what's your given name?'

'Marcas.'

'Meaning?'

'It's my father's idea. Something from a book he read.'

'Like Rambo said: you can't escape.'

The sound of a guard's footsteps approached Ghosh's cell door. The sound stopped, briefly. There was a jangle of keys. The footsteps started again, moving away.

'So,' said Ghosh, 'What are *you* going to do?'

'I want to go somewhere quiet, with simple stories.'

'Not back to China?'

'No,' said Nelson said. 'I want to retire now to a nice little country with lovely nice people who don't bother me and where there's lots of space to be on my own and do what I want. And I am twenty-six. I'm moving to Angola.'

'Do you know anybody there?'

'No. I'm going to be like your Rambo,' he said, meaning Rimbaud. 'I'm going forever and when I'm gone from here I'll leave everything except my favourite pink lampshade.'

'Why?'

'We can't escape the past. The lampshade was the first gift from my mother. When she was away it *was* my mother - a light in the dark of our bedroom. I was two years old. I've never met my father. I mean my *real* father. Now I only have the lampshade. It still lights up. It goes with me to Angola.'

'Why are you calling me?'

'I'm telling you to stop feeling and start thinking. I'm telling you'll be out soon, one way or another. I'll call you. What's your number?'

'I'm in a cell.'

'Tell me your cell number in England. I'll call you there.'

'OK, its 44 7758 0926 81.'

'Good. Starts like a nightmare and finishes fine.'

'Did you write it down?'

'Certainly not.'

Again there was the sound of a guard's footsteps approaching the cell. The cell door opened and a guard took the phone from Ghosh.

The guard said, 'Time's up,' and handed Ghosh a bowl of food to eat.

Ghosh sighed and looked hopeless.

The guard said, 'Eat, and if you can't do anything else now, sleep.'

CHAPTER 50
Day 4, Midnight

At midnight the door of Ghosh's cell was opened. The guard, Xiao Di, came in the cell and moved the door so that it was almost, though not quite, closed. From the outside it would have seemed, at a glance, that the door was closed, and the difference between being open and being closed is big. In the dark, it was difficult for Ghosh and the guard to see each other.

Ghosh asked the guard, 'How can I get out?'

The guard said, 'Start with your head.'

'Huh?'

'Your head looks cold. Stick this on.' Xiao Di handed something to Ghosh. Ghosh took it - a woollen balaclava.

Xiao Di said, 'See it's the only thing I'm doing. In winter. Lending a balaclava.'

Ghosh put it on and twisted it around his head so that his eyes were free.

'I see,' said Ghosh quietly. 'Thanks Xiao Di - Eddie.'

Xiao Di was standing by the far wall, examining it. His back was to the door. Ghosh moved to the door and started opening it, and as he did, Xiao Di also moved. Ghosh stopped. He turned his head. Xiao Di had his arm outstretched, and in his palm was the rat. He was offering it to Ghosh. Ghosh moved to take it. He refrained.

Ghosh said, 'The rat should live here. He has his friends, his place - and has you, too. I won't take him away on a whim just for my pleasure.'

The guard said, 'Yes,' and gently put the rat down on the floor. The rat ran toward the door, went out through the small gap and ran along the gloomy corridor until couldn't be seen anymore.

The guard said, 'You're a good man. I'm glad to have met you.'

They held each other's right hand for a moment. Ghosh turned and went out of the door. He walked along the corridor in the same direction the rat had moved and at the end of it came to a door that seemed to be shut, and almost was. He went through it. He was in a well-lit room, something like an entrance hall or a holding space. There were several doors, some glass, leading to other parts of the building. One door, at the far end of the room, was open to a cubby-hole office inside which there was a man with his head down on a desk, deeply asleep. Another door, to the left of the office, was almost closed. Ghosh went towards the door. When he passed the sleeping guard, the man opened one eye, made an 'O' with his mouth, and with thoughts of cash in a bag in a restaurant, closed his eye again. Ghosh went through the door. He was in a narrow corridor. Directly ahead, another ten metres, there was a metal door, slightly rusty. He went to it and found that it was almost closed, but not quite. He went through and was outside. It was cold. He was glad to be wearing a balaclava.

He walked and walked on snow and cinders. He walked past dormant building sites, industrial storage lots, and rows of workshops with metal shutters pulled down and locked, one after the other. Occasionally he saw another person, across the street, or in the distance, and he averted his eyes, looked down and tried to hunch his posture into obscurity.

After twenty or thirty minutes walking he turned a corner and just around the corner was a late-night eating place. Two red-faced men wobbled out, drunk and heavy, and one crashed into Ghosh.

'*Hà!*' shouted this man, who wanted to start a fight with a stranger. His friend didn't want to start a fight and pulled the first man's arm back. The two friends started to have a fight with each other, one saying, '*Hà!*', and the other saying, '*Nǐ!*', *you*, and each shoving the other in the shoulder. In the freezing, dry air their breath poured out in fiercely stinking mists of fried garlic and *bái jiǔ* - white spirits, 56% alcohol, *Red Star* brand. They looked like little pot-bellied dragons of winter drunkenness. The snorting dragons ignored Ghosh and he felt relieved by their unconcern. He knew that he looked anonymous to the eyes of two drunks, at night, in the dark, wearing his balaclava and down jacket, but he contained inside himself the knowledge of his appearance, his foreignness and his escapee status. He had to convince himself to have confidence in the ignorance of any who saw him.

The two men continued saying, *Hà* and *Nǐ*, more and more weakly. Drawn by their activity and the light from the open door of the restaurant, a taxi approached from far down the street, with its headlights off. Ghosh took the taxi. He pretended to be a bit drunk and sleepy and made his voice match, slurring the words of the address of his own apartment. He had no idea where *here* was and no idea how long it would take to get *there*. It took forty-three minutes by the clock on the dashboard, and when they reached his apartment building it was 1:04 am.

He asked the driver to wait, trying to make his Chinese both correct and drunk: 'Děng yīxià. Děng yīxià.' *Wait a minute*. The driver waited because he felt he had no choice. Ghosh went to the apartment building's gatehouse and shouted for the aged night watchman, again pretending to be a bit drunk. The night watchman was sleeping on a camp bed behind a cotton curtain. Ghosh called the man's name, 'Lǎo Wǔ! Lǎo Wǔ! Lǎo Wǔ! *Old Wu! Old Wu! Old Wu!*, and when the man appeared at the window of his tiny gatehouse, Ghosh said, 'Aiyā!' *Oh no!* 'Wàngjìle wǒ yàoshi!' *Forgot my key!* 'Bù hǎo yìsi!' *Really ashamed.* 'Duì bu qǐ, duì bu qǐ.' *Sorry, sorry*. Again and again.

The old man looked at Ghosh and didn't move and didn't say anything. Ghosh realised he needed to be himself. He snatched off his balaclava. The guard knew him and showed annoyance on his lips. Ghosh smiled, broadly. The guard got hold of some keys. They went up to his room. Ghosh found cash and his own spare keys and ran downstairs past the guard to pay the driver - putting the balaclava back on and slowing his walk before stepping outside. The driver was still waiting, of course. Ghosh paid the fare and another fifty RMB for waiting, which was too much though not ridiculously so.

Back in his apartment he took off the balaclava for the last time and saw it was brown and hand knitted.

He found his air ticket, his original air ticket to London, the one he hadn't used. He made a phone call to a company in England - it was nearly 6 pm there. He brought forward the date of his Beijing departure and the cost of the change was taken from his credit card. He finished the call and waited until 6 am when he called the number of a driver he knew and asked to be taken to the airport. He had breakfast at Beijing Capital International Airport, eating extravagantly at a stupid café where prices are ten times more than they should be.

At a flimsy neighbouring table a powerfully built middle-aged Chinese man in a dark suit was drinking black coffee. An iPhone was on the table.

'Excuse me. Sir,' said Ghosh. The man stopped drinking and held his cup without looking at Ghosh.

'Can I borrow your phone to send a text to my mother?'

The businessman looked at Ghosh from under his eyebrows.

Ghosh said, 'Very short.'

'Haven't you got a phone?'

'Er, I haven't got it with me. I'll give you the money.'

'Use it,' said the man handing his phone to Ghosh.

Ghosh texted his mother, giving details of his flight and arrival in London.

Ghosh returned the phone saying, 'Xièxiè nǐ,' *thank you*, and offered paper money.

'No, need brother,' said the man. He took his phone, got up and walked away.

Ghosh checked in early and his flight left on time.

CHAPTER 51
Day 5, 8 am

Four days after the deaths in the snowy field, in the morning at exactly 08:00:00, official news items were posted simultaneously on several media sites including the English-language *Global Times.*

50 Dead in Doomsday Cult Terror
Police Suspect Foreign Links

Xinhua/ Global Times
[8:00 February 8]

An act of mass terror by members of an illegal cult killed over fifty people in Beijing on February 4 and may be linked to foreign organizations seeking to destabilize China, authorities say.

The mass murder and suicide was one of the nation's worst ever terror atrocities.

Victims include government officials who were questioning the cultists about an illegal night-time gathering in suburban fields northeast of the capital, it was revealed by the Ministry of Religious Affairs.

As the bureaucrats went about their peaceful duties members of the criminal gang launched a violent and unprovoked attack leaving several dead. Following the pre-meditated killing, cultists resorted to a grotesque mass suicide to avoid lawful arrest.

Municipal police confirmed that all perpetrators were dead and did not pose a threat to the safety of the general public.

Destabilization Attempt

'The cultists' intentions are suspicious since we're coming up to the February 10 Security Council meeting,' said Li Weike, professor of Security and Anti-terror Studies at Beijing University, referring to scheduled monthly discussions of China's top government body.

The proximity of the New Year holiday meant the cultists also hoped to strike terror to the hearts of all Chinese, Li said.

'This horrific attack is a shocking reminder of the inflexible fanaticism characteristic of heretical cult activity', commented Li He, Director of the Beijing Anti-Cult Association (BACA), a nongovernmental organization undertaking anti-cult campaigns in the national capital.

Experts say some cults are home-grown while many have been introduced from the US or Japan.

CHAPTER 52
Day 5, 9 am

Party Secretary Zhao declared, 'I'm not resigning,' to nobody in particular and everybody in his outer office heard it with great attention. The deaths in the snowy field were now truths and the SLT was publicly blamed for them. But the real answers had not been found, not nearly, and somebody would have to pay for that ignorance. It was *threatening.*

Some of the officials in the outer office thought that despite the Party Secretary's words he would definitely resign. The others thought he would be fired. Neither group could guess they were both mistaken.

Of course, the Minister of Religious Affairs bore even more public responsibility. He was the face of the Ministry and had many awkward questions to answer. He wasn't in his office and he wasn't answering any of his cell phones. On the orders of the Party Secretary, based on concerns for the Minister's safety, his apartment door was kicked in and the rooms were searched. Nothing incriminating was found though the Party Secretary was puzzled to hear that the Minister owned seven functioning computers. He was not puzzled to hear that the Minister had fled.

Among all the offices at the Ministry of Religious Affairs, Party Secretary Zhao's desk had the least number of ugly ornaments. Unlike the Minister, who was in the regular habit of dashing knick-knacks to the ground in anger, he had no desire to destroy inanimate objects. On his smooth, clean desk there was only one non-functional item, a crystal pyramid, and it vexed him to see that somebody had put an ordinary envelope under the pyramid as if it were a paper weight. He snatched the envelope away.

Inside the envelope was a first class ticket to Seattle. Flight Air Canada 30, via Vancouver, departing 17:50 that same afternoon; flight time 13 hours 45 minutes. The passenger name was his.

'Who put this envelope on my desk?' he asked the people in the outer room.

'I don't know,' said the chief assistant. 'It was there this morning. I thought you, yourself - '

'You think I'm in the habit of leaving scraps of paper on my desk?'

'I did think it was curious.'

Attempting a show of normality, he asked the assistant to read through the list of this week's engagements. This was in fact abnormal because the Party Secretary always knew what he was doing. At that moment, he wasn't sure what to do.

'I'm going out,' he said.

'You're going out,' said his assistant.

Party Secretary Zhao walked through the corridors of the Ministry until he felt he was alone. With a clean key he opened the door of a storage cupboard that lead to a narrow passage between walls and rooms. He started walking around the building, listening to voices as he walked on his hidden path. Everything he heard was mundane. He didn't learn anything.

Almost as soon as he started walking he unconsciously thought of Bill, and of ending this walk by meeting him. But Bill was gone. Party Secretary Zhao had no friends or close family he could call on. His mother, who had dominated his early life and was the central figure for much that followed, had finally died, succumbing the previous winter to pneumonia at the age of ninety-four. It was pneumonia's third attempt.

His father had been dead for over five decades. He died - was killed - killed himself - under shame, imprisonment and pressure, when the Party Secretary was twelve years old. His father had been a gentle, weak and humiliated man who had carried secret loves for, amongst other things, violins. He had also fervently loved a certain pair of shoes, a tailored jacket and a hat, all French-made, that he had bought in Shanghai before the Revolution. And, most damming of all for Communist Party member, he owned a framed portrait of Mussolini.

He was denounced and divorced by his Party member wife, the future Party Secretary's mother.

The father took prison hard. He couldn't follow the rules of either the guards or the inmates. He was never visited. He attempted suicide by falling down a flight of concrete steps but wasn't immediately successful and it took him a month to die.

'It was cleaner for all of us, especially for you,' his mother had sometimes reminded him. He didn't like to hear it. Still he took his mother's name, Zhao. His father had been Xi. Only by his mother's assiduous Party loyalty and scheming plans had he, the only son, escaped the blot of the photo of Mussolini.

After twenty minutes of internal meandering he was back at his desk.

'I need to make some phone calls,' he said.

The assistant left the office. In fact, the Party Secretary had nobody to call. He had nothing to say to his superiors in the Party. There had been - there still was - a crisis at the Ministry. He had not been able to see it coming, he couldn't stop it, and he didn't know if it would happen again. Nearly three hundred people were dead and the government had only admitted to fifty. Things could still get much worse. It was difficult to see them getting better. Even if an answer and a solution was found, it would not eradicate the failings so far. His age meant he was coming to the end of his career. He was an easy choice of sacrifice. Not that he didn't deserve punishment, he realized. If he stayed and continued to manage the crisis there may be no benefit to him. There was the strong possibility of further demerit.

An official call came through to his office. The phone on his broad, glinting desk. A heavy desk, full of locked drawers, some lined with metal, the entire top surface covered in a plate of smoked glass. The call was from his best connection, his golden thread, a man who was going to get a seat on the Politburo, the nation's supreme decision-making body, the next time there was a change of guard; a man a decade younger than himself, a *friend*, whom Zhao had nurtured, taught, protected and at one time promoted, and who now had more power and seniority than himself and could help decide his future.

The man said, 'This is an official call.'

'That's clear.'

'You've been summoned to the State Council meeting on the tenth.'

'Will you be there?'

'Of course. You won't be required the whole time so you'll be made to wait outside until they want to see you. It won't take long, that part.'

Party Secretary Zhao was silent. It would be a trial and judgement.

He said, 'What's the sentence?'

'Listen, your record is good - outstanding. You've got a first class mind and better than that you're reliable - both loyal and able to complete every task.'

Zhao thought, 'He wants me to say: *except this one*.' So he did.

'Correct. As always, you are correct,' said the voice. 'And you also understand that this time I can't help you much. It's too big. You know that, don't you? You have more sense of responsibility than anyone else I know. It's an old fashioned virtue. You understand what's happening, don't you?'

'There's the Ministry itself.'

'Look, you of all people, you don't need me to tell you it's the Party that leads. And takes the blame. We can't blame the bureaucrats. Not in private, not at this level.'

'What will I keep?'

'Membership.'

There was a pause while the Party Secretary screamed in his mind: 'Membership! Party *membership*! All these years! All my life! All my effort! All my plotting and my mother's! All my mind flung at this Party and all they leave me with is membership! Forty-one years gone in a moment.'

The Golden Thread said, 'I don't think there's any question of house arrest. And there's one good thing. The talk on-line isn't as much as we expected.'

'No?'

'You were given the full four days - and I pushed for that - and now it seems that was correct. A full four day's silence to work.'

'Thank you for that.'

'Yes. There's really not much. That's why my four days idea was good. There's been popular reaction to this morning's news story: shock, horror, people saying bomb Japan, force Muslim women to marry Han Chinese, exile north-western Muslim men to the furthest parts of the nation - the usual banter. Nothing from the cultists.'

'Biding their time?'

'Keeping up with the internet isn't your strong point, is it? Nobody knows what they are doing. Anyway, it's quiet.'

'That's good.'

'Yes, until the foreign media gets hold of it.'

'Do you still care what foreigners say?'

'Yes, Party Secretary, we still care.' The Golden Thread was getting annoyed, particularly as he knew he could have done more to help his former protector, or at least been more sympathetic.

He said, 'It's on the tenth. You know where.'

'In the meantime?' Party Secretary Zhao had assumed a totally subservient role, as easily as a habit, although it was the first time ever in their quarter-century relationship.

'Make your calls. All the big potatoes you know. Plead your case.'

'What can I say?'

'Just pay your respects. Be mature. Take it like a man. Don't expect to escape punishment. You know it's coming. Be dignified like you always used to be.'

'Will I keep freedom of movement?'

'Now - yes. Afterwards - the details haven't been sorted yet.'

'A public trial?'

'No, no, no. Don't be ridiculous. We're not going to fight in public for the sake of giving more publicity to a cult - and to our own mistakes. Not now.'

'When?'

'I'm not saying when. Maybe never. You must know yourself - and this is completely private - between friends - we're still friends, isn't that right? Right?'

'Right, right.'

'You must know yourself that if - when - foreign media get hold of all this anything can happen. And I didn't say that. You already know all this.'

'Of course. I know.'

'Well, that's it. You've been summoned and, privately, you've been warned. So far you've been lucky. There are no secrets between us.' The call ended.

Party Secretary Zhao still did not know what to do next. He looked again at the ticket. He tried to calculate who bought it. He could only think of one person. What happened to the Minister? Where was that old bastard?

His phone rang - his personal phone.

The Party Secretary said, 'Who?'

A muffled voice said, 'Someone in the sky above you. On the way to hospital.'

'What? The line's bad.'

The voice replied clearly and un-muffled: 'No it isn't.' It went back to being unclear and muffled: 'Notice your desk is messy?'

'It was. I tidied it.'

'Indirect but short. Via Vancouver. That's in Canada.'

'I know.'

'Right - your wife lives there.'

'She doesn't live there - she's just receiving medical treatment.'

'Yeah, since 1996.'

'It's been a long malady,' said the Party Secretary.

'Sound sick yourself. Should go there. Get treatment. More important - families should be together. Ugh - nothing to do with you, of course - remember that old American was employed here?'

'Not sure that I do.'

'English teacher. Went back to America suddenly.'

'Foreigners are unpredictable.'

'Too right. And don't know when they're well off. In China he was blooming; over there he's fading.'

'How do you know?'

'Want photos?'

'You're joking.'

'Know what a webcam is? It sees lots of trees, old wooden house, mailbox at the end of the drive, bad weather, sick old man. Sad.'

'Are you watching?'

'Me? Don't have time. You've got time. Today.'

'Why?'

'Ugh. Families. What I said. Should be together.'

'No. I mean: why the envelope? For me.'

'End of our generation. End of work.'

'It would suit you if I were to go,' said the Party Secretary.

'Yeah, you can think of it like that if you want. Either way, you can live in peace.'

The call finished.

At that moment, in a draughty wooden house in pine woods ninety-five minutes drive from the suburbs of Seattle, a tired old man was pained by cold in his hands. The man was Bill. His hands were cold because he had them in the cold water of his kitchen sink and was trying to pull the plug out, unsuccessfully. He had filled the sink to wash some cups and the plug was stuck. It was the fourth time it had happened. Every day he would forget, put the plug in and fill the sink with cold water. Then he couldn't get the plug out. The water came from the bottom of a rain filled tank. The kitchen had no hot. It was a neglected summer house he had used on occasional visits to the US, and a fine place in beautiful Seattle Julys, though tough in February.

It was just after six in the evening; dark, hard and nothing to look forward to, and too early to go to bed. There had been no cups to drink from and that's why he ended up with his hands, red and white, in cold water. There were no neighbours, nobody to play basketball with, nobody to talk to, nobody to care for, and nobody to take care of him. Rain started again, pattering on the kitchen roof. He had bravely left Beijing to protect his friend Zhao, who he called Joe, and come back 'home' to emptiness.

Party Secretary Zhao could imagine all this and feel the pain in the most tender and hidden part of his heart. And he knew he should go, must go, had to go. He knew he would not resign, not be sacked, and he would this very day flee to his only *family* in the midst of a winter of another country which promised summers of such tranquil loveliness that even those less God-fearing than Bill might give thanks to the Creator and feel possessed with a thrilling joy of existence. If only their future together were in fact to be that way, he thought.

CHAPTER 53
Day 5, 12 noon

China>>Society>>Update

Cult Chaos Threat
Law's Tough Response

Xinhua/ Global Times
[12:00 February 8]

China's government is using the full force the of law in a tough response to threats of national destabilization made by doomsday cults, Vice Minister of Religious Affairs, Dong Bing, said today in Beijing.

The response comes after news of over fifty killed in a mass murder and suicide terror atrocity carried out by members of a criminal cult in the suburbs of Beijing. The cult has unexplained connections to foreign organizations, it has been claimed.

Public officers were sent to negotiate peacefully with the cultists in the early hours of 4th February following reports of an illegal gathering for anti-social purposes in the suburbs of the national capital. Several officials were murdered before the mob turned their weapons on themselves.

'This wicked stunt will not distract the government from its patriotic duty nor will it make cowards of the Chinese people,' declared Vice Minister Dong.

One of the first readers of the Chinese version of this article was the Minister of Religious Affairs. He had an update app on one of his iPhones.

He said, 'That performing poodle Dong Bing got his paws all over the thing now.'

'Is that the man always concerned about your health and strength?' asked Meiyuan, the Minister's favourite, and the elder twin Chen.

'Sickness and weakness, he means,' said the Minister.

'And now you're hiding in a hospital. He's right.'

'Not the point. I hate him.'

They had taken the 07:40 China Southern Airlines CZ5954 from Beijing to Fuzhou, landed at 10:15 and been driven in a car two hours up into the mountains to reach a small town with a hospital. After travelling sixteen hundred kilometres by air and sixty kilometres by road, they found themselves back in time twenty-five years, which, in a place changing as quickly as China, is some distance.

Minister Wang and Chen Meiyuan stood at the open window of a fifth floor room looking down at the centre of the town. Though it was much warmer than Beijing there was no difference in temperature between inside and outside because the location was, officially, the South, and there was no indoor heating. There were leaves on the trees and red lanterns strung up for New Year. Three grey roads met in a junction and on the roads were motorcycles, overloaded trucks, bicycles, dusty buses, hand-pulled carts full of garbage or cabbages, tractors and trailers, men and women shouldering heavy bags suspended on bamboo poles, and pedestrians walking or just standing. There was a bunch of motorcycle taxis, the riders standing by their parked bikes waiting for passengers to ride pillion. Some of the motorcyclists had helmets, some wore the hard hats of construction workers, though most had neither. Some of the people carrying or pulling heavy burdens wore wide peasant hats. Their clothes were fewer and older than those in Beijing, and their faces were darker. Bands of boys scampered about, happy, not in school. They were one thousand metres up and all around were mountains shaped like broken pieces of something. The sky was a cloudless blind white.

The Minister said, 'Why did you bring me to this desperate shithole?'

'Because it's the nearest hospital to where you were born.'

He said, 'These days kids get born in hospitals. Sad place to start your life. When I was a kid hospitals were for the wounded.'

'Like you.'

'Taking lessons from Dong Bing?' said the Minister. He looked at the white sky and blew a fart noise with his lips.

'Lost interest in the weather?' she said.

'The weather's done what it can do. No charm left. Not like you.' He pinched her cheek, gently. He turned to look into the room where some ceremonial cleaning was going on, a performance for their benefit rather than that of hygiene.

'Glad I'm not ill,' he said. The whole hospital had walls painted a pale green colour that made him feel lonely.

In Beijing the Minister played the bumpkin when it suited him. Back in the sticks he was shown up as a city slicker, to himself if not to everybody else. He was uncomfortable. Nobody called him. He had no office. He had nothing to do. Nobody to order or manage. People didn't know him. Sure, they knew he was a big shot and treated him obsequiously to his face. But he was nobody local, nobody famous. They saw a rough faced old guy with a young female paid companion.

Actually Chen, his companion, wasn't receiving pay. Not for being here, not for arranging the trip, not for choosing the location, not for getting the air tickets and the car from the airport up through the mountains, and not for getting the rooms at the hospital. It was her plan and she had carried it out, the Minister having lost something in decisiveness. She had started on the phone the evening before and called through the night.

She used the Minister's status, of course, while still protecting his identity and not using his name directly. She used his connections, navigating a network of people to contact the local party chief in the mountain town who in turn told the hospital manager that somebody big from Beijing was making the requests. The manager and staff in the hospital didn't even know if the man they now hosted was the real big shot or just somebody recommended by the big shot. They weren't used to the hospital being used as a refuge for people parachuting from as far away as Beijing.

When the Minister and Meiyuan arrived she had gone ahead to check the rooms while he waited in the Director's office. As she made her inspection, she didn't ask what kind of patients had been thrown out to make way for them. The rooms were satisfactory. She had paid for the service; nobody was paying her. In her relationship with the Minister, this was a change in the balance of power.

After the cleaners had left their rooms and they were alone together, she touched his arm and give it a gentle pressure.

She said, 'I'm going to propose something to you.'

The look in her eye and the tone of her voice was something he had not expected. She was getting ahead of him. He was not keeping up. He was too absorbed in his own defeat. He was losing ground.

Her finger was pointing to the floor.

'Stay here,' she said. 'And marry me.'

'Canada,' he said, weakly. It was a gasp, a curse, and an expression of desire.

'Live here,' she said. 'Retire. In peace. No more drinking *Canada*.'

'I need the heat.'

'Heating up a toad. It's unnatural. Throws you out of balance.'

'I'll die without it.'

'Then you'll live alone.'

This brief argument was enough time for him to recover. He thought about Beijing, and his job, and power, and the crisis, and her, and the remaining years of his life.

He said, 'My meaning is: go there. The *country* Canada. Travel. A month. Two. Us. I'll take Canada in Canada. That'll be the end of it for me. Then back here. To live. Like you say.'

'I say *no Canada*. Stay here together.'

'Ugh. OK. Whatever you want. Agreed. Together.' He put his arm around her shoulder. She moved near and put her arm around his waist. As one they turned to look again at the scene outside. There was calm in the chaos. This was the first time in decades for him to come back to the mountain area where he was born. It was not the triumphant homecoming he imagined as a young man, nourished on the ambitious plans of his mother and elder sister, both of whom had died too soon and not seen his greatest ascent, nor his return. Now he had a woman who knew him and would take him as he was and not push him to leave this place.

For Meiyuan the town was new and yet it felt like her childhood. Her life needed to change and this was the place for it. She knew she could live there. She knew she could manage it. She was satisfied. She was quiet.

He broke away from the view, the window and her.

He said, 'Ugh. Face it. No wedding, no end-of-Canada honeymoon. Can't work. I'm a dirty bastard playboy.'

She smiled and snuggled closer to him saying, 'We'll play games sometimes, old playboy. They might even be fun. Even after marriage.'

He smiled, too, and felt warm for the first time since their flight to the southern mountains.

He said, 'Not only am I wicked, I'm old.'

'Yes, you're nearly seventy. And I think you're a handsome old animal. Besides, you know I'm no maiden flower.'

'You look fresh to me. Ugh. And taste fresh, too,' he said, brushing aside her hair and sucking her ear lobe.

'Yah!' she said, pushing him away with a movement that showed she was happy.

Whatever he did or had done, she knew him thoroughly.

He thought: *I know exactly what she is. Or what she was.*

He said, 'Ugh. It's settled.'

She agreed.

CHAPTER 54
Day 5, 12 midnight (4 pm UK)

Seek knowledge even if it be in China. This was the message Ghosh saw on a sign after he ambled through customs and into the arrivals lounge of Heathrow Terminal 3. The sign was held by a middle-aged man with brownish purple rings under his eyes and a contrastingly yellowish complexion that seemed to say *liver ailment*. This man was Ghosh's father, RVS Ghosh, or what he wanted friends and family to call him, Jean-Jacques, or what he was actually called in England, Jacky, Indian Jacky and, when there was no attempt at flattery, Paki Jacky. He face looked ironical, superior, and discomforted at the same time.

Ghosh approached and said, 'I didn't expect - '

His father said, 'Come. Car parking is very expensive.'

Ghosh trailed behind as his father walked swiftly around a group of Nigerian businessmen, an extended Afghan family, and three sunburned white English couples.

Ghosh said, 'I didn't know - how did you know?'

Without looking back at his son, Ghosh's father said, 'The Prophet Muhammad.'

Outside the arrivals lounge, across a road, into a concrete car park, across the forecourt to a silver grey Nissan. They stood on either side. Ghosh's father said, 'Well, it is attributed to him. And that is what you seem to be doing. So it is an appropriate message I was sure you would notice quickly. And you did.'

'What?'

'*Seek truth even if it be in China.*' He unlocked the car doors. They got in.

As they were driving away from the airport, Ghosh's father said, 'A bombardment of phone messages from your mother insisting I come to meet you. Made her all worried about you. What's been happening? In your China?'

'It's been really hard. I - '

'Woman involved?' said Jacky Ghosh.

'No,' said Marcas. 'Well. It's not that. It's - '

'Ah! That's exactly what I told your mother.'
'It's not that, I - '
'No, of course not. Is she coming here?'
'I don't think so.'
'Very difficult - relationships at a distance.'
'It's not a relationship.'
'There's a writer - '
'French writer, yeah?'
'Yes, a French writer, and he said - '
'Balzac, right?'
'Yes, Honoré de Balzac, and - '
'It's always Balzac.'
'Not always. And there is in any case so much he says. In particular - '
'No, it's *always* Balzac. All my life - Balzac. Instead of reality: Balzac.'
'Marcas, *what* are you talking about? *What* do you know? *What* have you done? *What* have you made? *Il a créé un monde.*'
Ghosh had come back - come *home,* he'd thought - expecting safety and comfort. After five exhausting and frightening days he wanted restorative calm. He had longed for it. He had not dreamed that within five minutes he and his father would be skittering off into an irritated argument on his father's stupid favourite topic. The history of their behaviour patterns should have taught him it would be so. Knowledge of his own past would have told him his belief in finding nurturing harmony in his home country was an illusion.
Illusion lost, he hid in silence while there was so much to say.
Half an hour later, Jacky said, 'Do you know what kind of car this is?'
'Uh? No.'
'This is a 2004 Nissan Primera 2.2 2 with eleven thousand miles on the clock.'
There was a pause.
Ghosh said, 'And?'

'So you have been driven in this vehicle, the only passenger for thirty-three minutes, and you don't notice what kind of car or anything. You think you know everything. You don't notice anything except how you feel. Childish.'

'You would know.'

'What?'

'I said you would know.'

'I do know.'

Nothing more was said on the journey to Ghosh's mother's house. Ghosh got out. He didn't have any belongings.

Ghosh went up to his mother's studio flat on the third storey. The large room that contained her kitchen, bedroom and living room was light, airy and fresh. Outside was, of course, dark. Inside there were cream walls, pale blue paintings in frames, yellow curtains, and yellow light from lamps. After the tense and stale hour in a decommissioned taxi cab, being in his mother's room was a tonic.

His mother offered her cheek and as he kissed her she said, 'Did you talk to your father?'

'Ah!' He said. The tonic was contaminated. He was torn between wanting to use details of his last five days' ordeal to shock her and, because the true stories he might tell were like a weapon, not wanting to shock her.

He said, 'Yes, I had a nice flight, thanks. I chose beef over chicken for the main meal, and Western over Chinese for the light meal. I was met at the airport, and apart from trying to give me a lecture on a dead French writer - '

'*BalZAC*.'

' - the driver wasn't very chatty.'

'Marcas, don't try sarcasm, it makes you ugly. This was your big opportunity!'

'For what?'

'You know he's ill.'

'He looks sick. He always thinks he's ill.'

'Yes, he's hypochondriac. This time he is truly ill. And he doesn't want to speak about it. That's the big sarcasm. From God.'

Ghosh didn't say anything.

His mother said, 'Sit down, darling. I will make you coffee.'

Her coffee was French, the same brand her own mother had used. It was solid and unsubtle and high quality; she was meticulous about keeping it fresh. She had learned the correct way to treat and prepare coffee from her husband. As a young woman she had been a slob with coffee and bread. It was her husband who had started ordering the same coffee as her mother. She had asked him how he knew which brand her mother drank. He had answered: I asked her. He was careful with coffee as her mother had been and now she, the daughter, had learned from her husband to behave like her mother.

She said to her son, 'You are fine now, aren't you? I can tell. You've been in some trouble. I was anxious. That's why I asked him to pick up you. I sold my car.'

'Why?'

'It's an experiment. I don't know.'

'You love driving.'

'I do love it. There's nowhere I want to go. We'll see. Anyway, he's always going to the airport. I gave him money for the petrol. And I wanted you to talk.'

'With him? About what?'

'Anything. Nothing. Everything. Just talk. You don't *know*?'

'No.'

'That what happened in China - '

'It's - I was - '

'Marcas, we will talk about it. We will talk about it. First, you should know.'

'Know?'

'He's your father and he may be going to die.'

Ghosh sighed. He said, 'Can I have milk with this coffee? It's a bit strong.'

'Do they all drink coffee in milk in China?'

'Most people in China don't understand coffee.'

'Ah, so you'll be at home there. Are you returning to childhood through milk?'

'You take *café au lait* in the morning.'

'Yes, we all get babyish in old age. Though that's in the morning. Now it's the middle of the day. If it's bitter, use sugar. Your father might be dying.'

'What makes you think that?'

'The facts. Brute facts. You know he's had hepatitis for fifty years?'

'No.'

'No? Didn't you ever pay attention? That's why he's hypochondriac.'

'What? Because I didn't pay attention?'

'I meant the hepatitis virus - it's not all about you. But, now that you say that, it sounds true. He wanted attention from his flesh and blood.'

'Hepatitis - isn't that dangerous?'

'Have I mentioned he's dying?'

'Sarcasm - ugly.'

'So don't use it. What do you mean *dangerous*? For you?'

'Well . . . '

'He got hepatitis C as a child. In Bombay. It went unnoticed for years. And he has been drinking too much coffee, too much tea, he's had stress, stressful jobs, sitting down driving taxi cabs for the last ten years, he's a bit overweight - it's hard on the liver. When the symptoms come out clearly enough for English doctors to notice, it's too late.'

'Too late?'

'He's got cirrhosis of the liver. Fifty percent chance of dying in the next twelve months.'

'A year? That can't be right. Do you believe him?'

'No. It was his doctor who told me.'

Ghosh slightly raised the corner of his upper lip to make a sulky face.

He said, 'I'm not convinced.'

He looked down at the coffee cup he held. It was half empty.

His mother said, 'There's no more milk. You can't avoid this. Whatever troubles you have, everybody else in the world still lives, also has troubles, gets ill, maybe dies. Drink the coffee how it is. It won't kill you to think about more than your own feelings.'

Ghosh raised the cup and swallowed all the coffee, which still tasted bitter and cold. He shook his head and it was hard to say if that gesture was saying *no* to reality or to his own self-absorption.

He said, 'Really fifty percent?'

'And the chances get bigger and bigger. He's only fifty-three. It's not that old.'

'There's nothing he can do?'

'He can love himself.'

'He does, doesn't he?'

'You are mixing up. You think because he makes you unhappy that he makes himself happy. He doesn't. He's miserable. He divorced his wife. He can't speak to his son. He has no contact with his family in Bombay. He's a Francophile Indian driving cabs in Portsmouth. Now he's got a liver disease that's a hangover from his childhood. It's not want he wanted.'

'What can he do?'

'He can stop work. He can rest. He can let me take care of him. He can make friends with his son.'

'Will that make him live longer?'

'Longer? Better? Either? Both? Come on, Marcas! Have some care.'

'He must have made you unhappy.'

'My God, yes. Not as unhappy as himself. And I'm OK. I can manage. I have friends. I do things. I never had such big wishes as him. He hurts himself. He has moved again. He won't tell me where he lives - his address. Ridiculous.'

'Somewhere in Pompey?'

'Obviously. Somewhere.'

'What do you want me to do?'

'Marcas, talk to him. I know you've had trouble. You are young. You are OK. Your life is still fine. He might be dead soon. Maybe the next time you come back from China.'

'Talk about what?'

'If you want to talk practical things, tell him to move out of the *poxy* flat he lives in and take the flat on the second floor of this house.'

'How do you know it's poxy?'

'It's certain. Tell him moving here will save him money. It's warmer and cleaner and brighter and better - but don't tell him that. And say the main point is that I really want him to move in this house - but far too proud to ask him myself - because I am really desperate for the finances.'

'Is that true?'

'Of course it is fucking not true.'

Ghosh went downstairs to his own flat and despite his mother's strong coffee he fell asleep at 7:45 pm.

CHAPTER 55

Day 6, 12 noon (4 am UK time)

At 4 am, perhaps because of drinking his mother's strong coffee the evening before, Ghosh was wide awake. It was still a longer sleep than he had taken for weeks. He felt energised as if he'd just been running for thirty minutes. His heart was beating fast.

In his own kitchen he ate a bowl of breakfast cereal. He ate another. He had toast and marmalade. Tea and coffee. He checked his emails - nothing new. He looked at some clothes he had left unworn in a wardrobe for over a year. They were more stale and outdated than he remembered. He tried listening to the local radio: The Breeze 107.4 FM. He heard Lionel Ritchie's *Say You, Say Me* and Spandau Ballet's *True* sounding like his old clothes looked. He thought: *Dad was my age when these songs were fresh.*

It was 5:20 am. His father would be on the night shift. Ten pm till 6 am. He knew that because the previous evening his mother had told him, several times. And she had said: *Find him after work. After the end of his shift. He can't escape then.* She meant going to his unknown address. Ghosh was wide awake, impatient, and it felt to him like the middle of the day. He wanted to get it over with - the talk.

Ghosh went to his father's workplace, a scruffy little office next to a late night chemist with metal mesh over the windows. It was in a stubby cul-de-sac off a main road. There was a yellow lamp outside, and inside a tiny space for customers to stand and order cabs in front of a high, scuffed counter. Behind the counter the telephone operator sat on a high stool, and behind her were a few old seats for drivers. Two were seated and from the customer's position in front of the counter, only the tops of drivers' heads were visible. It was 5:55 am. Ghosh couldn't see the top of his father's head.

His father had tried to be a businessman - imports and retail - and failed. He tried to run a B&B, tried to be a driving instructor, and for the last ten years had been -

temporarily - driving a taxi. Critical and ambitious without the capability of realizing his ambitions, he had become increasingly dissatisfied with his life. He blamed his luck, his family, his nation, the nation he lived in, and his wife. Seven years previously he had demanded a divorce and had moved out - on principle - to a cheap tiny flat. Then another cheap small flat; and another. His wife had stayed in the family house that had originally been intended as the B&B. She borrowed from the mortgage, renovated the house, rented out the rooms as flats and paid off the mortgage. Ghosh's mother could look after herself, his father could not.

It was years since Ghosh's last visit to the taxi cab office. He been there to see his Dad, as a teenager, still living at home, sent by his mother with messages such as *tell him to answer my calls*, and, occasionally, some dish she'd made, in a plastic box, wrapped in a handkerchief. His father always refused the food. Ghosh had always hated the office.

Behind the counter the woman on the stool was talking to another woman standing beside her.

'I just will not buy a size 12. Like, if I see something I like in a shop, like a top or something, you know. I check the size. If it says size 12 I just will not buy it. I won't try it on. I am a size 10. Always have been. I'm not starting with size 12.'

'Oh you're lucky, Em,' said the other woman. She was the 6 am to 2 pm shift phone operator, the cushy shift. 'I don't remember when I gave in and started buying size 12. Long time ago. And it don't stop there.'

'That's what I mean.' The night shift woman slid off the high stool. She was younger than the day shift woman and was wearing black leggings. There were balls of nylon fluff on her bottom.

Ghosh said, 'Excuse me.' He had been waiting in front of the counter. The two women looked at him with faces that showed they were displeased with his intruding into their private conversation.

The younger one, Em, said, 'Can I help you with something?'

'Er, Mr Ghosh. Is he back yet?'

'Who?'

'Er, my Dad, Mr Ghosh. Jacky. He's a driver.'

One of the drivers at the back said, 'Indian Jacky.'

'Oh, *Jacky*,' said the woman, looking at the other woman.

Ghosh said, 'Yeah, Jacky.'

The second woman said, 'You his son then?'

'Yeah.'

Em said, 'You look, like, a bit like him, and like you don't.'

'Yeah,' said Ghosh.

The driver spoke. All Ghosh could see of him was a freckled bald head. 'He's got a fare, mate. Won't be long. Come back here and wait.'

'Is this your office?' said the older woman, turning to stare at the driver. She was the office supervisor.

'So let the boy fucking stand outside then blocking the way,' said the voice of the freckle-head.

'*You*'ll be standing outside,' said the older woman. 'Sitting around here giving orders. Haven't you got any work to do?'

'Language!' said the other woman, belatedly.

'Am on the fucking six shift same as you. Soon as a fare comes you'll be shot of me,' said freckle head.

'Language!' said Em.

From a back door, Ghosh's father entered the little office.

The supervisor woman said, 'Hijack-y?' It was her little joke. She used every time. It went like this: Indian Jacky to I Jacky to Hi Jacky to hijack-y. It was daily proof of her good sense of humour. So she said, 'Ha ha.' And because Ghosh senior did not have enough sense of humour to laugh at her joke, she said of him to Em, 'Cold fish.'

Ghosh's father didn't look at her and said, 'Good morning, Moggie.'

'Maggie!' she said to him.

'Sorry, Moggie,' he said. He sat down and disappeared from his son's view except for a bit of black hair and a circular bald patch.

He greeted the other drivers, 'Den. Micky.'

'Alright.'

'Alright, mate. Son's here.'

'What?' Ghosh's father stood up and saw his son. He said, 'I'm signing out.'

'It's not six o'clock yet,' said supervisor Maggie.

'It is now,' said Jacky Ghosh. He motioned with his chin for his son to go outside.

He said, 'Den. Micky.'

Micky said, 'See ya, Jacky.'

Den said, 'See ya. And take care of yourself.'

Jacky Ghosh said, 'Bye, Em. Moggie.'

'*Maggie!*'

He went through the back door. The world outside was still dark. Ghosh father and son got in the 2004 Nissan Primera.

When the dashboard light came on Ghosh junior said, 'Eleven thousand four hundred and forty-four.'

Ghosh senior said, 'Don't believe it. This car's speedometer's been doctored. It's worse than that. Much.' He drove away. He looked sicker than he had the afternoon before.

Ghosh junior was humbled to think his father was spending his life like this, working night after night picking up drunks, dealing with that little office and the people in it. Still there in the same place while he - his son - had graduated, moved on, made a different life. His energy was subdued by the sadness of it. He looked sideways at his father.

'What are you looking at?' said Ghosh senior.

'Why do you call her *Moggie*?'

'That's her name and that's what I call her. Always very conventional. That's me.'

'Her name's Maggie.'

'Ah, it could be that I haven't mastered local English pronunciation. Not having been born here. Like some.'

'Isn't she your boss?'

'She is in no way the boss. She creates schedules.'

'How is your schedule?'

'That woman is an antidote to anything improving or edifying for humanity and my schedule is malodorous. Cats look cute but have you smelled their excrement? Powerful poop. Every year without fail the Moggie sends me an email saying I've been sacked. On April Fool's Day as proof of her humorousness. Very British.'

It was a one-minute journey. They went down to a basement flat and entered. There was a smell of animal urine, stale milk and unwashed towels. The air was damp because every window was double glazed and locked shut.

Marcas said, 'What's that smell?'

His father said, 'The council are bloody useless layabouts. Never do a thing. Rats.'

'Rats?'

'Big and fat as moggies.'

His mother's judgement had been correct - it was a poxy flat. The ceilings were low and inset with circular downlights of which half the halogen bulbs were blown. The walls were bleak and white. There was a long corridor to the kitchen. There was hardly any furniture, and lying all over the floor were books, clothes, official letters and TV or DVD player remote controls. A patch of mould, as big as a ghost, speckled one bedroom wall. Ghosh saw the patch as he walked past because there was no bedroom door. At the kitchen sink, over a mound of dirty dishes and cutlery, his father gargled, violently, and started washing his hands like a surgeon. Ghosh went back to the bedroom to look at a small cage. The cage was divided in two by an amateurish arrangement of wire. There were two hamsters in there, one on each side. One hamster had a wheel and one had a metal sleeping box.

Marcas kept small pets as a child, when he, his father and his mother all lived together. He used to spend time with his pets when he didn't have friends or places to go to. Now, for his father, hamsters had become a reminder of more hopeful times that included a small son. Marcas felt sympathy, both for the hamsters and his father.

Back in the kitchen he said, 'Why've you got two hamsters?'

'Unless you keep them apart they fight each other. Hence I fixed the wire. Safety.'

'Yeah, I mean, why did you buy them?'

'What the hell makes you think I bought them? Den - cab driver - his grandkids were going to dump them. Needed a temporary home. I'm the mug.'

'Why?'

'Den's daughter wanted to move in with some worthless fellow and the fellow's condition was getting rid of the kids and animals. The pair of them compromised. Kids in; hamsters out.'

Jacky Ghosh had made tea; the milk tasted of onions. Marcas suddenly felt exhausted. He was supposed to talk about the illness and ask big questions and he hadn't.

His father said, 'You seem not here, mind somewhere else, in another place. How *is* China?'

'Well - '

'Don't monkey around with Panax ginseng. That's my advice.'

'Don't you make coffee anymore?'

'It's all gone. No time to shop. Sorry.'

'Milk's off.'

'There are some things you don't need to tell me.'

'You know why I'm here?'

'Tionnette - *maman* - sent you.'

'She says you're not well.'

'Balzac was dead at fifty-one.'

'Balzac? What was it you were saying about him and China?'

'I didn't say anything because you didn't want to listen. Balzac said that in a capital city, when money defines everything and everybody's relationships, the most valuable item is a woman's beauty.'

'Women's beauty? Isn't that a bit - '

'Marcas, the world is not run by primary school teachers. You're coming up to twenty-five years of age.'

'I won't be twenty-five any time soon,' said Marcas. He was twenty-seven last birthday.

'You say that now but you don't realise how quickly time moves,' said his father. 'Marcas, you are growing up. Time to start seeing and behaving as an adult.'

Marcas said, 'What about your illness?'

'I've been ill all my life. Blighted.'

'Yeah, this time though - the doctor - '

'You want to know what the doctor said?'

Marcas shrugged his shoulders.

His father said, 'I was in hospital and surrounded by tubes. Tests, tests, tests. This doctor, that doctor. Different specialists every day. Some of them Indian. After a week, they all gathered round my bed. The leader doctor said, Mr Ghosh. We have somethings to tell you. Good news and bad news, ha ha. Please, good news last, I said. And they said, well, the bad news, your disease is a new one and it is incurably fatal. Good news? I said. And they said, it's a new disease and as you are the first one we have named it in your honour: Bubonic Ghosh.'

'Dad. I was trying to talk to you.'

'No, no, no. Sorry. It was at the *Health Centre*. No GPs anymore. Don't know why they changed it. Never see the same doctor. It's not what it was, this country. Nobody eats marmalade anymore.'

'Don't they?'

'Except old age pensioners.'

'Wait, wait. What did the doctor say?'

'This young doctor said . . . He did say it was serious. He wasn't much older than you. More mature, of course. How serious? I asked him. I said, *please doctor tell me straight how serious it is and how long I have to live*. And he said, *ten*. I said, ten what? Years, months, *weeks*? I have a right to know. Informed consent and all. And he said, *nine - eight - seven - six - five* - Ha! Ha-Ha!' Jacky Ghosh was laughing loud.

Marcas Ghosh had a twisted half smile. He wasn't laughing. It was too difficult.

He said, 'I tried, I tried.' He was achingly tired. He wanted to go back home to sleep. And he had a secret: he wanted to love his dad.

CHAPTER 56

Day 6, 2:45 pm (6:45 am UK, 7:45 am Angola)

Ghosh got a phone call. It was Nelson.

'Are you free and safe in England?'

'Yes.'

'That's what I'm calling to hear you say. How's your father?'

'The same. Except he's ill and we can't talk about it.'

'Different generations have their different ways of talking.'

'That's over generalizing.'

'Believe too much in individuals and you start thinking you can escape your society.'

'Have you escaped to Angola?'

'I'm here and I haven't escaped anything.'

'I'm the escaper.'

'Now you've been in prison you've got *zīgé*, credentials. No one can say you're a know-nothing. I'm listening to what you say.'

'About your uncle.'

'Tell me.'

'Maybe he's not your uncle. Maybe he's your father. Maybe that's why you don't look like your cousin.'

Ghosh said this carelessly, because he was unhappy. None-the-less, he was correct.

Nelson said, 'You mean he loved my mother and pretended he was visiting her sister.'

'Love is more complex than amateur genetics,' said Ghosh.

Nelson kept quiet for a while and said, 'It's like what Rambo says: You can't escape what you really are.'

Ghosh said, 'How's Angola?'

'I see a beautiful dawn every morning.'

'What are your plans?'

'First, build a house on unoccupied land that makes a square fifty-eight kilometres on each side. Like a bigger Beijing and with only me living in it. Fifty-eight is a good number in many ways.'

'How?'

'You're not a number lover. You seem to be a walker - walking in and out of capture. So I'll explain it by saying fifty-eight kilometres is too far to walk in a day, through Angolan forest. And I'll have a lake there on the land and a hill for viewing. Everything will be spacious and peaceful.'

'Making a house. Is that all you're going to do?'

'That's not what I'm going to do, that's where I'm going to live. What I'm going to do is build roads.'

'Infrastructure development with Chinese investment?'

'Exactly. Right and left turns, banked corners, chicanes, artificial gullies, canyons, 30° cutbacks, pit stops and grandstands. And plenty of betting kiosks. Tracks all over Angola. Stock cars, BMW spec racing, showroom class endurance races, F3 Angola and so on. Adding up my talents in racing cars and numbers to make a state racing car gaming organization. My big ambition is to hold the Angola F1 Grand Prix by the time I reach the end of five cycles of the zodiac.'

'When you're sixty? Will you be driving?'

'A car? Of course not. It'll be the world's richest, fastest race with the most sophisticated gaming opportunities anywhere. I'll be driving everything.'

Ghosh said, 'I'd like to see your lampshade.'

'Visit me in Angola. You'll be welcome anytime. The lampshade will disappoint you. It's ugly and only I want to see it.'

'It's part of you.'

'Yeah - I'm ugly to myself. Listen: thanks for that insight about my dad. I was blind. Now I've got a home and a father. Let me tell you something to see when you're back in China.'

'Back in China? No plans to go back.'

Nelson said, 'You know you're going back to China even if you don't admit it. When you're there remember this: the tigers think everyone is proud, the pigs think everyone is greedy, the horses think everyone is ambitious, the monkeys think everyone loves a crowd, and the sheep think everyone loves their family. Only the lonely think nobody else is lonely. Remember this and people will be easy to manage.'

CHAPTER 57

Day 6, 3:45 am (7:45 pm previous day Angola)

The Minister's phone rang; he picked it up from the bedside cabinet and answered it.

Nelson said 'Good morning!'

'How do you know my number?'

'Numbers are mine to know. And I have your number: *sixty-nine.*'

'No proof of that.'

'Proof can be found. Like the proof of who is the father of the son, *Daddy.*'

The Minister knew absolutely that he was Nelson's father. He knew it from the start and so, of course, did Nelson's mother. Their affair was deep and lasting.

'All a long time ago. She - '

'She? My mother? My mother is not a long time ago. She was alive last week. And now: it's me and you.'

Minister Wang failed to deny it. He was relieved to let go of the secret. He was letting go of many things. The woman he had loved so long was dead. His career was finished. His age was apparent to himself. His curiosity was gone. There had been no miracle. Nothing came from heaven. A hundred and forty-seven SLT believers died in the snow and he wasn't interested anymore. He didn't expect to find anything in his future.

Nelson was interested in the new truth and he was still getting used to knowing it. He was amazed at how he had deceived himself. The original deception was performed in childhood and managed by adults - his mother and old man Wang. Nelson had carried the blindness forward into his own adulthood and had maintained it. He reflected on himself as a self-deluder and as the son of a man he had thought he knew. He wanted to know more about that man.

The Minister was exhausted, weak, suffering from chronic lack of sleep, and since being woken by Nelson's call, not sleepy at all. He knew there were more hidden things to let go. In confused moments of his own he connected all his shameful secrets to 1969. Nelson's call had woken him from a dream of that hell.

He said, '1969 was terrible. Nobody knew what they were doing. Nobody knows what we did.'

Nelson said, 'I wasn't born in 1969.'

'Ugh. Right. Why are you calling me in the middle of the night?'

'I know you're an insomniac.'

'Huh. Turning over new leaf. Healthy life. From tomorrow morning.'

'It's time you retired. At *sixty-nine*.'

'*Am* retiring. Whipper snapper nerd Dong Bing will take over the works. Me: changing my car to a quiet Mercedes Benz.'

'Hey! That's what I had when I was a kid.'

'I know that,' said the Minister. 'But for me it's rest and recuperation. Going away - far away.'

'Oh, don't be nervous, Daddy. No family reunions planned. I'm just telling you that I will always know where you are. And the new woman, the one you're with, I have *her* number, too.'

The Minister said, 'She's a good woman.'

Nelson said, 'Good? Good at what? Networking? I heard you had seven computers in your cosy and crowded apartment. Were you running a botnet?'

'No. There are people to do that for us. It wasn't for work. The computers are mine. I'll tell you the truth: I follow the weather.'

'Can you change it?'

'Can't change a thing. Can know what's coming. In detail. When and where.'

'Predictor? Like son, like father!' said Nelson.

'Not me. Computers do it. Make them pretend to be the heavens. See what's coming.'

'Why?'

'The will of heaven. That's what the SLT were waiting for. Beyond human will is the will of heaven. That's what Mao said in his final poems. The will is in energy and power, like earthquakes, or lightning, and when it touches you everything can change.'

'You believed it?'

'I wanted to see it. I wanted her to get the power. Or all of them.'

'Instead they got killed. And you knew they would.'

'I knew what was happening and I knew they all did what they wanted. She - all of them. Including Captain Ma. And now he's a hero. All those security guys were changed into heroes forever.'

'Did she know what would happen?'

'She knew there was a storm coming. She wanted lightning. She believed the religion. She was waiting for heaven.'

'Ha, ha! The heavens!' Nelson said, 'You know why people want religion? Lack of data. That leads to stories. Stories get fixed and they call it religion.'

'What do you know?'

'What do *you* know?'

'Case unproved. There wasn't an answer. Or the answer is death. Don't know. Too big for one mind to grasp. Even a very clever person. That's what I found out. And I've given up expecting anything. Even if I live till *jiǔshíjiǔ* - ninety-nine - *forever*.'

'You're a wise man, dirty Daddy.'

'You too, bastard son.'

CHAPTER 58
Day 12, 2 am (6 pm previous day in UK)

Officer Chen was back in England on another mission, the second within two weeks, and this time it was personal. This time she paid £95.55 of her own money to take a taxi from Heathrow Terminal 3 to Ghosh's home address in Portsmouth. She was headed for the same place and the same man as the first time though for different reasons and in a different mood.

She felt the lightness and relief she had felt in her Estonia days, only this time with more awareness and purpose. She was no longer living as a response to the love, demands or orders of others. Her feelings were clear and her actions derived from her wishes.

Once more it was night and England remained dark and shadowy. Her GPS app told her the route was 113.6 km, 1 hour 35 minutes, and by-passed the towns of Slough, Woking, and Guildford. From the back seat of the car she saw lights and vehicles moving on a black screen that was the world outside. Inside was quiet and warm.

She said, 'Driver, does your leg hurt?'

He said, 'No, it doesn't hurt. Knee's partly fused. I can't extend it. Fine for driving. Don't worry, never caused an accident and I've been driving with it ten years.'

'What happened?'

The driver told her of a car slamming into his taxi door as he returned home from a long night, looking forward to a week's holiday in Tenerife. He'd had six month's break instead, though it wasn't much of a holiday, he said.

'Silver lining, though, and all that.'

Chen drifted in and out of sleep, as the driver told her of the compensation he'd got and the wish he'd fulfilled by building a pub in his back garden.

'Just one room like, but got all the optics, dartboard. Pals come over, I stand behind the bar, serve 'em.'

Chen heard slices of speech and in her head formed the idea that language was breaking down.

'Wife loves it. Keeps me out of trouble. Not far to stagger home. Limp home in my case. Ha, ha. You might laugh. But it's what we like to do. Managing my own private pub: it's what I'm good at.'

Officer Chen was good at managing everything; her difficulty was in opposing her duty and, by extension, her own ambitions, and, by implication, her government. That was why it had taken time and effort for her to leave her home village and plan to free Ghosh. Once she had set out she had been completely determined and did not delay.

On the day Ghosh had walked out of his captivity Chen had gone back to the Ministry of Religious Affairs headquarters. She hadn't known Ghosh was gone. When she found he had gone *even before* her own attempt to free him the previous evening, she was surprised and glad. She knew she should control her wish to contact him. Ghosh would flee to his own country as soon as he could and if he was still in China, people would be looking for him, and they could be watching her in the hope she would lead them to Ghosh. Also she had needed to wait until after the State Council meeting on 10th February. At the meeting the highest handful of men in the country would decide the strategy for investigating the snowy field deaths, and, following the collective failure to anticipate, prevent or explain the deaths, the fate of all Ministry officials, including herself. Now that meeting had been held, all the decisions had been made, and the consequence, personally, for Chen and Ghosh, was favourable. That's why she was in a taxi, asleep, with a stiff-legged driver steering calmly through the night.

When she arrived at Ghosh's house this time she didn't wait outside in the street. She knocked, Liam opened the door and he said, 'What a pleasant surprise, it's Miss I-Spy, from MI5, on the Chinese side.'

Chen followed him down the corridor to the kitchen. Liam went back to his own room. Ghosh was sitting at the table, as before, elbows on the wooden table top, wearing a fresh white T shirt and black sleeveless down jacket. Golden hairs on his forearms. Chen felt a warm energy spread in all directions inside her body from a point five centimetres below and three centimetres behind her belly button.

Ghosh gestured to an empty chair at his side and as Chen sat down he said, 'You've come back.'

She had been afraid before she saw Ghosh's face, eyes and expression. Now she could see him and she caught again that memory of the scent of chicken blood and star anise, and she knew it was right.

For the second time in ten days she said to him, 'Come back to China.'

She said, 'My village. My family.'

Ghosh said, 'Let's go.' He smiled for the first time in nine days. 'Is everything arranged?'

'No. This time you need a visa. I'm here as Chén Yǐng, not Officer Chen. In personal matters we have to be like ordinary people.'

'And be extraordinary.'

'Only to ourselves.'

'It's enough.'

After the golden glow of that first moment in which they spoke a fluent language of symbols, there were hours of direct concerns. Of course, Ghosh was frightened about going back to a place he'd just run away from. There was the visa, his safety, and what to do in China. Chen repeated Mao Zedong's words about escaping jeopardy by running to a hard place.

Ghosh had been coming to the end of the contract with the International Red Cross. It wouldn't be renewed and it was a prestigious loss.

'Not a good way to finish, going missing completely,' he said. 'I contacted them to say I'm OK, and don't worry, and I'm sorry. It's too much to explain. I said I won't be coming back. I guess there was a huge sigh of relief on the other side of the email. Part of my brief was to contact lower level government officials, if possible at ministries. Talking to them now, I feel like Christopher Columbus talking to the Queen of Spain. Hey, you sent me out to reach Asia and I ended up discovering a whole new continent. And the

Queen doesn't care because it's not India and it doesn't make sense.'

Chen had never heard of Columbus.

She told him all she heard about the State Council meeting. From the Council members' point of view, their big decision was to switch emphasis from investigating the details of how the two hundred and ninety-seven people simultaneously died, to a policy of destroying the SLT. *Digging the roots to stop the fruit.* Anybody connected to the SLT was to be arrested, more effort was to be made in blocking SLT-related messages, and in tracing and arresting all message posters. The target was total annihilation of the SLT and that was what would surely happen.

More immediate for all Ministry officials, including Chen, was the decision to dissolve the Ministry, absorbing its functions into a department of the Culture and Education Committee of the State Council itself. This meant direct control from the top and the centre of government.

Chen told Ghosh of the rumour that the senior leaders of the Religious Affairs Ministry had been infected with a foreign virus: New Orleans flu.

'Is that true?' said Ghosh.

'I don't know whether it's a cover up or a lie. They've disappeared - that I do know. It's said they're ill. All this information is coming from the Vice Minister, Dong Bing.'

'Closing the Ministry - isn't that a disaster for Dong Bing? Sure to be next Minister - that's what you said.'

'It depends how ambitious he is. Everyone's thinking for themselves and I'm sure he isn't the slowest thinker. The only thing other officials are thinking about is their money. The Ministry closing means everybody's status goes down. Less chance to work as paid consultants or take official trips abroad when you unofficially buy luxury goods and sell them back home for big profits. By the way - I have to get some cases of whiskey.'

Ghosh laughed.

'Yes,' she said, 'It's a joke. I'm one of them. Or was. I've been thinking about something nobody is thinking about:

all those dead people. Those dead security guys, I knew some of them, they were good men. And the cult believers - I saw the photos - I can't believe what's been said. They were so ordinary, like anybody you see on buses. I can't believe they were terrorists, criminals, dooms-dayers. Photos when they were lying there dead. No one thinks about all those people. Nobody cares about all the dead souls.'

And she said, 'Another thing nobody is thinking about is you. Nobody is looking for you. All that went before in the last two weeks is forgotten. Forgotten means you're safe. You don't matter. It doesn't matter that I was sent here to find you. That I was ordered to stay in my home village. That I defied the order and came to England. Soon I'll be missed but now there's too much change and confusion for any action to be taken. If I go back quickly I'll still have my job, or I have a job under the new set up. I could carry on as before. That's not changed. The thing that has changed is not my job. It's my thinking about my job. I betrayed you and I feel I was betrayed,' she said.

'It's everything you prepared for,' said Ghosh. 'You'll be *out*.'

'I'm not middle aged. I'm young enough. Many things are changing. Opportunities are coming. I can take some of them. For example, Dong Bing was sure to have been the next Minister. Now he'll be looking for another ladder. I could cling to his skirts and climb with him. The Ministry has gone. Who knows what might go next. One day even this government - this way of government - might change.'

'Are you serious?' said Ghosh.

'There's no evidence. We can't guess. I'll live a long time. Many things can change.'

'Can you imagine things being better?'

'I can,' said Chen.

'Good.'

'Yes. Can't you?'

'Not for my country, not for the world. Maybe for myself. With you I can.'

'Too pessimistic. Except maybe too optimistic about me.'

They talked for hours because there was much to say and they were too tired to stop. Chen spent the night at Ghosh's house. They were alone in the dark and naked, thinking only of themselves and with nobody in the world thinking of them. Only they know what they did.

The next day they were wearier and less adrenaline excited. There was a trip to London to get an express visa for Ghosh. He'd been deported and brought back to China with passing through immigration; as far as standard airport procedure was concerned, the whole journey never happened. His multiple entry Category Z work visa had been cancelled on the orders of the Party Secretary when he'd been taken out of China; when he left the second time he'd been able to do so based on that final cancellation.

Chen also wanted to find Britney. So when they went to London, in the six hours between lodging a visa application and receiving the visa, she and Ghosh visited Chinatown restaurants looking for Britney who had no visa and no chance of applying. They saw plenty of exhausted women pushing dim sum trolleys. Working a trolley was one possibility for Britney, without language or documents. More likely she would be back of house as a cleaner, or cutting veg, or washing dishes. Chen walked into five restaurant kitchens and was thrown out of three of them. They visited many more restaurants. Chen tried to ask questions. Some staff would not speak, some spoke frankly. Nobody knew Britney though it was hard to say who she was without a photo or real name. It was a hopeless mission. They had made the mistake of believing their own joy, luck and optimism would spread around the world wherever they wished.

Chen said, 'I thought about Britney the last few days. She recognized me because she thought I was my sister. She couldn't guess I had a twin. She helped me know what we had done, my sister and I. So I want to help Britney.'

'She's lost,' said Ghosh.

'She's lost to us,' said Chen. 'We'll never know if it's good lost or bad lost.'

The journey back from the capital city to the southern coast of the country was inconceivably short by the standards of a nation as vast as China. Chen looked out of the train window to see the landscape and saw only her own reflection. It didn't comfort her and she felt unhappy and exhausted after the hard and unsatisfactory day.

She said, 'How can Britain allow this?'

'What?'

'Britney.'

Ghosh said, 'So it wouldn't happen in China?'

'China doesn't claim to be free and fair. China is too big.'

'Any problem? *China's too big*. So split it up. Make thirty Britains.'

Chen was patriotic and not by nature sceptical and so they found territory to argue. It was part of discovering each other and they were putting the borders in place.

Chen gestured at the carriage and the darkening world outside, 'Is this freedom? We're freer in Beijing.'

'I wasn't.'

Chen Ying touched his arm. 'I'm sorry. What I said was wrong. What happened to you was wrong. What I did was wrong.'

'OK, OK. You didn't know what they were going to do to me when I came back.'

'I didn't. I should have thought about it. I didn't want to think about the truth. And they could have killed you.'

'Don't hurt yourself too much.'

'I've hurt the people I want to be closest too. And I can't find Britney.

'We did what we could,' said Ghosh. 'And we found each other.'

Early next morning Ghosh made breakfast for two. He had dreamed wishfully of such a moment while he had been imprisoned.

He said to Chen Ying, 'This is my mother's mid-afternoon treat. Don't tell her I gave it to you for breakfast. She calls it *lost bread*.'

Their cosy, enclosed mood was ended by a knock on the kitchen door from outside. It was Ghosh senior, Jacky, the father and taxi driver, having just finished his shift.

He brushed past Marcas and addressed Chen, 'Please forgive an old father, Miss - Miss - Miss?'

'Chen. Chen Ying,' she said.

'Miss Chen Ying.' He held out his hand and took hers. 'At my age I probably shouldn't be holding the hand of a beautiful young woman so please excuse me.'

Marcas said, '*Dad*.'

Jacky kept Chen Ying's hand and did not acknowledge his son.

'Don't compromise,' he told her. 'Choices you make now will last forever. Don't settle for second best. Be strong willed. Human will is the world's most powerful force - that's what Balzac says.'

He held her hand and attention for a moment longer. He turned to his son.

'What are you burning in here?' he shouted. 'Ah! *Pain perdu*?'

He looked and smiled theatrically at Chen, saying, 'The Punjabi rickshaw driver's dream!'

She didn't understand him but she laughed because his face and posture were comic.

To Marcas he said, 'Oh it's soft, limp. Heat! Heat, man! You need to turn up the heat. Don't be such a coward!' He turned up the gas to maximum.

'At the end: crisp, brown and tasty - like me. Not white, wet and soggy, boy.'

Marcas said, 'What are you doing here? You never come here.'

'But I wanted to meet her,' said his father in a loud whisper.

'Who?' said Marcas.

'Who?' Jacky turned to Chen. 'Who? *Who*, he says!'

He picked up a whole slice of bread from the pan and popped it in his mouth as he skipped out of the door flashing his eyes at Chen with the French toast hanging over his chin. She laughed again, which was what he wanted, and he was gone.

When the day was light Chen and Ghosh walked around the town in the cold. It was her first time in the country with nothing to do except look. All the buildings Ghosh pointed out looked the same and she couldn't tell which were four hundred years old and which were forty. Anyway, they were all old.

She said, 'Your father is so funny. I like him. You should talk to him more.'

'You can't talk to him.'

'And they say he's going to die? He must be frightened.'

'He's impossible.'

Chen said, 'He's your father.'

Ghosh said, 'Just because - ' and did not go further. He sighed and made a silent promise to see his father, again.

CHAPTER 59
Day14, 11 pm (3 pm UK)

After lunch Ghosh fell asleep with residual jet lag and when he woke he called his mother. Chen Ying was still sleeping.

His mother said, 'I'm making coffee. Are you downstairs, Marcas? Come up.'

He went outside, up the fire escape, knocked at her door and heard his mother's voice say, 'It's open.'

She was at the sink pouring boiled water into two cups to warm them before putting in the coffee. On the round table in the centre of the room was her notebook diary, open with the pages facing down. The plain front cover had her name, *Tionette*, and on the back cover she had written, *«Apprends à écrire tes blessures dans le sable et à graver tes joies dans la pierre.» Lao-tseu*. Her handwriting looked like her - small, neat and light, and almost too Spartan to be attractive.

She brought the coffee and said, 'Is it warm down there? Do you have the heating on? Are the blankets enough?'

'I'm fine, mum. Fine.'

'Yes, it's the poor girl I'm concerned about.'

'I'm sure she's tougher than me.'

'You mean you treat her tougher than you treat yourself.'

'Give me a break, maman.'

'What's this about?'

'It's Dad. She wants me to talk to Dad. How?'

'My God knows I have that kind of problem myself. Maybe one way is not to treat him tougher than you treat yourself. In any case, that girl has the right head on her shoulders. Talk to him about what he wants to talk about. Ask him about China.'

'China?'

'*Aaask* him.'

Ghosh walked towards his father's basement flat. He wore clothes he'd had left behind in England, the kind of clothes he wore as a student: track top, track pants - wide at the thigh, tapering to the ankle, and clean white trainers. The Portsmouth pavements were wet with damp; the sky was one grey entirety. To Marcas as a boy, Portsmouth had seemed an isolated place. When his parents had taken him on trips, even to places nearby, he had felt their difference. It wasn't that he liked Portsmouth more, it was more familiar. That familiarity remained, connected to his parents, his childhood and the past.

He had to ring the doorbell three times before his Dad opened the door, on a chain. His father said nothing, unlocked the chain, opened the door, and quickly glanced left and right. Inside, he said, 'Welcome to the dungeon, my boy.'

They went past the door-less room with the hamster cage. Marcas could see the hamsters were gone.

'Where are the hamsters?'

'In the bin, my boy.'

'What?'

'The council does nothing about the vermin issue. I told you that. Dead.'

'What?'

'The bloody rats ate them up. Most of them. Left parts.'

'Oh wow! That's - that's - '

'How expressive,' said Jacky. A look passed across his face which meant he was not going to allow any further conversation about hamsters.

He said, 'I was just getting up to do my bits and bobs.' He picked up a glass and started gargling, spitting out the water over unwashed trays of ready meals in the kitchen sink.

Marcas said, 'Er, you know, I was thinking. What was that you were saying about China and everything? It was right. What did you say?'

'It wasn't me that was right, it was Balzac. Revolution, chaos, glorious wars, reaction, restoration. He wrote it all. As I told you.'

'Yeah, you did. Some people say the Chinese way of answering the phone comes from French.'

'What's that - *oui*?'

'No, *wéi*.'

'Only a B-class villain answers the phone *oueh*. I answered the phone to a Chinese villain last week.'

'What?'

'Oh, wide and far is the taxi driver's knowledge. Kidnapped women, factories and farms. There's one near here. Starts work at 11 pm. Through the night. Usually. I told him the woman went to Cambridge.'

'Cambridge?'

'Slaughterhouses. Very quick thinking on my part. Fact is, she cabbed it away to London. Good luck to her. Anything can happen there.'

Marcas found out that his father was indeed talking about Britney. As he told the story of that evening from his point of view his dad listened attentively. He carried on listening with attention and pertinent questions as Marcas went on to tell about his return to China and the days he spent in prison and his midnight escape.

His father said quietly, 'My boy no longer: a man. You remind me of what Nelson said.'

'Nelson? You know Nelson?'

'Of course I know Nelson because we learned more about your pirate heroes in Bombay schools than you ever do here. *Aft the more honour: for'ard the better man*. Go back there. China is the making of you. Escape from gaol! Man! That's enough adventure for the rest of your life. You've found a place and you're luckier than me.'

'I didn't do anything. Those things happened.'

'That's talk and nothing more. See what you are doing in China. And what you and your Chen Ying did for that girl here.'

'It might not work out well for her.'

'Probably won't. But you took risks and gave her a chance.'

'I was naïve. Didn't know what I was doing, really. Didn't think the danger was real. Not in here, not in China. That's why I got into trouble in the first place.'

'You know who was fascinated by China? Balzac's father.'

Marcas didn't say anything.

Jacky said, 'So, what are you here for?'

'Talk.'

'*She* sent you. It's true, isn't it? Tell me it's true.'

Thinking of Chen Ying, Marcas said, 'Yeah.'

Thinking of Toinette, his father said, 'I can see it. Talk? I can talk. Talk about what exactly? Were there any helpful suggestions?'

'She said hobbies.'

'Do you read anything?'

'I read reports.'

'Any *literature*? Lord of the bloody Hobbits, is it?

'That was a good book.'

'No it bloody wasn't. *Isn't.* You know your mother's from Tours?'

'Yes, Dad. We went there nearly every Christmas.'

'Best spoken French anywhere, Tours. As if your *chère maman* cares about that. Do you know my mother was Karhade Brahmin? Do you know what is Karhade Brahmin?'

Rain began throwing itself at the dirty kitchen window.

Ghosh's father poured on, 'You know what's going wrong with this country? Constant spraying of table tops with squeezy sprays in a belief that this causes cleanliness. Then they're saying with a serious face: *You can use my washing up water.* What the bloody fuck is that? Save our water. Rain's hammering down, filling in the silence in human speech. I'm the only one talking. Everyone's keeping quiet and saving themselves for the three holy topics: football, shopping, porn.'

'Dad, shut up. Talk properly. Come on. We're worried.'

'Worried? Why now? It's not the first time I've been told I'm going to die. And there's been more than once I *have* wanted to die. Who's the most worried? Stop worrying me with your worries. You and her. Your worrying is not welcome. I've haven't got time for them. Now go. Go back to her. Then go home to China.'

CHAPTER 60
Day 15, 11 pm

Vice Minister Dong Bing tasted the bitterness of being the most senior official in a Ministry that did not exist. The Minister and the Party Secretary Ministerial Branch had both 'retired' due to ill health; Dong was the remainder. He was no longer an equivalent rank to Vice Ministers at existing ministries and could not move upwards, or even sideways. Nor could he descend the ranks to begin a fresh career climb within the new structure that held the former Religious Affairs Ministry as a mere department under the State Council's Culture and Education Committee. He seemed to be washed up, stuck on the bank as the river of power flowed on without him.

Every day he was contacted by his official or de facto superiors to be asked questions about the former Ministry and its operations. Usually these questions came late at night, after the important meetings were over, a timing that showed something of his real rank. He was asked about informants and eventually the questions came to Nelson, including how much he was paid, what he was working on, and whether he produced results. Dong Bing said Nelson was paid nothing, at least not money. His superiors found that hard to believe. He agreed and said he suspected some other payment, as well as a family link between Nelson and Minister Wang.

'That we know about,' said the State Council official.

Dong Bing said that Nelson had been working on the map.

'Map? Ah, that scrap you sent us. We think there's nothing in it. Now, apart from your colleagues, this scammer was talking to a foreigner. How much was *he* paid?'

'He gave information without knowing it and without getting paid for it.'

'A fool, then. Even lower than a scam artist. He's been got rid of, we expect.'

'He's gone.'

Dong Bing knew that at least two Ministry officials had wanted Ghosh to escape and that their reasons were different - love and fear. He knew Ghosh had in fact escaped because of an unknown third person's efforts. Dong Bing did not know exactly the reason Party Secretary Zhao was afraid of Ghosh though guessed at the general source. He knew of the relationship between the Party Secretary and Bill. He knew why the Party Secretary flew to Vancouver. He also knew that Minister Wang escaped to his own old mountains. He could have prevented both flights.

When these men's air tickets were registered with the airline by name, a computer signal appeared showing a code. The airline bookings operator reported to a superior who found the code related to the government and required reporting to the company's internal security section. This he did and the company's security section reported to the government's security bureau who in turn reported to several places, including, through a contact, to the Ministry of Religious Affairs, that is to say, Dong Bing.

As they were falling, Dong Bing had no need to pursue the Minister and Party Secretary. He was not vindictive and he was sympathetic to the extent of being aware that eventually he too would fall or slide from power completely.

Dong Bing was working towards solving the puzzle of the deaths in the snowy field. He now believed the two top officials had been too fretful of the exposure of their own secrets to solve the snowy deaths secrets. He now understood the SLT believers' purpose in gathering, holding hands and waiting. He knew the identities of all those dead, security personnel and believers both, and he knew that the woman at the centre of the dead was either the lover or the sister of the lover of Minister Wang. Dong Bing had the impression of the Minister's deeper involvement in the deaths, though from that dark impression could not grasp any tangible evidence. He held information on many details of the SLT and of the Minister's actions, and was frustrated by the smoothness of the data. He found no links or hooks to catch the Minister; he would never know that the

Minister was his father and that Nelson was his younger half-brother; nor did familiarity with the SLT make him religious. Dong Bing had his own philosophy.

When he was a university student, fiercely learned, full of political strategies and empty of experience in the world, he was taken by members of the Communist Party Youth League to a nightclub. The Youth League members were his seniors, in their mid-twenties. They knew his qualities and they expected him to go far. His earnest manner camouflaged a powerful personality and they called him *Lǎo Bīng* - Old Bing, old soldier - with a mixture of familiarity and respect. They took him to a Beijing bar with an English name: *Return*. Dong Bing knew of such places but had never been in one and until that moment had never wanted to be in one. He had a slightly naïve trust of his seniors, and when they said, 'Hey, Old Bing, you'll learn something of the world,' he believed them. They sat around a table and began to drink. Old Bing was given a tall glass of sugared sodas and colourful syrups swirling around a column of ice cubes.

He was amazed at the customers' dancing. From their clothes, haircuts and the price of drinks, he knew they were wealthy and, possibly, important members of society. Their dancing was grotesque and unaccomplished. They were, he thought, paying money to expose themselves to public ridicule. He did not also fail to notice that they seemed to be thoroughly enjoying themselves.

Customer movement stopped when two white women began pole dancing. They were professionals, imported from Russia, engaged and trained by the nightclub. Their faces, hair, and bodies were thrillingly beautiful to Dong Bing. Their costumes were so small and their actions so fully sexual that he was frightened. He blushed; he couldn't look away; his eyes traced paths all over the women's bodies, returning again and again to a line of sequins sewn along the lower hem of one of the women's panties, next to her upper thigh.

One of his seniors nudged another and pointed at Old Bing with laughing eyes. He didn't notice. The crowd of customers shouted and laughed at the dancing, as did members of Dong Bing's group. He stayed silent, staring and intense.

When the pole dancing finished, Dong Bing hung his head in exhaustion. He looked up and a girl was sitting next to him. Her face was close and covered in a mask of make-up. He could see that underneath it she was young, even younger than him, and smaller. He couldn't tell if she was the pole dancer, not without seeing her whole body.

She said, in mesmerizingly imperfect and entirely comprehensible Chinese, 'Do you want something? I can do anything for you.'

Dong Bing looked at her eyes - grey, streaked with lines that reflected lights, red around the rims, and delicate. He felt her physical *human-ness*; he felt in his mind her insides of tissue, flesh, organs and blood. Her location, employment, make-up, costume and questions were proof of a life very different from his.

One of his mentors shouted, 'Hey! Get out of it! He's just a boy.'

She immediately stood and left for the next table. Dong Bing was shocked by the encounter, the shock destroyed his confidence, and the loss of confidence made him deeply unhappy. He wanted to say, 'She might be eighteen - or less. She should be in school.' He knew it sounded stupid and he hated that. He hated himself for being magnetised by the erotic dancing. He felt powerless.

In the encounter, his innocence and his values, both nurtured in a life of ignorance and patriarchal protection, clashed with the values and knowledge of the world worked by money. He didn't like it but he grew to understand it more, and also to understand the attraction of sex, and how the attraction and was linked to money, consumption, and, amongst other activities, pole dancing. He wanted to change what he didn't like. He became ambitious for more than just himself.

One of his old values was that the movement of history is progressive and just. To be a member of the Party was to be a part of history and of making things better. That's what Dong Bing believed and he kept that belief, hidden behind his daily habits.

The disestablishment of the Ministry of Religious Affairs forced him to be more adventurously ambitious. He began scheming to become Vice-Minister in another ministry. There were twenty-eight ministries to aim for and he narrowed his focus to three: the Ministry of Education, the Ministry of Supervision, and the Ministry Public Security. Though assiduous and skilful, as the highest officer from a disbanded, discredited minor ministry, his chances were small.

Meanwhile, he had the time to complete his list of Chinese inventions. The whole list was short and easy to read. He added an afterword, and kept it simple.

'I made this list without references. I used no more than the patriotic knowledge that is shared by all Chinese. This list could have been made by all of you that are giving your busy and productive lives to shape our economy, society and families. I made it on your behalf and for you: all Chinese people, everywhere.

Patriotism was my motivation to make this list as it is your motivation to read it. Chinese patriotism is silent. We need to break the silence and readdress patriotism. To protect our Chinese nation, society and families, let us all fill the silence with our truly patriotic voices!'

Dong Bing's list was expertly packaged by a leading public relations and publishing company. It appeared simultaneously as charming pocket-sized paperback, subtly echoing Mao Zedong's so-called little red book, and as a downloadable app; there was a webpage, a campaign on QQ and Weibo, accounts on Renren and Douban, interactive links to myMei, and a snowstorm of marketing tweets.

Within a few weeks, it was a phenomenon. All profits went, vey publically, to a charity paying for the primary education of children in deprived, disputed, ethnically diverse and strategic border provinces. Dong Bing received donations, gifts, and offers of many kinds. He appeared in TV interviews as a strong, serious and self-effacing person - a studied presentation that made him appear heroic. On-line clips of the interviews spread like wind through the sky.

Dong Bing became popular. Of course, popularity is a dangerous asset. It draws attention and jealousy from one-party governments. Dong Bing understood this and yet believed he had found a reasonable exchange for what he had lost. Popularity for a ministry. A shield for a sword. The man with the list became a man with a powerful future, a future in power.

CHAPTER 61
Day 21

The State Council's strategy was to hunt and exterminate the Shining Light of Truth. To carry out the plan the Ministry of Public Security was ordered to cooperate with the Ministry of State Security. The Ministry of Public Security with its huge manpower and nationwide neighbourhood Public Security stations, and the Ministry of State Security with its cutting edge surveillance technology from domestic suppliers and Israeli exporters, combined to form an overwhelming force. The SLT was officially blamed for the murders in the snow though the number of deaths was to be forever 'about fifty'.

Mass arrests removed the SLT from public life. Anyone who could be linked to the SLT from internet trawls or footage from internet café webcams was taken. Other religions, especially smaller and newer groups, were checked and SLT sympathizers were taken. They were held and questioned, and while they were held they could not communicate by text, phone or email, and every effort was made to prevent physical meetings with other alleged members, and, if at all possible, any other prisoners.

These measures did not prevent an outbreak of chanting. Prisoners chanted the name *Shining Light of Truth*. Three Chinese characters, pronounced with equal length, the first a falling tone, the second and third level tones: \ — —. A three tone rebellion. Chanted over and over. The chant became a punishable offence. Prisoners were gagged with old rags. They beat the rhythm with their hands. They were beaten and their hands were tied. They used their feet; they were shackled. They hummed. Their noses were broken. They scraped their limbs on concrete floors. They were beaten again. It was an inexplicably contagious show of defiance.

The order came from the Security Council: chant-signalling would stop. Repeat offenders were to be charged, convicted and shot. The government was pleased to note that within a few weeks, from supporters of the SLT in prisons, all public places, and on the internet, there came silence. The phrase *Shining Light of Truth* was blocked from *weibo* and could not be searched for. The cult was killed. Calumnious articles appeared in the media, one after another.

CHAPTER 62
The Following Spring

Time went on; weeks and months. The weather changed; spring moved ahead in the capital and the air became warmer, the sky lighter and green leaves appeared. There was no snow and no storms were forecast.

Storms are hard to forecast and their effects, such as lightning, even harder to predict. Yet it can be done, just as the time and place of SLT gatherings could have been predicted, by careful monitoring of data.

Expert weather-watchers also know that some places on earth are more storm prone than might be expected, such as the countryside around Beijing. Once a storm starts, its movements can be tracked in real time by government operated satellites linked to classified access computers.

Mao Zedong said that the movement of anything affects all the other things around it but that things change because of *internal contradictions.*

Lightning is born from the violence that occurs when contradictions emerge in the atmosphere: warm air meets cold. For example, when sub-zero winds from the frozen northeast blow in high over Beijing. Opposing fronts are attracted to each other and rush together. In the rush the tiniest parts of air and ice bang into one another causing excitement and mutual damage. The excitement is electrical; the damaged parts are negatively charged and congregate in clusters inside clouds in the sky. The earth turns positive in contradictory logic. The two forces repel and attract. The sky force seeks its contradictory and complementary opposing force on earth. The negative downward surge meets an upsurge of positive energy channelled through a place, an object, or people.

The forces smash together in a flash from sky to earth: a lightning strike. The flash is two centimetres wide, hotter than the surface of the sun, and carries ten million volts, thirty thousand amps. The earth returns the strike - even brighter - along the same track. At the peak of a storm, lightning strikes once every twenty seconds.

This is the way lightning is born, and lightning can be anticipated and waited for by somebody such as the Minister of Religious Affairs, with his computers, his technical experience and his interest. That is what he did. He anticipated lightning on the stormy night of the SLT gathering in the snowy field north of Beijing. He told Yonglan, once Honglan, Nelson's mother, of his anticipation. He also told her that lightning can never be predicted with certainty. Perhaps it can only be brought into being by the two forces that influence universal laws: the force that Mao himself identified - human will, and the force that Mao acknowledged only as he was dying - the will of heaven.

After midnight, on the 4th February, one hundred and forty-seven believers of the SLT stood on frost-crusted snow, holding hands in twenty-one expectant groups of seven. They were waiting for someone or something to transform their lives. A radical power with the potential to destroy, cleanse and renew.

They believed it was a moment of possibility and of risk. They were there by choice. They did not want the security personnel to join them because those armed men were ignorant of what they were doing. So Yonglan warned them. They did not listen. The men had entered the field and approached the believers as the sound of thunder grew loud.

At the same time in the Ministry compound, the women on the balcony of the Minister's apartment ignited fireworks. The Minister made them do so because the noise concealed the thunder from the ears of everybody in the Ministry, and because fireworks excited him.

As he anticipated, but could not predict, lightning struck the field.

The power of lightning is electrical and it moves through air and it can move through the crust of frozen snow, especially snow that has crystallized in dirty city skies around the toxic soot of metals, chlorides and other pollutants. From a single, lightning-struck point - say the exposed metal wire of a fence half-buried in the snow - the massive pulse of lightning energy flashes across the frozen surface in an electrified sheet. This is what happened.

Everybody standing in the field was instantly and simultaneously shocked by a tremendous electrical force. Electricity sets the heart quivering - just for an instant. It soon stops. The heart is a system that switches from limp to hard in a regular beat because of its own internal electrical contradictions. Lightning contradicts the system and in a split second struggle a new system is born: from old unity to new. Blood stops moving; there is no breath. The power of lightning is so immense and its motion so speedy that it makes no burn, bruise or mark; it does nothing more than end life. If by some remarkable chance a person is not immediately dead, muscles spasm and blood bulges from the brain to lie trapped under the skull. If they are not already dead, a person dies from lack of oxygen in every part of the body unless someone gives them *the kiss of life*. If they are not already dead, a person will die soon, lying unloved on frozen snow, in freezing weather, and with fresh snow to fall.

CHAPTER 63
Day 25 11 am

At an aeroplane window seat, Ghosh opened his eyes, raised a shutter and saw crinkly dry hills far beneath the wings. It was a landscape that seemed to be without buildings or people.

'That's where I live,' said Chen Ying. Ghosh and Chen had spoken English in England and she had now switched to Chinese as if to acknowledge they were back in China.

Thirty-seven minutes later they were walking through Beijing Capital International Airport, along miles of spotless arcades full of menial staff who have never used the services they provide, never, for example, bought a Large Café Latte costing one tenth of their monthly wage, never had a purse haphazardly full of Euros, won, baht or dollars, never taken an international flight or been on any kind of aircraft anywhere, and never peed in a marble bathroom with a uniformed attendant standing by holding a rag and humming to piped Mozart.

From the airport they went to a downtown bus terminal and got on the first bus they could to Chen's home village. The bus was already almost full so they had to sit apart, Ghosh on a flip-down seat in the aisle. When all the flip-down seats were taken the bus started its seven-hour journey.

The passenger to Ghosh's left was a man who snacked continuously at a supply of food passed by his wife, sitting to Ghosh's right. He was a noisy eater, slurping at liquids, sucking at meat products, and smacking his lips at everything. At the same time he talked on his cell phone in a voice like a distorted megaphone and using a blurred version of Modern Standard Chinese. Beef congee in a paper bowl was split on Ghosh's trouser leg. Ghosh also suffered from a minute's burping, followed by hiccoughing, and then the man started sneezing. Ghosh soon hated his neighbour.

The other passengers were quieter, checking phones or dozing in their own heat, not out of the habit of wearing many layers of clothes in winter. Most men had a dozen keys on the belts of their pleated trousers; women wore trousers but kept their keys hidden.

There was a meal stop at a scrappy place on the edge of the highway where the stinging stench from the urinals sent Ghosh into a sensitive state unable to order any food. He sipped tea from a little cracked cup.

Chen ate noodles in soup and said, 'You feel bad now but if you don't eat you'll feel worse later.' She was correct.

It was dark when they arrived at their stop and the snacking man and his wife followed them off the bus. They stood together. It was cold and there was nobody else around. A car horn sounded.

The snacking man said, 'Hey!' and waved his arm. The car came towards them with the passenger shouting greetings to the snacking man. The driver was Chen's cousin but the car belonged to the passenger, a businessman from the township of which Chen's village was part. He was the friend of the snacking man, who was a government official, *gànbù*, the township's bureaucratic leader. The official acted as if he had just seen Ghosh for the first time and offered him the front passenger seat, three times. Even without seeing the look in Chen's eye, Ghosh knew it would show ignorance to accept.

The township *gànbù* was at the lowest point of the government's national structure and had high status in this local area, higher than the businessman who owned the car and had wealth but depended on the official for permissions and legality. And both were much higher than the driver of the car, who was not wealthy and had no official position. However, the driver was Chen's cousin, and Chen was an official at a government ministry in Beijing, though she was currently way out of her territory and jurisdiction. Ghosh was an outsider, connected to a Beijing ministry official, and a foreigner - a wild card in the status game.

For a fourth time the official offered Ghosh the front seat. He was being magnanimous, conceding to Chen's higher theoretical rank. Ghosh refused again and he and Chen sat on one side of the car's back seat, recognizing the official's de facto power on behalf of her whole family. The middle of the back seat was taken by the businessman, the official's wife got the other half to herself, the official kept the front passenger seat, and Chen's cousin drove.

Over the rocky road in the black night, the official focussed on Ghosh, giving face to Chen. The official said he was hungry and that there had only been one meal break on the bus, which his wife heartily confirmed. And he said and the foreigner only had a cup of tea the whole journey. The businessman said foreigners can't eat our food. The official said you don't know anything. In Beijing there are tens of thousands of foreigners eating nothing but Chinese food. Americans, Japanese, Africans. Every tenth man is a foreigner. The businessman said, 'Is that so?' and looked at Ghosh as if he were about to suddenly multiply.

Ghosh and Chen rode on, squashed together in the back of a car in the back of beyond on a bumpy road in the dark. At that moment they both turned to look at each other. They would know more, but they knew enough. They were both strong; she was the stronger. She was slightly older, more finished in personality and behaviour; he was slightly more flexible, and had only just started on his path. There was a big journey ahead, with risks and many rewards.

The car stopped by a wobbly gate, made of wood. A little yard, a heavy door, inside a fire and a family - Chen's home.

There were seven people sitting in a circle around a fire in centre of the room, faces lit by the flames, each face shining at the couple on the threshold. The edges of the room were impenetrably dark. Ghosh's eyes adjusted. There were four women, two men and one child. They were all wearing several layers of clothes, some with two jackets, one on top of the other. Three of the women were old, that is, over sixty, and two of them wore tight fitting knit hats. The eldest man, aged thirty-nine, was smoking a cigarette and sitting on the only chair. All the others sat on little three-legged stools - irregular, not a matching set - except the child, seated on his mother's knee, and Chen's mother, sitting on a plastic crate.

There were wooden planks on the floor and the rectangular fireplace in the centre was contained by clay walls two hands high. Inside the fireplace was a deep bed of grey soot and glowing chunks of wood under a big black kettle on a metal tripod. Smoke rose to the ceiling.

The man with the cigarette stood up and gave his chair to Ghosh; the man took the stool of the woman with the child, who sat on a plank. Chen was pushed to a stool and one of the women with knit hats stood.

Five voices started talking at once. Chen taught Ghosh who the people were. The standing old woman was her mother. Another woman was Chen's aunt, her mother's younger sister. The eldest woman was the mother of the smoking man. The smoker was the husband of the woman with the child. That woman was Chen's elder cousin, the daughter of the aunt. The younger non-smoking man was also Chen's cousin, the last and only male child of Chen's aunt, and brother to the woman with the little child. The little child, thirty months old, was the baby son of the woman and the smoker.

Chen's mother was wearing black leather boots with high heels and she was telling Chen that this was *fashion*. As they talked Ghosh saw more of the room. There were blue-grey walls, and hanging from the ceiling on strings in the smoke was dry meat, like black rags. The voices went silent. Everyone stared at the fire. A shout. Alcohol was brought out. It was *báijiǔ*, a distilled white spirit, purchased from a shop, for special guests or Spring Festival. To Ghosh it had a viscous quality, a whiff of ethanol, a taste of the smell of a mouth that has vomited, and it burned his insides.

'*Gānbēi!*' said the smoking man. It was a real bottoms up: dry glass. They were soon drunk. The man offered Ghosh a cigarette. He wasn't a smoker but he took it; the man lit it for him. Ghosh coughed and the man laughed and Ghosh smiled.

The man asked him which nation he was from. Ghosh told him England.

'Oh,' said the man.

'My father was born in India.'

'India? India is poor but good. Pakistan is bad.'

'Pakistan is next door to India.'

'Next door!'

'Pakistan is also next door to China.'

'Liar! *Gānbēi!* '

'*Gānbēi!*'

Ghosh had a headache. He asked for the toilet. There was laughter.

Chen said, 'I'll show you.' There was even more laughter. She took him outside - the cold was a shock - round the back of the house to a pit between two chest-height walls.

'Don't fall in,' she said. She went back inside.

When he came back to the room somebody seemed to be shouting, 'Don't marry him if he's from Pakistan!'

Ghosh sat on the only chair and fell asleep.

He woke up next morning on a bed that had not been there the night before. He felt a pain like he'd broken his neck. He was cold and sweating, very thirsty and bursting to pee. Chen's mother was cooking something on the fire in a black pot. It smelled bad. Chen was also busy, cutting spring onions on the top of a tree stump that served as a chopping board. She was using a cleaver.

She said, 'We have to take that bed back to my cousin's house.'

Ghosh was still in his clothes. He took a spoonful of rice porridge and burnt his tongue. He drank warm water and felt sick. He pushed his feet into his shoes and with Chen carried the bed through the village. Children laughed at them. Ghosh didn't laugh. He was concentrating on his body's many aches.

Chen laughed, 'They say we're getting divorced after one night in the village.'

They stopped twice for Ghosh to retch, throwing up nothing.

His nose was running.

'You've caught a cold,' said Chen, laughing again.

On the way back from the cousin's place, Ghosh began to get his breath back and he looked at the village in the daylight. Pink tissue papers hung in tatters from doorways, celebrating *Spring Festival* - the new year. Bits of blasted fire crackers were swept in corners together with strips of unusable waste plastic, grit, dust, dried dog shit and twigs too small to be burned. There was no paved road and they walked on cobbles. He hurt his ankle.

It was cold and raw. A wind was scrabbling the dust. Although the Spring Festival had passed there were no signs of spring in the air. But from the ground, green shoots were poking up and cracking the dried mud, and there were catkin buds on trees and a purple tinge at the end of branches.

Back home, Chen's mother was working on her flags. The room was full of them and they were all the same. Ghosh sat in the chair. *Māma* moved to the black pot on the fire and from it poured a black liquid into a thick glass. In the pot remained a residue of twigs, leaves, roots and fat seeds. She gave the glass to Ghosh.

She said, '*Hē*', sounding *hurgh*, meaning *drink*, with a quick raise of her chin. She went back to her work.

Ghosh said thanks, downed the bitter medicine, winced at a spasm of pain in his head, and started laughing.

Chen said, 'The medicine was fast or the wind has blown you crazy.'

'Do you know what flag this is?'

Chen said, 'No.'

'Good. Does your *māma* know?'

'I don't know,' Chen's mother said. 'I just make them to the pattern and I take them to Old Wu's house and they get picked up and I get paid nearly nothing. This is the last one.'

It was the flag of *East Turkestan*, a non-existent country imagined by some people in the far western part of the People's Republic of China. A flag of rebels, an illegal flag, of sky blue, crescent moon and single star.

Ghosh said, 'It's a flag for the future or it's an enemy flag.'

Chen said, '*Your friends will be your enemies and your enemies your friends.* Mao Zedong said that.'

Chen's mother gathered the finished flags, tied them in a bundle and took them on her back to Old Wu's house.

Ghosh and Chen stayed in. Chen did household tasks, knowing from childhood habit exactly what to do. And while she worked, they talked.

Ghosh said, 'Enemies and friends. Have you changed?'

'I've changed because of what happened to us and what we had to do, and because of what kind of heart I have. *External causes are the condition of change and internal causes are the basis of change.* Mao said that, too. I memorized it in politics classes.'

'You use Mao to describe yourself?' Ghosh said. He had memorized Mao's behaviour.

'A bad man can be correct,' said Chen. 'And he was saying very old things.'

That afternoon a different cousin brought a different bed for Ghosh to sleep on and in the evening there was more drinking of *báijiǔ* as relatives gathered to celebrate the two guests from Beijing. Ghosh drank, which calmed him, and showed he'd learned how to drink without getting drunk. He was able to step outside to toilet without asking for or needing help.

He was followed outside by the hungry township *gànbù* who smirked beside him as he peed and said, 'Having fun playing with that girl?'

Ghosh couldn't turn at that moment; he was embarrassed and angry.

He said, 'What's the meaning of that?'

The official walked away saying, 'Well, well, you know . . . '

When Ghosh could follow he ran after the man and said, 'What? What do you mean?' He pulled at the official's shoulder to make him turn around and face the question.

'No, no. No meaning.'

They faced each other. Ghosh was panting a little and still had his hand on the other's shoulder.

The man said, 'You understand. I'm a peasant. No culture. Not a big city guy. This little place - I'm somebody. These people are my people.' He gestured at the house behind him in the dark. There was a cigarette and a fried chicken leg in his hand.

'She's their daughter. Supports them all. Big family in the village. Anything happens to her. Anything happens to them. Comes to me. I need to speak.'

'Nothing's going to happen.'

'I know. You are good people. Nothing's going to happen.' He slapped Ghosh's bicep five times, once with each wish: 'Good luck. Good fortune. Good health. Long life. Many children.'

He turned and said, 'Let's head in. I'm starving.'

In the morning Ghosh and Chen carried the cousin's bed back. It was a heavier bed than the first and a longer journey though easier because Ghosh didn't have a hangover and the village was more familiar and friendly.

Ghosh watched Chen Ying's face as she exerted herself to carry the load. He thought back to her face the first time he saw her in his kitchen. She had looked brave, hard and radiant: irresistible.

He thought of her face the second time she had walked into his kitchen with a request *come back with me again*. She had looked like a defiant child prepared for unjust punishment; brave enough to know that honesty would hurt and still ready to say what she had to.

The name *Yìng* signified hard, obstinate and tough as a stone - like jade. Her heart was loyal and not sceptical. She would love Marcas Ghosh for a long time and she would love him generously and unpossessively. This was not articulated in her mind but it was real. Neither would she give spoken demonstrations of her love. Ghosh sensed all that.

They left the village at noon. They had arrived to shouted greetings and departed to mumbled goodbyes.

'You're going? So, see you.'

Ghosh felt that the villagers were anchored in place, that Chen was anchored to her extended family, and that without her he would be drifting.

There was no car available and they walked out of the village to a bus that took them to a river they needed to cross by ferry. The Beijing bus could be picked up on the other side of the river. The river bed was wide and, being winter, the water flow reduced to a central channel, fast and deep. The ferry was a flat-bottom metal platform that was winched on steel cables from one bank to another. There were no seats. The platform crowded with passengers from three buses. Ghosh and Chen were among the first to get on and were gradually pushed to the railings on the river side, standing side by side, holding hands. The sun shone straight at them and they started to sweat in their winter clothes. Chen opened her coat. More passenger pushed on. Chen and Ghosh were packed in place now, unable to hold hands. The ferry started to move with an unannounced jolt. People behind them tumbled and they were all rolled around without hurt or pain or falling down.

The squeeze, roll and jolt pulled the button from the top of Chen's jeans. She was pressed into the railings; Ghosh was pressed into her right shoulder. He saw the jeans had pulled undone and the zip had slipped. He pressed tighter and covered the open zip with his right hand. Without turning to look at him, Chen Ying seemed to smile, a little. The ferry was floating.

Ghosh put his hand under the open zip, inside the jeans. His fingers touched white cotton and rested there, slightly cupped. Chen showed no change of expression. She looked out across the water. The ferry slid smoothly; the crowded deck was hushed; there was the sound of straining cables and squeaks of friction.

He thought *this is a liberty, but if I don't take it that would deny my attraction*. She did not want to seem to encourage such a liberty but could not truthfully feel or demonstrate a rejection. So they stood like that in a motionless turmoil.

When the people on the far bank became clearly visible, Ghosh took his hand away and Chen twisted to cover her jeans with her coat. They carried on their journey.

In Beijing, over the next few weeks, they had many things to do and one of the most important was finding a place to live in the future. They wanted to deposit money on an apartment not yet built. Like other first-time buyers this gamble was their only option.

Every weekend and many evenings were spent visiting construction sites and model homes.

One Sunday afternoon the pair of them were seated at a wooden desk waiting for a housing company representative to return with the floor plans of apartments for sale in a projected property. Beside them was an empty chair for the rep. The desk was outside, standing on a wide area of muddy ground in the middle of a building site. Around them in the clay were puddles of water made by spring rain, slabs of wet concrete and piles of rusting rebars. Framing the area were three-metre plywood screens with a dreamy-blue-skied-computer-produced impression of the finished product tagged with the slogan, in English, *Trust your choice*. Behind the screens was the actual building-in-progress - an eleven-storey wall of nearly one hundred and sixty-five future homes. It was a modest development. The property company rep was over there getting the plans from somebody.

Chen and Ghosh thought this would be the one: it was the location and the price and the size and the completion date they wanted.

They believed possessing their own property would bring stability and hope and they sat in optimistic silence. Mild sun came from behind gentle clouds. Chen was relaxed enough to be scratching the middle of her back with her left hand as she said, 'You forgive me and forgive China and you're staying here.' She was smiling.

Ghosh said, 'China is the same and it won't change but I can make my own life good.'

Chen said, 'And we have a life, not like all those people killed in the snow.'

'We do,' said Ghosh. 'And more luck than Britney.'

'We do,' said Chen. 'Which apartment are we going to choose? What are you thinking?'

'Nelson told me something,' said Ghosh. 'He said numbers are important and it's good to choose the right one. He said some numbers sound like something else, or their shape is like something good. People come to believe in it and act differently and it changes their luck. But he said don't try for a perfect number. '

Chen Ying said, 'What's wrong with perfect?'

'Nelson told me eight times eight should be a perfect number: eight lucky eights. But eight eights is sixty-four. A number ending in four - *sì*. Death. Perfection ends in death.'

The property agent came back to the open air desk with a creased and folded floor plan of the various apartments available to buy. Marcas Ghosh and Chen Ying studied the plans carefully, considering daylight, directions the windows faced, potential views, height above ground, orientation of entrances and exits, and also numbers. For their new life together they chose apartment number sixty-three.

CHAPTER 64
Day 44, 00:44 am

Chen Meiyuan, who was the elder twin, the one-time favourite, and now the new wife of the ex-Minister of Religious Affairs, slapped the mattress of the hospital bed she was lying on and said, 'It's late. Come to bed.'

She wanted a child.

Retired Minister Wang was standing by the window drinking *báikāishuǐ* - plain boiled water. The spring nights were cool in the mountains.

His wife said, 'You'll die of cold. Come into the warm.'

Their two names were together on a marriage certificate. She was now an ex-Minister's wife. Yes, a disgraced, internally self-exiled, out-of-favour, over-aged, retired Minister of the most minor and now disbanded ministry with a reputation muddied by failure, but still, in a little mountain town, that was something. Now the thing she didn't have was a daughter or a son.

Ex-Minister Wang already had three sons that he knew of and one that he didn't. The prospect of another failed to inspire him with hope; by the time the son was a man, he'd be dead. He understood and supported Meiyuan's desire, though for him sons had not brought fulfilment. For her sake he tried sometimes to think of it like this: making a new son was a chance to re-meet and remake his own father - he would be that father, and the son would be himself and live the life he wanted. The thinking did not succeed in creating the wish.

The newly-weds did not go to Canada but the ex-Minister had stopped drinking *Canada*. Since starting internal self-exile in the mountain hideaway his sleeping had become fitful. His mind worried in two ruts. First there were rumours of him being dragged up to Beijing for investigation. It could even go public. And he had anxious night thoughts about the days decades ago when he took food from a young woman in the countryside at a time they were all extremely hungry and that woman later died after trying to break into a cadre's house and being beaten up by people who ran to the scene of the cadre's cries. She flew in his mind at night, just off the ground, looking at him, in a marsh, in the evening, flitting, like clouds.

'You're standing in a draught,' said Meiyuan. 'Come away. Warm yourself here.'

Chen Meiyuan liked the hospital suite with a view. She'd lived in dozens of places during her ten Beijing years, mostly the northern outskirts of the capital - Tangjialing, Shahezhen, Xiaoyuehe, so-called villages inhabited by three thousand villagers and fifty-thousand unregistered migrants from the countryside. She had been one of the migrants. She had shared thin-walled rooms, bathrooms, toilets, sinks, and the noises and smells of neighbours. When, in the last two years, she'd had more money to spend, she'd relocated centrally to prestigious, extravagantly furnished, expensive places, much larger and lonelier, lost in a glut of new buildings.

She now delighted in the fresh air and scenery of their new mountain home. After years in Beijing it was like being in her childhood environment although among these southern hills the air was more moist and fertile, and the soil less dry. Soil feeds growth and allows roots to form. She was reinvigorated and her life was changed. This was the unspoken theme of the happy chats she had every day with her younger twin, Little Sister, Chen Ying.

And every morning she went to the market, sent fresh things to the hospital kitchen and managed what she and the ex-Minister ate because he complained of the local food: dishes of pickled radish, pork fat, salt and vinegar; snacks of dried sausage, boiled roots and cabbage. He was used to the wealth and variety of menus served to Beijing government officials. At least that was his excuse for eating less.

The Minister was not thriving on his home soil after decades away. He looked five years older than two months ago. He needed care.

He gulped some hot water and put the lid back on the cup. It was after midnight. He saw clouds flashing across the stars, hiding and revealing them. Sudden gusts slammed into the window and he could feel the pressure. An early typhoon was coming.

He'd heard nothing of his long-time sparring partner in politics, the Ministerial Branch Party Secretary, though he knew he'd gone, gone to his 'family', the reason for his fear of the young foreigner. And that foreigner - British drunk, idiot spoiler - that catalyst for disaster, whose weapon was he? The Minister had first suspected the Party Secretary. He soon saw that was wrong. And next Dong Bing. But he'd lost the Ministry. That was the only good point of all that happened: Dong Bing would never be Minister of Religious Affairs. Destroying the Ministry had made sure that Wang was the last Minister. *I am the last Minister*, he thought. *I will be forever the last, and last forever*.

His phone vibrated. Removing it from inside a cardboard toilet roll tube, he found there was a one-word text from ex-Vice Minister Dong Bing. The single logograph电 *diàn*, the first character in every word related to electricity - *electron, electrode, current, volt, circuit, resistance, computer, generator, electrify*, the *yīn* and *yángdiàn* of *negative* and *positive electricity*, as well as *electrocute, shock*, and *lightning*.

From habit ex-Minister Wang looked at a weather monitoring satellite site. Closing that, he remotely accessed an office computer in a police station, clicked on weibo, and signed in with one of his pseudonymous account names - the account with the most followers.

He looked up to sky and closed his eyes. He typed without seeing:

midnight stars Shining
near death Light
birth of Truth

John Francis Cross

Born in Lancashire, England, he left school at seventeen and worked for several years in Israel, Holland, France and Australia before taking a BA in Chinese and becoming a reporter for a Japanese news agency in Hong Kong. Following an MA in linguistics, he was employed at a key university in China, later moving to a British university where he taught Chinese-English translation and Chinese Studies. He has published a variety of literary, academic and journalistic writing, and has been a frequent participant in spoken word events in Tokyo and Brighton. Currently he is living and working in Tokyo and his next novel is *I Was Baldomero Xeluco de Nazo*.

johnfranciscross@hotmail.co.uk

41310871R00171

Made in the USA
Charleston, SC
24 April 2015